Praise for No Hallowed Ground

"With crackling dialogue, fast action, and a compelling mystery, Steve Hockensmith leads readers into a wilderness of bitter grievance and unpaid debts. I couldn't put it down!"

— Richard Prosch, author of *Hellbenders*

No Hallowed Ground

ALSO BY STEVE HOCKENSMITH

Double-A Western Detective Agency Adventures

Hired Guns

No Hallowed Ground

Holmes on the Range Mystery Series

Holmes on the Range

On the Wrong Track

The Black Dove

The Crack in the Lens

World's Greatest Sleuth!

The Double-A Western Detective Agency

Hunters of the Dead

Black List, White Death: Two Holmes on the Range Novellas

Dear Mr. Holmes: Seven Holmes on the Range Mysteries

Partners in Crime: Five Holmes on the Range Mysteries

No Hallowed Ground

Double-A Western Detective Agency Adventure

Book Two

Steve Hockensmith

ROUGH
EDGES
PRESS

No Hallowed Ground
Paperback Edition
Copyright © 2024 Steve Hockensmith

Rough Edges Press
An Imprint of Wolfpack Publishing
1707 E. Diana Street
Tampa, FL 33609

roughedgespress.com

Paperback ISBN 978-1-68549-509-1
eBook ISBN 978-1-68549-508-4
LCCN 2024943418

No Hallowed Ground

PART ONE

SOUTH VS. NORTH

CHAPTER 1

"I'll grant you this much, Appelbaum," said Echols. "You did pick a good spot to rob a train."

Echols was up on the slope beside Appelbaum and Landry, looking down on the railroad tracks. The tracks wound around a big knot of rock that jutted up like a raised fist at the west end of Donner Lake. The mountaintops in the distance were covered with snow.

"Thank you. That's quite a compliment, coming from you," Appelbaum said with a smile. "So do we have a deal?"

Echols and Landry looked at each other. They were unshaven men in shabby coats, but the stocks, side plates, and barrels of their well-polished rifles—pulled from scabbards after they'd tied their horses beside Appelbaum's—glinted in the bright mid-morning sun.

"Let's ask the boys," said Landry.

Echols nodded.

"Of course. Talk it over," said Appelbaum. "Don't forget, though—after this Tuesday you'll have to wait another month for…"

Appelbaum's words trailed off.

Landry had swiveled to the left and lifted his rifle over his head, the barrel pointing up straight like the staff of a flag. He waved it slowly three times over his flap-eared muskrat cap.

A signal.

"…your…next…chance," Appelbaum said as Landry lowered his rifle. "Uhh…if you will recall, gentlemen, I had asked for a meeting with Mr. Landry alone. It's all right that Mr. Echols came along, as it's well known that you two assumed joint leadership of… your organization last year. But please—remember my request for discretion. I took a terrible risk just contacting you. I'd really rather not be seen in your company, even by your most trusted compatriots."

Landry and Echols looked at each other again.

Echols shook his head and snorted. It was unclear if he was amused by Appelbaum's erudite discomfort or something else.

Noises echoed out of the snow-dusted pines and boulders to the northeast. Voices, whinnies. Then distant clops that grew steadily louder.

"Sorry, Appelbaum," said Landry. "Too late."

Appelbaum turned toward the sound of approaching men and saw that he was right.

The rest of Landry and Echols's "organization"—the gang known as the Give-'em-Hell Boys—was riding toward them, their horses moving slowly over the jagged shale lining the train tracks.

Appelbaum recognized Cyril Axton, Early Jones, Alberto Segura, Fuzz Witten, and Oscar Martinez immediately. They were famous men. Each with his own Wanted poster. Apparently, the Give-'em-Hell Boys had been recruiting because Appelbaum didn't recognize the two men—both younger and slightly cleaner-looking than the rest—riding drag.

At least Tidy Tom wasn't with them. If he had been…

An eighth rider came trotting out of the trees.

Tidy Tom Post.

Appelbaum gritted his teeth and threw a quick glare heavenward. For just a second, blasphemy flashed in his pale-blue eyes.

He forced himself to give Landry and Echols the nervous smile that fit the situation. The nervous part came easily. The smile, not so much.

"Not to imply anything insulting," he said, "but if I go missing before the Tuesday run—"

"Take it easy, Appelbaum," Landry said. "You've got nothing to worry about."

Echols gave Appelbaum a long, disdainful look.

Or do you? it seemed to add.

"Come on," Landry said, starting down the slope.

"Um…well…really…I…"

Echols's scornful look turned into a glare.

Appelbaum took a deep breath and followed Landry. A moment later, Appelbaum heard Echols following *him*. Closely.

They gathered on the other side of the tracks near the big, rocky rise and the fallen fir that Landry, Echols, and Appelbaum had hitched their horses to. The Give-'em-Hell Boys—once the country's most successful and feared train robbers—circled Appelbaum. The men still on horseback took in his double-breasted Ulster coat and black Homburg. His purple paisley ascot and silver stickpin. His oiled, graying hair and wire-frame spectacles and prim little businessman's mustache.

They clearly didn't like what they saw.

Appelbaum gave some of the men another nervous smile. Not Tidy Tom, though. His gaze Appelbaum avoided.

"All right, boys," Landry said. He nodded at Appelbaum. "This is Mr.—"

"Please!" Appelbaum cut in. "Are names really necessary? With everyone, I mean?"

"Appelbaum," Landry went on.

Some of the Give-'em-Hell Boys chuckled. Appelbaum couldn't tell if Tidy Tom joined in. Appelbaum had turned his back to him, and the only sound he heard from that direction was the creak of saddle leather, as when a man leans out to look at something from a different angle.

"What'd he want with you, Marty?" asked Oscar Martinez. He was a tall, barrel-chested man with a reputation for using his big fists to shatter railroaders' jaws whether they resisted during a robbery or not.

"It was like the note he gave Ada said," said Landry. "Had a proposition for us. Idea for a job." He waggled his thumb at the bend in the tracks behind him. "We'd hit it right here. Next Tuesday. The 11:20 out of Truckee."

"What's so special about the 11:20 out of Truckee?" asked Early Jones. Of all the Give-'em-Hell Boys, he still looked the most like a farmer, with a droop-brimmed hat and stained sack coat and creased, leathery face. Almost all the gang had been sodbusters or drovers-turned-small-time-cattlemen before a shared hatred—of the voracious, rapacious Southern Pacific Railroad—had steered them to a new career.

Appelbaum threw a glance at the two new recruits and saw that they were different. Barely more than kids, really, with the same thin faces and buck teeth and eager expressions. Brothers, it looked like, thrilled to have started a life of adventure. Not knowing yet how much death that life would bring. Or not caring.

"You all know the Olympic Club in Tahoe City, right?" Landry said.

Most of the men answered with chortles and hoots.

"Know *of* it, sure," said Cyril Axton, flashing a snaggle-toothed jack-o'-lantern grin. "Haven't managed to get inside it yet. I think my tuxedo's not up to their standards."

He brushed imaginary dust from the shoulder of his equally imaginary tuxedo.

His emaciated frame was covered by a fraying brown poncho that looked like it had spent its first few years of life as a homesteader's rug.

"What's the Olympic got to do with it?" Appelbaum heard Tidy Tom ask. It was obvious from his terse tone that he hadn't been one of the men laughing.

"Appelbaum says it's owned by some operator back in San Francisco named Ned Foster," Landry said. "The first Tuesday of every month, they send the rake-off from all the gambling and girls up to Truckee so it can catch the 11:20 westbound out of the mountains

and into Foster's pocket. We hit that train, we hit the jackpot. Appelbaum says."

One of the young brothers leaned closer to the other.

"Carl...what's a 'rake-off?'"

"Shut up, Sam," the other brother said.

"Why not grab the money on the road outta Tahoe City?" Early
Jones asked Landry.

"The Give-'em-Hell Boys rob *trains*," Echols snapped.
"Southern Pacific trains."

"They took our land, we make them pay," Martinez said
somberly. "That's why *I'm* out here."

Jones rolled his eyes. "Oh, come on. That battle's long over, and
you know it. It stopped being a crusade when we started robbing the
passengers. Nah—we're just talking about grabbing some cash here.
So why not do it where—?"

"Damn it—how many times do I have to say it?" Echols cut in.
"The Give-'em-Hell Boys fight the S.P. We ain't bandits. We got a
cause."

Jones just gave that a sour, skeptical frown. Clearly Echols could
say it a thousand more times, and Jones still wouldn't be convinced.

As they argued, Appelbaum's eyes darted toward the slopes to
the north and the trees to the west. He couldn't see much of them,
though. There were too many men crowded in too close
around him.

Beads of sweat popped out on his forehead even though it was
nearly cold enough to freeze them into salty pellets.

"Look, Early—someone *could* try it on the road. Yeah," Landry
said diplomatically. "But that someone would have to take out half a
dozen guards armed with shotguns. Risky. And definitely messy.
When it goes on the train, though, it's put in a special mail sack that
travels with a single, solitary postal inspector. A crooked postal
inspector. Who works for Foster...and now says he wants to work
with us."

One by one, the men turned to look again at Appelbaum.

Appelbaum gave them another limp smile and raised a trembling finger.

"Another advantage for us all, gentlemen," he said, voice warbling, "is that a train robbery would look like happenstance. You are, as Mr. Echols points out, the famous Give-'em-Hell Boys. You'd be doing what you do...this time with a supposedly unexpected windfall. But if you attack those guards on the road, Mr. Foster will know that someone in his employ has betrayed him to you. Sooner or later, he'd come after us all."

One of the brothers—Sam—barked out a dismissive hee-haw guffaw.

"We ain't scared of no 'Mr. Foster' in San Francisco!"

"The Give-'em-Hell Boys ain't scared of nobody!" his brother Carl threw in.

They looked around at the rest of the gang for approval.

The other men ignored them.

"Well...it makes sense to me," Fuzz Witten said, scratching at his prodigious neck beard. "I say we give her a go. We been freezing our nuts off up here too long with nothing to show for it but fresh whorehouse crabs."

Martinez swiveled in his saddle to survey the western bluffs. "Plenty of cover up there. More in the trees. Blind turn here around this rock. Yeah...perfect place for stopping a train."

"Or for an ambush," said Tidy Tom. "How'd you know Ada could get a note to Landry, Appelbaum? How'd you know we was anywhere nearby?"

Appelbaum couldn't keep his back to the man now. It would be too obvious. He forced himself to turn and look up into Tidy Tom's grimy, mud-flecked face. (The "Tidy" in his nickname was ironic.)

"It's well known that Ada Gill and Martin Landry...share a special friendship," Appelbaum said. "So when Miss Gill takes up her trade in Truckee, it's a safe bet Mr. Landry will do the same in the vicinity sooner or later."

Tidy Tom glared down at him with contempt but—it seemed—not recognition. Not yet.

"'Share a special friendship,' huh?" Tidy Tom snorted. "First time I ever heard what those two do called that."

He glanced at Axton.

"Well, of course, it's 'a special friendship,' Tom," Axton said. "Ada gives Marty freebies."

Both men burst out laughing.

They peeked over at Landry to see if he was offended.

He glared back at them. He was.

They laughed harder.

"You two idiots satisfied?" Echols growled.

Axton, still cackling, just nodded.

"Okay, okay," said Tidy Tom. He jabbed a hand at Appelbaum. "The man'd be crazy to come out here like this if he didn't mean it."

"How about you, Early?" Landry asked Jones.

Jones shrugged. "Sure, why not? I never seen a postal inspector before, but this bird's pretty much what I'd imagine." He put his left hand to his privates and gave them a vigorous scratch. "Plus I'm sick of sitting around itching at crabs, too."

There were snickers here and there, and Fuzz Witten pawed at his beard and said, "Well, there we go."

Appelbaum didn't try to hide his relief.

"Excellent, gentlemen, excellent," he said. "I've proposed to Mr. Landry and Mr. Echols a quite reasonable finder's fee of—"

"Hold it," someone said.

The voice—one Appelbaum hadn't heard before now—was a strangled whisper. Appelbaum turned toward it.

Alberto Segura sat atop an Appaloosa beside Tidy Tom's pinto. He was a lean, neatly bearded man with a brown fedora and a little unlit stub of cigarette tucked into one corner of his mouth. His yellow duster was unbuttoned, the right flap thrown back so as not to cover the black-barreled Remington he'd used on railroaders, passengers, and lawmen alike. A long red scar creased the left side of his neck—a memento from a Nevada posseman's bullet two years before.

"Yes?" Appelbaum said.

Segura stared at him silently. Then he slowly moved his gaze around the circle of men on horseback. He stopped at Fuzz Witten.

"Give him your hat," he croaked.

Fuzz stopped rubbing his whiskers. "What now?"

Segura jerked his head at Appelbaum. "Give him your hat."

Slowly, bushy brows beetled with bewilderment, Fuzz took off his Stetson—a dusty yellow one with the brims curled up at the sides—and tossed it down to Appelbaum.

Appelbaum caught it with a look of confusion and disgust, as if someone had just thrown him a dead cat.

"Put it on," Segura told him.

"If you insist." Appelbaum looked over at Fuzz. "I'll keep my Homburg, if you don't mind."

"Damn—I thought I was about to get me a fancy new lid!" Fuzz said.

Only Sam and Carl, the young brothers, laughed.

Appelbaum took off his Homburg with his left hand and plopped the Stetson on his head with the right.

"Does this make me an official Give-'em-Hell Boy?" he said, stretching both arms out wide.

"Now take off your glasses," Segura said.

"Excuse me?"

Segura's breathy, wheezy voice didn't get louder, but it did get harder. "Take. Off. Your. Glasses."

"All right…if I must."

Appelbaum reached up and unhooked his spectacles from one ear, then the other. He squinted up at Segura—though now he could see better than ever.

"Any more fashion tips?" Appelbaum stretched his arms wide again and turned this way and that. "From any of you? Perhaps I should trade coats with Mr. Landry? Or trousers with Mr. Echols?"

"Put a finger over your mustache," Segura said.

Appelbaum froze, arms still outstretched. "What?"

"Put. A. Finger. O—"

"I heard you. I'm just beginning to find this ridiculous, if I may say so."

Appelbaum lifted his right hand, still clutching the spectacles, and stuck out the index finger so that it covered his thin, gray-brown mustache.

"Would you prefer me with a Van Dyke?" he said. "A goatee? Muttonchops?"

Segura looked at the man to his right. Tidy Tom.

"That time outside Winnemucca," Segura said. "When those three Southern Pacific bastards almost got you."

"Yeah?" said Tidy Tom.

"And they didn't see I was with you cuz that gopher hole slowed me up."

"Yeah?"

"And I followed the White one back to town to see who he'd been talking to, and I got his name out of Willena Rostrup before I killed her."

Appelbaum stopped squinting. In fact his eyes were starting to go wide.

"Yeah?" said Tidy Tom.

"Well?" Segura pointed at Appelbaum. "Ain't that him?"

"You mean the White S.P. man?"

"I don't mean Willena Rostrup."

Tidy Tom stared down at Appelbaum, cocking his head first one way, then another. "I didn't get a good look at him, Al. Could be, I guess."

"Can I take my finger down now?" Appelbaum asked.

Segura didn't answer him. He turned to Landry and Echols instead.

"There's no 'could be' or guessing for me," he said. "This man's name is Oswald Dial, and he works for the Southern Pacific Railroad."

Appelbaum lowered his hand and began shaking his head.

"No no no no," he said. "I assure you you're mistaken."

He was even telling the truth.

His real name was Oswin Diehl, and he hadn't worked for the Southern Pacific in eight months. He was with the A.A. Western Detective Agency now.

"I mean, really, gentlemen," Diehl said. "Do I look like a railroad detective?"

He stretched his arms out so wide this time he could've been

Jesus on the cross.

"Why do you keep doing that?" Early Jones said.

"Hmm? Doing what?"

"Putting your arms out like that."

"I don't know what you're talking about," Diehl said blandly.

He didn't lower his arms.

"It's a signal!" Echols said.

"Oh, please...not you, too," Diehl said. "I'm telling you this is ludicrous."

Yet his arms stayed up and out. Because it *was* a signal.

Shoot! Shoot now! Start killing people before they kill me!

And still nothing happened.

Echols began to lift his rifle.

Diehl couldn't keep waiting, couldn't keep bluffing. The time had come to run.

He'd had a few minutes to watch the men around him—Echols and Landry on foot to the right, the other Give-'em-Hell Boys in a tight encircling "C" on horseback—and plot the best route out. He'd had time to figure his odds, too, but he couldn't think about that now. If he did, he might not bother trying.

"Die, scum!" he cried, and he whipped the only weapons he had —his fake glasses and Homburg hat—at the men directly across from him, the young brothers, Carl and Sam. Then he spun, ducked, and darted between Segura and Tidy Tom's horses.

Segura clawed at Diehl as he went past but only managed to knock the borrowed Stetson off his head. Tidy Tom went for his gun.

So did Carl and Sam—just as Diehl had hoped. Startled, the young men jerked back in their saddles. Their horses, flustered by the commotion (and the spectacles that bounced harmlessly off one's muzzle), began to stamp and spin.

"I got him!" said Carl, raising his shiny Colt Peacemaker.

"*I* got him!" said Sam, bringing up an identical Colt that looked like it had come in the same package from Montgomery Ward.

Segura spat out a curse that his choked voice made it impossible to decipher.

"Don't, you dumb——!" Tidy Tom barked.

The brothers began firing.

Carl's shot went high, zipping off toward Donner Lake in the distance.

Sam's shot plowed into a muddy smudge over Tidy Tom's left eye and made a mess of the back of his head.

"Oh, no! Tom!" Sam blurted out as the dead man slid sideways from his saddle. He blinked once, then turned to his brother. "Look what you did!"

Carl was fighting to control his panicked horse but managed to get out, "What *I* did?"

The other horses were spooked, too, jerking back and jostling each other and threatening to trample the two men still on foot in their midst — Landry and Echols. Only Cyril Axton was able to keep his mount steady enough to draw his gun and try to get a bead on Diehl, who was zigzagging toward the big rock at the end of the lake.

As Diehl ran he threw his arms out wide again. It looked like he was either making a desperate appeal to heaven or trying to take off like a bird.

"Shoot! Shoot!" he yelled.

"Happy to oblige, ya son of a bitch!" Axton yelled back.

There was a *boom*, but it wasn't from Axton's Colt. Instead the slug came screaming in from somewhere in the distance. It smashed into Axton and sent him flying off his horse with a gaping hole in his buckskin coat.

Diehl didn't look back but knew what the sound meant.

"Finally!" he cried, still zigzagging.

As he lowered his arms, another shot rang out—this one sounding sharper, closer—and Fuzz Witten clutched at his right shoulder.

"Aw, hell, boys!" he said. "I'm hit!"

Then he was hit again from the same direction. He couldn't tell the boys about it because the second bullet went straight through his heart.

Fuzz went stiff and toppled over backward.

"There's at least two of 'em," Oscar Martinez said. "One in the trees, the other up on—"

There was another distant boom, and Martinez grunted and dropped off his horse. The other shooter had put a bullet into his big body that went in the right side of his belly and exploded out again on the left. He landed on his side—what was left of it— groaning. The groaning didn't last long.

Only four of the Give-'em-Hell Boys were left in the saddle now: Carl, Sam, Early Jones, and Alberto Segura.

"What do we do? What do we do?" Carl asked Echols and Landry.

Both were flat on their backs, Echols knocked there by Tidy Tom's runaway horse, Landry by Axton's.

"Shoot back, dammit!" Landry yelled.

"Shoot at who?" said Sam. "I can't see nobody!"

Jones and Segura were crouching low now, trying to keep their heads behind their horses' necks. Their eyes met.

Without a word, Jones pointed his mount toward the trees to the east and dug in his heels.

Segura spat out a bitter *"Mierda."* But then he did the same.

Carl and Sam gaped at each other wide-eyed as Jones and Segura fled.

"Are they running away?" said Carl.

"Yes!" said Sam.

"Why, those damned cowards," said Carl. "Should we go with 'em?"

"No!" said Landry. "Stay! Fight!"

He needed cover so he could get to a horse and flee himself.

"Let's—" Sam said.

A bullet thumped into his left shoulder, sending him spinning from his saddle.

"Ow!" he said when he hit the bare, rocky ground. "Ow ow ow ow ow!"

"Sam!" Carl cried.

He dismounted and ran toward his brother.

Landry immediately hopped up, got on Carl's horse, and raced away.

"Hey," Carl said.

"Ow ow ow!" said Sam.

Echols ignored all this. He'd sat up just enough to spot "Appelbaum," who was still snaking his way toward the big fist of rock overlooking the lake.

"Dial!" Echols yelled.

He raised his rifle and fired.

The slug clipped a branch from a pine tree a foot to Diehl's left.

"It's pronounced 'deal!'" Diehl yelled back.

If someone was going to shoot him, the least the man could do was get his name right.

Echols levered another round into his Winchester and got off another shot. This one tore through Diehl's long Ulster coat six inches below his crotch.

Diehl yelped but kept running.

He was almost to the rock now. Once he got around it, he'd be safe…so long as no one followed him.

He looked back.

Echols was following him.

"Killllllllll!" Diehl bellowed. "Himmmmmmm!"

There were two shots in the distance.

Both of them slammed into the fleeing Martin Landry a hundred yards away. He fell forward limp as a rag doll yet somehow stayed in the saddle.

"I meant him! Him!" Diehl shouted, pointing back at Echols.

Echols was still coming at him, hunched over but moving straight and fast.

"Dirty sneaky sons of bitches!" Carl cried behind him, popping off a shot at the slopes. It had the same effect as shooting at clouds. "Show yourselves like men!"

"Ow ow ow ow," Sam moaned.

Echols fired at Diehl again. This time the bullet smashed into the mound of rock to Diehl's right, sending a spray of chipped stone into the side of his face as he passed.

Diehl cursed and kept running. That was all he could do. He'd been carrying a little twenty-two Blue Jacket revolver in his coat pocket when he arrived that morning—the sort of gun a postal inspector might have—but it was there to be found and taken. And it had been. It was in Echols's pocket now. Not that Echols needed it.

Echols levered his Winchester again as he followed Diehl into the pines around the rock. The trees were sparse, but there was enough cover and shade to make a long-distance shot from the northern slopes nearly impossible. And from the woods to the west there'd be no "nearly." The rock now blocked any shots from that direction.

Diehl was on his own.

"It'd be a big point in your favor if you surrendered!" he called over his shoulder as he weaved around trees and boulders.

"A big point with who?" said Echols.

He'd been rushing straight ahead while Diehl zigzagged this way and that, allowing him to close the distance between them to less than forty yards.

"The court! The judge! The law!" Diehl said.

Echols spit out an acid laugh. "You think I'm worried about the law or judges now? There ain't gonna be no trial for me. I've known that for a long time. Only one thing matters—making the S.P. pay as much as possible before I go."

He got off another shot that kicked up sparks and shards of rock between Diehl's flying feet.

"I'm not the S.P.!" Diehl said.

"You may as well be," Echols said, levering his Winchester yet again. "Killer-whore."

There were two echoing shots behind them followed by a here-and-gone scream of horror and pain. None of it slowed Echols for a second.

"All you believe in is money," he said as he hurried after Diehl. "At least I stood for something. At least I'll die for something. Unlike you."

"I believe in stuff!" Diehl said.

He was too distracted for a better answer. He just wanted to keep Echols talking while he searched frantically for a place to hide, a weapon to grab, any kind of plan, any kind of hope. He'd rounded the big rock, so for a moment—surely not a long one—he'd be out of Echols's sight. He stopped and whirled in a circle, but all he saw was more rock and trees and, a hundred yards off now, the long, smooth, indifferent blue of Donner Lake stretching on and on into the distance.

"'Stuff,'" Echols snorted as he drew closer. "That's still nothing. A man's land…the sweat and blood he soaks into it. That's something."

"*Shit*," said Diehl.

There weren't enough trees to lose himself in. Not nearby. And pine branches and pebbles aren't much to fight with.

Once Echols got around the rock, Diehl would be exposed and helpless. And Echols wouldn't keep missing Diehl forever. He probably wouldn't keep missing Diehl another thirty seconds.

Diehl glanced up at the cloud-smeared sky over the lake and seized the opportunity—his last, most likely—to send a quick prayer to the creator he'd soon be seeing face to face.

"Well, thanks," he said. "Bastard."

He turned to look for the largest, sharpest stick to lunge at Echols with—hell, even a big pine cone would be better than nothing—and found that he wasn't alone. A figure was striding toward him out of the tree shadows to the west. One that seemed berobed and ghostly gray.

"When you work the soil, you become part of it and vicey versa," Echols said. He was mere feet away now—about to round the north side of the big rock. "That's what farmers understand."

Diehl kept watching the figure as it approached. Dappled sunlight revealed not robes but a heavy shawl over a long checked dress. The figure—the *woman*—glared at Diehl, muttering angry words he didn't understand. The long-bladed knife in her hand glinted whenever the sun hit it.

"That connection…it's a sacred thing," Echols said. "And when it's destroyed for the sake of greed, that's a blasphemy."

He was so close it sounded like he was speaking directly into Diehl's ear.

The woman was close now, too—arm's length.

Diehl reached out for her knife.

Onawa—wife of Diehl's partner Hoop, sister of his partner Eskaminzim—skittered around him.

"I'll do it," she said. "And next time you won't tell me to stay back with the horses."

She swept on, knife still in hand, and disappeared around the rock.

"That's why I keep killing railroad men," Echols said. "And I won't stop till I've drawn my final...who the hell are you?"

Those were Echols's last words. Screams and gurgles don't count.

When Diehl came back around the big rock, Onawa was already marching off toward the railroad tracks. Echols's bloody body was behind her. Seven more bodies lay here and there over the loose shale and hard, scrubby earth ahead.

Quite a morning's work for the Double-A Western Detective Agency. And it wasn't over yet. Not for someone in their line of work.

Reap what ye shall sow.

It was harvest time.

Diehl sighed, took hold of Echols's ankles, and began dragging the man toward the tracks like a horse in harness pulling a plow.

CHAPTER 2

When Onawa reached the cluster of bodies not far from the tracks
—Sam and Carl a little to one side, Martinez and Axton and Tidy
Tom and Fuzz Witten to the other—she stopped and called out in
her language. She shouted first at the woods to the west, then at the
slopes to the north. Diehl didn't understand her exactly—even after
all these years, his Mescalero Apache was pretty bad—but he knew
she was saying what he himself might have, with one or two important differences.

Where were you?

What took you so long?

Why did I have to come out and save Diehl's ass myself?

The woman's words echoed off the bluffs, bouncing back over
the lake and into the forest. For a moment, there was no reply. Then
a man with long, dark hair and a red bandanna around his forehead
—Eskaminzim—stepped out of the trees and shouted back, also in
Mescalero Apache.

The only answer from Hoop was a little cascade of rocks and
dirt from a high ridge four hundred yards away. He was climbing
down to join them, but he'd be in no hurry. Not when there was so

much body-piling to do—and with his wife down there in the mood she was in.

Diehl kept dragging Echols toward the other Give-'em-Hell Boys. Echols had been a tall man, but a thin one, almost gaunt. It was hard to stay fat living as a bandit. So the man wasn't that hard to pull. Diehl just had to be careful not to spill anything.

Onawa, knowing their business and the importance of recognizable corpses, had kept Echols's face pristine. His stomach, not so much.

Onawa jerked her head back at Diehl and said something that made her brother laugh as he drew close, rifle in hand. Diehl didn't ask for a translation—he knew from experience that some things he'd rather not understand—but Eskaminzim gave him one anyway.

"My sister has a new name for you after seeing how you run," he said. "'*Gah.*' Rabbit."

Usually Onawa called Diehl *Ba*. Coyote. After the trickster whose schemes sometimes helped the Apache, sometimes hurt them.

Diehl dropped Echols's feet and threw his arms out wide.

"You couldn't see this?" he said, flapping his hands. "I wouldn't have to play rabbit if you weren't blind as a bat."

Eskaminzim didn't stop grinning.

"We had to hide for a while," he said with a shrug. He pointed at Fuzz Witten, then at Tidy Tom. "You didn't notice those two checking my side of the woods a while ago?" He shifted his finger to Martinez. "Or the big one and those two kids checking the bluffs near Hoop?"

"Oh," said Diehl, letting his arms go limp. "No."

Eskaminzim laughed again, shaking his head. "I'm not the one who's blind."

"Hey, I was a bit preoccupied. You know—being the sitting duck? Standing around out here dressed like a banker waiting to see who was going to show up and shoot me?"

"I told you to let me be 'Appelbaum,'" Eskaminzim said. He put a hand on the lapel of his blue pea coat and struck a dignified pose. "I think I would make a wonderful whatever-you-call-it."

Diehl picked up Echols's feet and went back to dragging him toward the other bodies. "There aren't many Apache postal inspectors."

Or black or female ones. Which was why Diehl had to be Appelbaum by process of elimination.

He wondered, not for the first time, about recruiting a junior partner. A young, White, not-too-bright one who wouldn't give him a hard time about everything.

"I'll bring up the horses and make lunch," Onawa announced. She glanced back at Diehl. "Don't get shot while I'm gone, Rabbit."

She went striding off toward the trees her brother had emerged from a minute before.

"I told you it was a good thing she was coming with us," Eskaminzim told Diehl. "Now there'll be hot hominy...and you'll be alive to eat it."

"But will I be alive *after* I eat her hominy?" Diehl replied.

Onawa had turned out to be a skillful scout and now—much to Diehl's chagrin—bodyguard. As a cook, on the other hand...

"You'll be alive," Eskaminzim reassured him. "You just might be missing some teeth."

When Diehl had Echols with Sam and Carl and the others, he let the man's feet drop again. Eskaminzim had gone off to collect Landry, who'd toppled from his horse not far from the lake.

Now there were logistics to consider. They hadn't come prepared for so many bodies. The whole gang wasn't supposed to show up until Tuesday morning, when Diehl and Hoop and Eskaminzim would have a small army of US marshals and sheriff's deputies and Southern Pacific Railroad Police with them. Today they'd intended to bait the trap, not spring it.

The downside: Diehl had almost died.

But there was an upside.

"We must have four-thousand dollars lying here," said Hoop as he crossed the tracks in his big buffalo coat and beaver hat. He gestured at Sam and Carl with the barrel of his Sharps rifle. "Don't recognize the pups, though. Probably not worth shooting."

"It's appreciated all the same, even if you take a loss on the bullets," said Diehl.

Hoop grunted, then glanced to the east. "Too bad Segura and Jones got away. That would've been another thousand."

"We'll make it up on the horses and saddles. No percentage on that."

Hoop grunted again, grimacing at the word "percentage."

Whatever side money they made, they could keep. Rewards they had to split with the A.A. Western Detective Agency.

At least they could say they weren't bounty hunters. They were "operatives." "Agents." "Detectives." For all the difference that made when there was killing to be done.

Hoop turned toward a palomino that was staring at them expectantly from a few yards off. Other than the three still tied to the overturned fir nearby, there was only one other horse—the one Landry had taken from Carl—in the rocky clearing by the bend in the tracks.

"The mounts scattered pretty good," Hoop said. "Bet some ain't coming back."

"Hey—come help me with this one!" Eskaminzim called out. "Feels like he ate an anvil for breakfast!"

He was bent over Landry with a grip on the dead man's limp arms. Most Apaches avoided handling the dead. Too much chance of riling up a ghost. But Eskaminzim had gotten used to it over the years. He'd had plenty of practice.

Hoop held up a hand—*Gimme a minute*, the gesture said—and turned back to Diehl.

"Gonna be hard to get all the merchandise moved with the horses we got left."

"So let's not use the horses," Diehl said. "We'll flag down the 11:20 train. I can talk the conductor and the mail car man into helping us out. They should be thrilled to see our baggage. You and Eskaminzim can gather up the animals and gear and sell it all in Truckee."

"While you ride in style down into San Francisco."

Diehl shrugged. "One of us has to. *And* talk to the S.P. *And* collect the bounties. *And* wire the agency's split to Ogden and yours to your relatives in New Mexico. You wanna do all that? Or would you prefer to have Eskaminzim take care of it?"

Hoop said nothing. What was there to say?

Only one of them could pretend to be a postal inspector. And while maybe—maybe—Hoop could've done all the rest to get their money, it would be a *lot* easier for the same one.

"Hey, look at the silver lining. I'll be doing all the paperwork," Diehl said. "By the time you and Eskaminzim and Onawa get back to the Mescalero reservation, your shares'll be there waiting for you. And Crowe doesn't have another job lined up for us. All you'll have to do for a while is sit back and enjoy your money."

Hoop snorted. "If Onawa *lets* me sit back and enjoy it. Most of it'll be spread around her family before I can so much as buy myself a new pipe."

"What do you need a new pipe for?" Eskaminzim called out. "You know how to roll a cigarette."

He'd stopped trying to move Landry and was now entertaining himself going through the dead man's pockets.

"Meanwhile there you'll be in San Francisco all by yourself," Hoop said to Diehl dryly. "How lonely you will be."

Diehl smiled for the first time that day. "Just one of the little sacrifices I'm happy to make for my partners."

Hoop snorted.

Diehl had several old acquaintances he could look up in San Francisco—and one or the other would either be between marriages or in one with enough flexibility to accommodate a little time with him. He wouldn't be lonely long, he figured.

But he was wrong about that. Wrong about Hoop sitting back and enjoying himself for a while, too.

Neither of them would have time.

Chapter 3

The Western Union Telegraph Company Incorporated
 Received at 200 Sutter Street, San Francisco
 10:14 a.m., March 26, 1894
 From Ogden, Utah
 To Oswin Diehl, Hotel Miramar, 683 Geary Street, S.F.

Proceed immediately Kansas City. Client JJ Featherston en route. Will communicate via Western Union K.C. Utmost urgency. Discretion imperative. Identical instructions sent Hoop et al.

P.S. Congratulations re: Give-'em-Hell Boys. Monies received. Publicity noted. Segura and Jones escape disappointing.

P.P.S. Diana insists I add quote warmer unquote conclusion

DESPITE EXTRA EXPENSE. SO: DOG DOING FINE. WE ARE WELL. GOOD LUCK.

P.P.P.S. NOT WORTH THE EXTRA FIFTY CENTS.

COL. C. KERMIT CROWE

CHAPTER 4

THE WESTERN UNION TELEGRAPH COMPANY INCORPORATED
RECEIVED AT 101 SOUTHWEST BLVD., KANSAS CITY
2:40 P.M., MARCH 28, 1894
FROM JEFFERSON CITY, MISSOURI
TO OSWIN DIEHL, GENERAL DELIVERY, K.C.

ON THE MOVE WITH ASSOCIATES. HEADING SOUTHWEST. EXPECT
NEXT COMMUNICATION GENERAL DELIVERY WESTERN UNION CENTRAL
MISSOURI. RENDEZVOUS POSSIBLE CLINTON OR HERMITAGE.
FOLLOW WITH HORSES AND GEAR APPROPRIATE FOR YOUR WORK BUT
DO NOT ATTRACT ATTENTION. NEED FOR SECRECY CANNOT BE
OVERSTATED.

JOHN JAY FEATHERSTON

CHAPTER 5

The Western Union Telegraph Company Incorporated
Received at 311 East Young Street, Clinton, Missouri
4:50 P.M., March 29, 1894
From Hermitage, Missouri
To Oswin Diehl, general delivery, Clinton

Bearing still southwest. Expect approach Butler or Lamar tomorrow. Look for mounted party of six. Speed and caution critical. Mum is the word.

John Jay Featherston

CHAPTER 6

Diehl—

Veering south. Pace quickening. Destination Joplin? Hurry.
(Discretely!)

—J.J.F.

Diehl refolded the note and slipped it into a pocket in his sheepskin
coat.

"And when did he leave this with you?" he asked the Western
Union clerk.

"About two hours ago. The gentleman walked in at 3:05."

Diehl glanced at the clock ticking away on the office wall.

4:58.

He looked at the clerk, meeting the young man's steady but
incurious gaze.

Too steady. Too incurious.

The clerk had obviously read the note and was working hard not
to seem intrigued.

Diehl choked down a bitter laugh.

Discretely! indeed.

Still—may as well go through the motions.

He pulled out a silver dollar and dropped it onto the clerk's tidy, uncluttered desk.

"Thanks. It's good to know where my father and his friends are heading," Diehl said. "Apparently there's some mighty good fishing over on the Sac River. We'll just mosey thataway and join them."

The clerk slid the coin off the desk and into his vest pocket. "Thank you, sir. Lots of bass and catfish just waiting for you, I'm sure. Good luck."

He gave Diehl a smile. Within five minutes, he'd be telling everyone in town about Diehl and which way he was really heading.

Not that there were that many people to tell. Lamar, Missouri, was so small Diehl had worried when they rode in that it wouldn't have a Western Union office at all.

He gave the clerk a little farewell salute, then rejoined Hoop, Eskaminzim, and Onawa outside. All three were still on their horses, studiously ignoring the stares they were getting from the few passing townspeople.

Diehl let himself chuckle unhappily about the *Discreetly!* now. The *Mum is the word* from the message the day before, too. Whoever their client turned out to be, Diehl already knew this much about him: He was the kind of man who put "The need for secrecy cannot be overstated" in a telegram to Kansas City. That was like having a love poem printed in *The Chicago Tribune* under the headline "NO ONE READ THIS BUT AGNES LARSON OF 527 WEST BELMONT AVENUE!!!"

A White, a Black, and two Apaches—one a woman—are supposed to ride through Missouri heavily armed with no one noticing or taking an interest? Angling down toward the Indian Territories like Blaze Bad Water or some other outlaws scurrying toward their hideout in the Cherokee Nation? Right.

Diehl locked eyes with one of the townsmen— a snow-bearded geezer sauntering past the dome-topped bandstand in the park across the street. The old man's stare turned into a glare.

Diehl tipped his Stetson.

The old man spat in the street.

"There must be something wrong with the water in Missouri," Onawa said dryly. "So many of the people we see spit when we pass."

"That ain't a problem with the water. That's a problem with the people," said Hoop. He looked at Diehl and jerked his head at the Western Union office. "So…?"

"No telegram this time. We're close enough for a handwritten note. Featherston's two hours south of here."

Hoop scratched at his beard, then glanced to the west. The horizon beyond the bandstand was starting to turn the burnt-orange of twilight.

"Two hours south for him. Not for us," Hoop said. "We can catch him not long after dark if—"

"We hurry," Diehl finished for him. He raised one finger. "But discretely."

"That in the note?" Eskaminzim asked.

"It was."

Eskaminzim laughed. His sister did, too, though there was no amusement in the harsh sound that came out of her. She muttered a single word in Spanish—another language she could speak fluently. Diehl had never had a knack for languages, but he didn't need a translation. He'd heard the word directed at himself from time to time. Now it was being applied to their client.

"*Tonto.*"

Fool.

They were two hundred and fifty miles west of St. Louis, the self-proclaimed "Gateway to the West." But this wasn't the West they knew—the sparsely populated West of canyons, arroyos, and mesas that made hiding easy (for those with skill and patience anyway). Even clawing its way from the cold clutches of winter, this Missouri "West" was a lush one, with white- and pink-flowering dogwood trees and fields of greening grass. Its well-worn roads ran through tightly packed woods and countless hamlets and farms.

You could leave the road and move discreetly here, but then you couldn't hurry. Or you could stick to the road and hurry, but then you wouldn't be discreet.

Diehl wondered how discrete John Jay Featherson's "mounted party of six" was being. Probably about as much as a circus caravan.

"Who's the bigger fool, Hoop?" he asked. "The fool or the fool who works for him?"

"The fool," Hoop replied without hesitating. "The fool who works for him is getting five dollars a day."

"Good point."

Diehl unhitched his horse, mounted, and led his own little circus south out of town.

———

"Thank you very much, ma'am," said John Jay Featherston as the wizened little woman in the gingham dress poured coffee into his cup. "We'll remember your Missouri hospitality as vividly as your beautiful Missouri countryside."

The woman eyed him coolly and set the coffee pot down by the fire.

"If you want more in the morning, that'll be another fifty cents," she said.

She turned and stalked away from the fire, heading across the farmyard toward the cabin forty yards off.

"Of course, Mrs. Moss. That'll be fine. Good night!" Featherston said.

Mrs. Moss said nothing more.

The four men huddled around the fire waited for her to go inside. They were all well-dressed and gray-haired, with black suits and Masonic watch fobs beneath their Prince Albert coats. Not usually the sort to approach a remote farmhouse to negotiate for a night in the barn and a pot of coffee. The same could be said of the other two men they'd ridden in with—the ones who'd gone into the woods in opposite directions to "see a man about a dog." With their rifles.

"I think she suspects," said hunch-shouldered, shivering Bill-heimer, the oldest of the old men, when the door closed behind Mrs. Moss.

"They all suspect something," said Pixley. He was the youngest of the bunch. A spritely 53. "They just don't know what to suspect."

"We hope," said Klein.

The three men shared a dark look across the fire.

"Steady there. It's under control," Featherston said. "I've got these people fooled. No one's any the wiser."

"Yes, well...that could be," Klein said slowly. "But they don't have to know the specifics to know they don't like us."

Billheimer nodded grimly. "These Southern country people... who can say? They might slit our throats in the night just for fun."

"Damn it, Peter — I said *steady*," Featherston snapped. "If old farm crones are going to leave you quaking, how can I depend on you when it comes time for the real fight?"

Billheimer lowered his head so far his bristly gray chin whiskers brushed his chest.

"Sorry, John," he said.

"By god, steel yourself," Featherston said. He looked around the fire so the other men knew he was talking to all of them. "You know what's at stake."

He took a slurp of his coffee...then recoiled with a grimace.

"Good god," he muttered, scowling down into his cup.

"Chicory and potato peels," said Pixley. "Or maybe worse."

He'd poured out his own cup after one sip, but Featherston hadn't noticed.

A warbling whistle pierced the silence of the dark woods to the west. If the notes had been an octave higher and twice as fast they would have sounded like the night call of a whip-poor-will.

It was a signal. One of the men on watch—Hosford, given the direction—was returning early.

"Whip-poor-will," a man said to the east, toward the road.

The other man on watch—Stringer, who was even worse at imitating birds than Hosford—was also returning early.

If there'd been danger, they were supposed to sound out like owls. (Or, in Stringer's case, say, "Who-who.") The whip-poor-will call was the all-clear. Yet Pixley, Klein, and Billheimer slipped their hands to the revolvers in their coat pockets.

Why were Hosford and Stringer coming back at the same time?

Featherston just watched the shadows for their friends, unalarmed…until their friends stepped into the flickering firelight without their rifles. And with dark shapes behind them. Two strangers.

The one behind Hosford was black, in a shaggy buffalo coat and beaver hat. Ira Hoop.

The one behind Stringer was white, in a sheepskin coat and gray Stetson. Oswin Diehl.

Diehl smiled. Hoop didn't.

"Good evening, gentlemen," Diehl said. "We saw your fire from the road and decided to join you. We didn't want anyone getting too nervous about unexpected guests, though, so we made our introductions to your doormen here first."

"It's all right, John," Hosford said to Featherston. "They're from Col. Crowe."

Diehl tugged on his hat brim. "The A.A. Western Detective Agency, at your service."

Billheimer and Klein relaxed and smiled and slipped their hands out of their pockets.

Hoop focused on Pixley.

"That means you can let go of that gun now," he said.

Pixley swallowed hard and eased his hand out into the open.

"Excellent! Excellent!" said Featherston. "You can bring the rest of your men in. It's safe here."

"Oh, we know. We've made our own little reconnoiter," said Diehl. He turned toward the darkness to the south. "Eskaminzim. Call in 'the rest of our men.'"

The Apache stepped into the light.

The men around the fire gasped.

Eskaminzim grinned at them, pleased by the reaction.

He turned to the road, puckered his lips, and blew out a perfect high-pitched trill.

"That," he said, turning back toward the fire, "is how you do a whip-poor-will."

In the distance, a horse whinnied. The sound of creaking leather and slow-moving hooves on hard sod soon followed.

The old men watched the road expectantly. When a single person appeared leading four horses, the reins for two in each hand, their shoulders sagged. When the person was close enough for them to make out long, dark hair worn loose and a checked skirt over wool leggings and a shawl draped across slight shoulders—make out that it was, in fact, a woman—they jerked up straight again, their eyes wide.

Featherston stood and peered past Onawa. But there was no one else to see.

"Do you mean to tell me this is it?" he said. "Three men and a woman?"

"You were expecting the Tenth Cavalry?" said Hoop.

"I was expecting something equal to the task. This will not do!"

"Will not do for what, Mr. Featherston?" Diehl replied mildly. "If you tell us why we're here, you might find we're equal to whatever the task happens to be. I'm Oswin Diehl, by the way. These are my associates Ira Hoop and Eskaminzim."

Featherston didn't acknowledge the introductions or make any of his own. Instead he glared at Onawa as she entered the farmyard. She passed by without a word, leading the horses toward the barn.

"And that's Mrs. Hoop," Diehl said. He turned to the three men still sitting around the fire. "Would you gentlemen be so kind as to help her with our horses? The sooner she's done, the sooner she can make us all coffee." He dropped his voice to a whisper. "Hers isn't the best, but I'm guessing it's better than what you just got."

Onawa growled something in Apache. Diehl would have to lower his voice even more the next time he talked about her cooking.

Hoop cleared his throat.

"My wife's coffee is very good," he said woodenly.

Eskaminzim checked to make sure his sister wasn't watching, then looked at the men around the fire and shook his head.

Diehl held a hand out toward the barn.

"If you please?" he said. "I'm sure you're all familiar with what-ever Mr. Featherston's about to tell us."

Klein and Billheimer looked at each other uncertainly, then—grunting and groaning as they slowly rose—shuffled off after Onawa.

"John…?" Pixley said, eyes on Featherston.

Featherston nodded.

Pixley was able to get up and leave a little faster than the older men. But he didn't look like he wanted to.

"Thank you," Diehl said as Pixley headed toward the barn. He walked to the fire and took Pixley's place on an overturned log. "Eskaminzim—why don't you give these other gentlemen their weapons so they can go back to sentry duty?"

Eskaminzim nodded and brought Hosford and Stringer their rifles—in Hosford's case a gleaming, slight .22 that looked fresh out of the case at the general store, in Stringer's a Springfield old enough to have seen service in the Civil War. The old men looked wistfully at the fire, both obviously hoping for a "No, stay" from Featherston. When they didn't get one, they walked off into the dark in opposite directions.

Diehl waited until they were gone—leaving him, Featherston, Hoop, and Eskaminzim by the fire—before speaking again.

"So," he said, "we know you're following a group with a wagon that's headed toward Indian Territory. Who are they, and why are you after them?"

Featherston was a tall, lean man—standing there with gleaming Oxfords beneath the straight lines of his black coat, he looked like an exclamation mark—and now his spine snapped so straight he shot up another couple inches.

"How do you know that?" he said. "We haven't told a soul!"

"Your trail done all the talking once we got on it," said Hoop. "Every crossroads, there's been your tracks over the same wagon ruts and hoofprints. Taking whichever turn they do."

"Except when you lose the trail and have to double back… which happened twice in the last ten miles," Eskaminzim added. "Fortunately for you, I'm here now."

Featherston seemed to accept the explanation begrudgingly, as if he couldn't quite believe his actions had been so easy to read. (He also eyed Eskaminzim in a way that suggested he didn't feel himself fortunate to have the Apache eight feet to his right.)

"What has Col. Crowe told you about me?" he asked Diehl.

Diehl shrugged. "That you're a client we need to find."

"And you've never heard of me?"

"No. Should we have?"

Featherston had a prim gray mustache much like the one Diehl had grown for "Appelbaum," then shaved off in San Francisco as soon as he could. The thin lips beneath it puckered.

"No," Featherston said.

But his eyes said *Yes*.

"I," he went on, "am the president of the First Bank of Springfield in Springfield, Illinois. Four days ago, one of our employees betrayed us, and thieves gained access to our vault. They took our customers' valuables, papers, and, of course, money. Tens of thousands of dollars. I've been able to call in enough debts and secure enough credit to cover the bank's operating costs for now. But that won't last long. If we don't recover what was taken within a few days, the First Bank of Springfield is ruined."

"And so are you?" Diehl said. "Which is why you're out here with your chess club instead of a posse...?"

"I told you," Featherston snapped. "I am trying to save the First Bank of Springfield. If it fails, many of our depositors will lose their life savings. Everything they have. It is vital that this incident remains a secret. If it were to get out, the bank would never recover even if we manage to get the money back."

Diehl nodded silently a moment, his gaze flicking from Featherston to the fire to Hoop before returning to its starting point.

"What do you know about the robbers?" he said.

"There are seven on horseback and two with the wagon," Featherston said. He seemed relieved to be talking about something other than the bank—and himself. "They're all men of a certain age. Fifties, sixties. All with dark hair." His lips puckered again, and he threw another quick glance at Eskaminzim. "Swarthy. The wagon says 'Lee Creamery Pure Ice and Ice Cream' on the sides."

Eskaminzim laughed. "I hope they've got strawberry! That's my favorite."

Hoop and Diehl ignored him. They clearly had practice.

"How do you know all this?" Hoop asked Featherston. "Folks along the roads tell you?"

"That's right. In Illinois, after we first found the trail. Since we crossed over into Missouri, people have been less willing to help."

"That's no surprise," Diehl said. "A bunch of heavily armed men riding down from the North. They'd think you were Pinkertons or the Army of the Potomac if you didn't look like you should be hobbling into the druggist's for your rheumatism medicine."

Featherston reared back as if he'd been slapped.

"I am fit and ready to fight," he said. "Crowe should have told you. I'm—"

He stopped himself. After scowling at Diehl a moment, he began again, his voice softer.

"Col. Crowe and I served together during the war," he said. He nodded toward the barn. "My friends—they served, too. All of them. We may look feeble to you, Mr. Diehl, but I assure you that within each of these breasts, there still beats the undaunted heart of a patriot and warrior. When the moment comes, you won't find us flinching. Or reaching for our rheumatism medicine."

Diehl and Hoop shared another quick look.

Diehl had goaded the man and gotten what he wanted. Less discretion, more information.

So Featherston had been in the Army. Surely an officer, probably high-ranking. Even when they've been out of the uniform for decades, you could still tell.

Diehl forced himself to appear contrite.

"I apologize, Mr. Featherston. I should've stuck to the point. We're south of the Mason-Dixon and heading...south-er. Toward the Deep South. A group like ours—Yankees and mixed company —won't be able to count on much assistance. Not from the locals and perhaps not even from the authorities. And certainly not if we can't even say what we're really doing."

"I am aware of all that. Why do you think I asked Col. Crowe to send me his best men?" said Featherston.

He paused for a glance at Hoop and Eskaminzim. He didn't try to hide what sort of impression Col. Crowe's "best men" had made so far.

"Now," he went on, focusing on Diehl again, "what do you propose to do?"

"First, we rest," Diehl said. "We had to ride hard to catch up to you. Then…"

He turned to Hoop and Eskaminzim.

"The wagon's not that far ahead," Eskaminzim said. "If we start out again in a few hours we should be able to find it by first light."

"We oughta get a good look at the men with it before we make more plans than that," said Hoop.

Diehl turned back to Featherston and opened his mouth, about to repeat everything the other two men had just told him. Bringing their recommendations up the chain of command, as it were.

It suddenly struck him as silly, and instead he just waved a hand at Eskaminzim and Hoop in a "What they said" sort of way.

"But you will strike?" Featherston asked him. "You will deal with the thieves quickly and safely secure the wagon?"

"Of course," Diehl said. "When we know who we're striking and the best place to strike them. I'm sure an experienced military man like yourself appreciates the importance of reconnaissance and planning."

Featherston scowled at him, searching for sarcasm.

It was there. But Diehl was good at hiding it.

He had to be. He'd been a military man, too.

"Fine," Featherston said. "What time do you suggest we move out?"

"*We* will go at five o'clock," Diehl said, nodding at Hoop, then Eskaminzim.

"Four," said Hoop.

"Four o'clock," said Diehl. "As for you and your friends, get up at your normal time, whatever that's been, and proceed along the road as if nothing's changed. When we need you, we'll find you."

He really meant *if* they needed Featherston and his friends, but he knew better than to say so.

Featherston folded his arms over his chest and gave Diehl a brusque nod.

"Fine. Do that," he said, his voice a little louder, more stern. As if giving an order rather than receiving one.

Pixley, Klein, and Billheimer were returning, following Onawa back from the barn.

"We will forgo that other pot of coffee," Featherston announced, turning toward them. "Tomorrow's an important day. We need rest to be ready for it."

The old men nodded.

Onawa walked straight up to the fire and began kicking dirt onto it.

"Good," she said. "You never should've started this in the first place unless you *wanted* your throats slit in the night."

Once the fire was out, she spun on her heel and marched back toward the barn. Pixley, Klein, and Billheimer scattered to get out of her way.

"I'd better help her fetch the bedding," Hoop muttered, starting after her.

Featherston watched Hoop and his wife move off with a frown.

"And where will *she* be tomorrow?" he asked Diehl with a jerk of the chin at Onawa's back.

Diehl didn't answer until she was back inside the barn.

"Mr. Featherston," he said, "that woman will be wherever the hell she wants to be."

CHAPTER 7

The sides of the wagon—white around the words *LEE CREAMERY PURE ICE & ICE CREAM*—practically glowed under the light of the full moon. That's why it was so far from the main road, parked for the night in a hollow off a rocky side lane. The camp around it —seven softly snoring shapes curled under blankets—had no fire.

A man led his horse slowly up the lane toward them. He had a rifle in a scabbard, a pistol in a holster, and a tomahawk tucked under his belt. He didn't jump when the voice came out of the darkness to his left. He'd been waiting for it.

"Something going on, Ned?" the voice said softly.

The approaching man nodded. He still couldn't see the source of the voice, but he knew he'd been watched for at least the last two minutes.

"Better wake the major, Eli," he said. "The Yankees finally got them some help."

CHAPTER 8

"You don't believe it, do you, Hoop?" Diehl said.

They'd been back on the road an hour, and dawn was still just a dull glow of promise on the horizon's thinnest edge. Diehl and Hoop were riding side by side while Eskaminzim and Onawa, three horse-lengths ahead, trotted along with their eyes on ruts and hoof-prints Diehl couldn't even see. Every mile or so Onawa said something in Apache that seemed to annoy her brother. Diehl got the feeling she was critiquing his tracking style.

"The story about the bank?" said Hoop.

Diehl gave him a groggy nod.

He was still waking up. Getting up in the night and climbing atop a horse and riding off after men who'd probably kill him if they could wasn't as easy as it used to be. And it had never been easy for Diehl.

He wished, far from the first time, that he'd been born with other skills. Other interests. Ambition. *Something.*

That wish—for him to be different—was the one thing Diehl and his father had shared in common. Which was why his father had arranged for him to go to West Point all those years ago. Now

here Diehl was two decades later, still making his living with a gun…
and hoping that didn't bring his living to a sudden stop.

Thanks, Dad!

"Are you even listening to me?" Hoop said.

"Sorry…lost in thought."

"Man asks someone a question, least he can do is stay awake to
hear the answer."

"I'm awake! Go ahead!" Diehl said.

Onawa looked back and shushed him.

"Go ahead," Diehl said again. Quietly.

"What I was saying was nope. I do not believe Featherston,"
Hoop said. "But I don't not-believe him either."

"Yeah…that's how I feel," Diehl said. "I mean, the story's not
implausible. It's happened before. A bank gets cleaned out, and the
men who run it keep it quiet. That's not so hard to swallow, right?"

Hoop shrugged. He'd summed up his thoughts on the matter
already. More talk without more facts was just blather.

"But for the bank president to trail the robbers himself?" Diehl
went on. "With a 'posse' that looks like it should be falling asleep in
church? It makes you wonder, doesn't it?"

Hoop didn't say whether it did or didn't. This time he didn't
even shrug.

"How come you're not asking if *I* believe it?" Eskaminzim said
without taking his eyes off the road.

"You're busy," said Diehl.

"I can do two things at once. Look."

Eskaminzim took out his knife and—still not looking up from
the ground—balanced it on his palm, the blade tip pointed at
the sky.

"See?" he said. "You can ask me what I think."

Diehl stifled a sigh. "All right. Do *you* think Featherston's telling
the truth?"

"How should I know?" Eskaminzim said. He flipped the knife
end over end, caught it, and tucked it away again. "White people lie
so much I've stopped trying to figure out when they're telling the
truth."

"Very helpful. So glad I asked."

Diehl had known it was a trap. Some traps aren't worth the effort it takes to ride around them, though.

"I don't know if he's really a bank president, but he is a businessman," Onawa said. "His friends are the same. Soft hands, weak backs, barely know how to unsaddle a horse. One thing is sure, though. Whatever they're really after, it's important. Because they don't want to be out here. They want to be in warm, soft beds waiting to die in their sleep."

Diehl sat up straight in surprise. It was the most he'd heard Onawa say in English in years.

"Excellent points. Thank you."

"*I* can make excellent points," Eskaminzim said with a petulant frown. "Like does it even matter if Featherston's telling the truth? We get paid either way, don't we?"

Diehl saw an opportunity to cheer himself up. He smiled and took in a deep breath.

"Uh oh," Hoop muttered. "Here we go."

He knew what was coming.

Charles Swain, English poet, 1801-1874. Diehl's favorite.

"'The want of feeling—temper—trust. The want of truth, when hearts are sought,'" Diehl recited. "'Gold, linked to these, is worse than dust. With no such gold will I be bought.'"

"Now *there's* a lie!" Eskaminzim laughed. "I've seen you bought with twenty dollars in blood-soaked greenbacks."

"It's aspirational," Diehl said. "Like so much of Swain."

"It's horseshit," said Hoop. "Like all of Swain."

Onawa laughed.

"Philistines," Diehl grumbled, slumping again.

"No no no—how many times do I have to remind you?" said Eskaminzim. He thumped his chest. "Mescalero!"

Diehl didn't bother stifling the sigh that came to him now. Or the others that followed as they trotted on into a cold Missouri morning.

———

They reached the turnoff at dawn. By then Diehl could see the tracks, too.

"So they spent the night somewhere off thataway," he said, nodding at the path that branched westward from the main road. He looked back down at the fresh ruts and hoofprints that exited the side trail, heading south again. "And now they're back on the move."

"Got started a while ago. Middle of the night," said Hoop. "But with that wagon they can only go so fast."

"We'll be close enough to smell their farts soon," said Eskaminzim.

Diehl could never tell if he was joking when he said things like that.

Eskaminzim and Onawa started down the main road again, following the fresh tracks. The morning dew had left the dirt moist, so they wouldn't have to worry about kicking up a dust cloud the men ahead could see. Yet the Apaches were moving more slowly now, so Diehl and Hoop did the same. None of them wanted to trot round a bend and come face to face with a gang of bank robbers. Or whatever they were.

The road wound on past more forests and farms, rising and falling at times, weaving around bluffs and gullies at others. After half an hour, Eskaminzim lifted his nose high and sucked in a big sniff.

"Beans and cornbread for dinner," he said.

He took in another whiff.

"Ooo—canned peaches for dessert!"

He looked back at Diehl and grinned.

Onawa spoke to her brother disapprovingly in Apache. His grin instantly disappeared, and he snapped something back at her. No one seemed to irritate him quite like his own sister.

A few minutes later, she spoke again, insistently this time. She pointed down at a pile of horse turds in the road. It glistened moistly under the morning sun.

"Fresh," Diehl said. "Within the hour."

"It's not just that," said Onawa. She glanced back, focusing on her husband. "Look close."

Hoop stopped his horse and swung down from the saddle. He kneeled to inspect the tracks they'd been following, tilting to peer at them first from one angle, then another.

Eskaminzim looked back at Hoop and grimaced, then did the same thing—dismounting to study the road more closely.

After a moment, the two men looked at each other. From the expression on Eskaminzim's face, Diehl knew that whatever he said next would be in either English or Spanish.

The Apache language has no curse words.

Eskaminzim opted for English.

"*Shit.*"

"What is it?" Diehl asked.

Hoop straightened up. "Some of these tracks are identical."

Onawa said something to Eskaminzim in Apache. Though she wasn't smiling, she looked smug enough to make it obvious she was gloating.

"From the same horses?" Diehl said. "Riding over the same stretch of road?"

Hoop nodded.

"So some of them peeled off and circled to make it look like the group had stayed the same size…" Diehl said.

Hoop nodded again. "While others went we don't know where."

"And we missed it," said Diehl.

"Until now," said Onawa.

Diehl looked at Eskaminzim.

"You're fired." He pointed at Onawa. "She's hired."

Eskaminzim took in a deep breath. There was an expression on his face Diehl had never seen before.

Embarrassment.

"Missouri doesn't like me," he said. "The land won't talk to me."

The others let him have his rationalization. Diehl didn't even entirely consider it an excuse. Missouri *was* different than Apacheria or the Sierras. Maybe it really wouldn't tell Eskaminzim its secrets.

Hoop moved his gaze to the road ahead. A high-sided ravine

about three-quarters of a mile off held his attention for an extra-long time. The road cut right through the center.

Eskaminzim said what he was thinking.

"Perfect place for an ambush."

Diehl gave that an unhappy nod. "We've forced their hand. They must've known Featherston and his friends were behind them, but they weren't too threatened by it. Maybe they were counting on them to hang back and keep their mouths shut about the robbery. But then we showed up."

He looked back at the road winding northward through the gently rolling hills. There must be other routes north. Side roads, creek beds, railroad tracks. Something locals would know. A way to circle around.

Back toward Featherston's group.

"Now they have to deal with us," Diehl said. "All of us. In one fell swoop."

"We don't *know* that's their plan," said Hoop.

"We split our forces, so they've split their forces." Diehl shook his head. "We know."

"Well, what are you waiting for then?" said Onawa.

The men turned to look at her.

"Someone has to go back and warn Featherston while you deal with whoever's up there," Onawa went on with a nod at the ravine ahead.

"You're right," said Diehl. He looked at Hoop. "What would you think about having Onawa — ?"

Onawa wheeled her horse, galloped past them, and carried on northward up the road.

"Oh," said Diehl. He gave Hoop a sheepish look. "I *was* trying to ask you."

"Better that you didn't," said Eskaminzim. "He might've said no because he doesn't like it...but it's the only thing to do."

Hoop just silently watched his wife riding off to find Featherston, his expression grim.

After a moment he pivoted, turning that grim look toward the hills to the south.

CHAPTER 9

Young Duck squinted down at the road. Then squinted harder. Then squinted even harder. Then cursed.

Despite his name, Young Duck wasn't young. He was, in fact, old. And he didn't like to admit it.

Sometimes you have to do things you don't want to, though. That's what the old know. You have to pay your taxes (at least some of them) and eat more greens if you want to stay regular and tolerate your children when they grow up and start thinking they know as much as you.

And—if your eyes aren't as sharp they used to be—you have to turn to a surly SOB like Mink Winkleside and say, "You see someone on the road?"

"What are you asking me for?" Winkleside sneered. Of course. "You and Crump are supposed to be the crack shots. I thought you could pick a fly off a hog's ass two counties away."

"I can. I'm not sure if I saw someone coming, that's all."

"Great," Winkleside growled. "A blind sharpshooter."

He walked to the edge of the ridge and leaned out for a look north.

"Don't show yourself!" Young Duck said.

"'Take a look at the road, Winkleside…I can't see for shit!'" Winkleside mocked. "'No, no, Winkleside—don't take a look like *that!*'"

He shook his head in disgust and stepped away from the edge.

"I don't see a damn thing," he said. "Why didn't you tell the major you need spectacles, old man? Afraid he wouldn't give you a pat on the head?"

"Watch who you're calling 'old man,' old man," Young Duck muttered.

He wasn't looking at Winkleside, though. He was looking across the ravine, at the hazy shape that had emerged from the bushes there. Young Duck could make out just enough detail—brown sack coat, gray hair spilling from a shapeless hat, trousers too short for spindly legs—to know who it was.

Jesse Crump. Falling Pot, the man assigned to wait with Crump on the other side of the road, was a foot shorter and thirty pounds heavier.

Of course, the real giveaway was the long Whitworth rifle Crump held in his hands. And then the voice, too.

"Keep out of sight."

Young Duck shrugged and tried to flap a hand back at Winkleside—a *Tell it to him* gesture.

His own Whitworth was cradled in his arms.

"You see someone on the road?" he asked Crump.

"No. Now stay down and shut up."

With a single step back Crump disappeared into the shrubs and shade across the ravine.

Young Duck tried to do the same on his side, but his right toe caught a knotty tree root, and he barely managed to keep a "Dammit!" from popping out of his mouth as he stumbled.

He wasn't the man he'd been thirty years ago. Hell, he wasn't the man he'd been thirty months ago. Thirty *weeks* from now they could be shoveling dirt into his two-by-six hole in the Spavinaw Baptist Cemetery. If he even lived *that* long.

Cheerful thoughts.

That was something else you had to get used to as you got older.

Seeing death coming at you so slow and steady it could be a farm mule in front of a plow. Breaking a little more of the ground between you all the time. Gouging your grave out of the earth with each new step, each new day.

Yeah…cheerful thoughts indeed.

He eased himself down, leaning back against the tree that had just tripped him, and went back to watching the road. Or at least the nearest two hundred yards to the north. That was all he could see clearly. When he heard Crump firing, he'd pop up and fire, too—that was his plan. Whatever blurry smudges were out there to kill, he'd kill. Just like in the war, after he became a sharp-shooter.

Sending lead into a blue dot. Watching the dot stop moving. Finding the next dot and doing the same again. It sure as hell beat marching across an open field toward men whose faces you could see. Men with rifles aimed at the big gray line—and you in it—as it proudly, defiantly, stupidly made itself a bigger and easier target.

Keeping away from those men—keeping them smudges and dots—had been how Young Duck had survived the war. And hope-fully how he'd survive this, too…and the new war to come after it.

A mourning dove cooed on the other side of the ravine. One on their side answered.

Young Duck glanced over at Winkleside to see if he'd noticed.

Winkleside was sitting against a different tree twenty yards away, picking his nose, his shotgun across his lap.

A man in a blue coat stepped out of the bushes beyond him.

"Hello," the man said. Grinning, friendly. "I'm supposed to keep one of you alive, if I can. Any volunteers?"

The man had long black hair and dark skin and was younger than Young Duck and Winkleside—forty-ish to their sixty-ish.

The Winchester in his hands pointed at Young Duck's stomach.

"Shit!" Winkleside blurted out.

He jerked his hand away from his nose and down to his shotgun.

Young Duck jumped to his feet as the man in the blue coat swiveled, fired his rifle, worked the lever, fired again.

The first bullet slammed into Winkleside's chest. The second splattered his brains over the dark bark behind him.

"All right. Not him," the man said as Winkleside's body slumped over sideways. "How about you?"

His Winchester was pointed at Young Duck again.

"Young Duck! What's—?" Crump shouted.

That was all he got out before there were more shots, followed by shouts from different, unfamiliar voices.

"The other one—!"

"I see him!"

"He sees *you*!"

And the blast of a shotgun that made Young Duck wince.

"So," the man with the Winchester said to him, "are you going to drop that rifle?"

The gunfire on the other side of the ravine continued. Revolvers, it sounded like now.

Maybe Crump and Falling Pot were having better luck than Young Duck and Mink Winkleside. Maybe they were fighting off whoever had bushwhacked their bushwhack.

"Don't worry about all that fuss over there," the man said mildly, still smiling. "What matters to you is how *our* conversation goes."

Young Duck looked him up and down, taking in the red bandanna around his head, the breechclout draped over the top of his buckskin trousers, his moccasin boots. Then he looked him in the eye.

"What are you?" Young Duck asked. "Some kind of Comanche?"

The man's smile disappeared, and he looked Young Duck—and his battered felt hat and frayed jacket and heavy farmer's work boots —up and down in the same way.

"What are *you*?" the maybe Comanche said. "Some kind of White man?"

Young Duck didn't try to point his rifle at him. But the way he tightened his grip on it, scowling, suggested he might.

The man shot him.

The slug tore into Young Duck's right shoulder, and he staggered back a step, his left hand jerking away from the barrel of his
rifle.

The man levered his Winchester.

"Drop it," he said, "or the next bullet will—"

But Young Duck was still stumbling backward, the muzzle of his
Whitworth dragging along the ground now. His heel caught the
same gnarled root that had tripped him minutes before, and
suddenly instead of just teetering he was flying. Balance gone, feet
coming out from under him, he plummeted backward—right over
the edge into the ravine.

His scream lasted little more than a second. It ended with a thud
and the crunch of bone and wood.

Young Duck would grow no older.

───────

For a moment, there was silence. Then a whip-poor-will cooed.
When one cooed back, Eskaminzim walked to the edge of the cliff.
Hoop and Diehl stepped out of the brush on the other side of the
ravine. They looked at each other, then looked down at Young Duck
and his shattered Whitworth rifle.

Eskaminzim spoke a few solemn words in Apache.

Hoop provided a translation for Diehl. It probably wasn't exact,
but it got across the gist.

"Oops."

"He thought I was Comanche," Eskaminzim added, as if that
provided all the explanation necessary. "How about on your side?"

Hoop shook his head.

"Oops," said Diehl.

"Just two over there? Like over here?" said Eskaminzim.

"Yup," said Hoop.

"Which means—," Diehl began.

Hoop and Eskaminzim were already spinning away and
hurrying off into the woods. They needed to get to their horses fast.

They'd been right about the first trap. So they were probably also right about the second—the one for Featherston and his friends.

The one Onawa was riding straight into.

CHAPTER 10

As usual, Featherston wanted his group moving by the time the sun came up.

As usual, they got moving—slowly—about an hour afterward.

Also as usual, Featherston and Pixley were the first to be ready. Which made sense. Featherston was the leader. Not just the ranking officer, back in the day, but the pillar of society now. The big man. The one who called congressmen and titans of industry friends. (Though perhaps not as many as he wanted people to think, and certainly not as many as a few years before. Even congressmen and titans of industry grow old and die.) He had to be ready first. He was leading the way.

And George Pixley—he was the lad of the group. Back still straight, brown hair graying but not thinning, hands steady and free of liver spots. He hadn't even had his first kidney stone yet, and he couldn't join in when the others grumbled about their gout and lumbago. Getting up was easy for him. Or easier, at least. He was barely over fifty. Practically a kid.

The other men treated him like it, too, though they weren't aware of it. They thanked him when he helped with their bedrolls and saddles, yes, but they also expected him to do it. Expected him to help them mount up, too, though there were no thanks for that. It was too embarrassing to speak of. There were simply silent nods before one-two-three-four Klein and Stringer and Hosford and Billheimer rode out to join Featherston on the road.

Mrs. Moss didn't wave or call goodbye as the old men left. She just dumped out what remained of the "coffee" she'd brought them that morning—she certainly wasn't going to drink any of the thin brown swill herself—and went back inside. Her sulky, skeletal husband had passed by wordlessly as the men saddled their horses a little before, headed to some far pasture for chores perhaps. Or to dig out a hidden bottle with which to forget Mrs. Moss. Or to tell the neighbors about the strange Northerners they'd bilked ten dollars from for one night's use of the barn and a pot of boiled barley and molasses they'd called "coffee."

Yet compared to some of the people Featherston's group had encountered since crossing over from Illinois, Mr. and Mrs. Moss were downright gregarious. Others they'd talked to about a place to sleep had heard their story about heading south for an old comrade's funeral — first to Columbia, then to Osceola, now to Fort Scott — with skeptical scowls and terse words.

"Best keep moving."

"No room for you here."

"Ain't staying on my land."

"Nope. Go."

The further south they went, the worse it got. Pixley could only hope they wouldn't have to go much further. Not now that Col. Crowe's detectives were finally there.

Pixley looked at the road—golden sunlight dappling the dark ribbon of dirt that wound off through the trees—and imagined Diehl and the others ahead, catching up to the wagon. Dealing with the scum who rode with it.

Yes, Crowe's men would be outgunned. But they were professionals, right? The ones who fought not for their country but for their supper. Bloodshed was their business—and it was one Pixley had no interest in being part of, if he could help it. He'd had his fill of that when he was truly a young man, thirty years before.

Yet here he was, riding south with a Bull Dog revolver resting heavy in his coat pocket and his slender .22-caliber rifle—occasional killer of garden-raiding groundhogs and rabbits—in a new-bought scabbard by his right thigh. He hoped both could stay where they were until he was home again, and one could go back in its drawer, the other back on the wall.

"Think we'll pass through a decent-sized town today, John?" Stringer asked Featherston. "I'd love to get my hands on a fresh newspaper."

The other men gaped at him.

This could be the day their fingers went back on their triggers—the day duty put them in the line of fire again—and he was worried about keeping up with the news?

Stringer noticed his friends' incredulous gazes.

"I want to know what's happening in Washington with that silver bill," he said.

Billheimer blew a derisive snort out through his bushy beard.

"Good luck finding a Republican paper down here," he said. "Good god, Alvin—we're practically in Arkansas."

Pixley looked around at the oak trees and sumac shrubs and distant, rocky bluffs.

"Reminds me of Tennessee," he said.

That quieted the others.

Being reminded of Tennessee reminded them of Shiloh…and everything they'd seen there long ago.

Featherston, trotting jauntily twenty yards ahead of the rest, noticed the uneasy silence.

"No time for newspapers," he said. He swiveled to show his friends an attempt at a reassuring smile. "Keeping things *out* of the papers—that's what we're here for, hmm? And today, God willing, our reinforcements from Col. Crowe will help us do it."

He turned back to the road ahead.

The others looked at each other. None of them seemed reassured.

"'Our reinforcements'?" said Hosford, careful to keep his voice low. "Pretty grand way to talk about three men."

"They snuck up on our sentries pretty easily last night," Klein pointed out.

Hosford and Stringer glared at him. They'd been the sentries.

"Sneaking and fighting are two different things," Stringer grumbled.

"I don't doubt they can fight. They wouldn't work for Crowe if they couldn't," said Hosford. "I just wish there were more than three of them."

"There are," said Pixley. "By one."

"Oh, yeah. The woman," said Stringer. He grunted out a sour, scoffing chuckle. "She's actually the scariest one of the bunch."

"The look she gave me in the barn last night…" Klein shivered melodramatically. "I was relieved to wake up this morning with my scalp still attached."

Billheimer pointed at the receding hairline half-hidden by Klein's flat tweed cap.

"How could you tell the difference anymore, Andy?" he said.

The men laughed, even Klein.

Featherston started to turn to look back at them again, and Pixley expected the equivalent of "Quiet in the ranks." "This is no laughing matter" probably. Featherston had hit them with that more than once already. Whenever they forgot, even for an instant, the momentous importance of what they were doing or the vow they'd taken to see it through no matter what the cost.

"Perhaps—" Featherston said.

He stopped. Something up ahead had caught his eye.

The other men craned their necks to look past him.

In the distance, a lone figure on horseback was cresting a rise in the road. Riding hard.

Billheimer cursed under his breath and pulled out a pair of spectacles. By the time he had it on, the figure had disappeared behind the rolling hills.

The other men turned to Pixley, assuming the youngest among them would have gotten the best look.

Pixley shrugged.

"Whoever it is, he's in a hurry," he said. "That's all I could tell."

"Who'd need to be in a hurry out here at eight o'clock in the morning?" said Klein.

The men turned again. This time to Featherston.

He straightened his back and set his jaw, looking like he could be posing for a portrait or a marble statue.

"George—ride ahead and see who it is," he told Pixley. "The rest of you draw your weapons."

"Sidearms or rifles?" Stringer asked.

"Your pistol, Alvin," said Billheimer. "Unless you think you can get a Springfield rifle loaded on horseback without falling off."

"It's not a stupid question," Stringer muttered.

Then two things happened at once.

Pixley spurred his horse forward, and the other men began pulling out their revolvers.

A second later, a third thing happened.

The firing started.

It began in the trees about a hundred yards ahead on the left. Pixley could see the puffs of smoke as the first volley rang out. Then there were more booms and puffs of smoke from the other side of the road.

A bullet buzzed past Pixley's head like an angry bee.

Others slammed home. Into Featherston, who slumped and clutched his stomach. Into Klein and Billheimer, who toppled off their horses with bloody holes in their chests. And into Hosford's left leg and Stringer's right shoulder.

Pixley's horse charged on—straight toward the killers hidden in the woods ahead. There wasn't enough room for a galloping turn. The forest was too close on either side of the road. Pixley had to pull back hard on the reins, fight the animal to a stop, then jerk its head to the side and force it to wheel, whinnying, stutter-stepping, panicked. Pixley expected the next volley—expected death—the whole time.

The shots came just as he managed to turn back toward his friends. Featherston was hunched over in the saddle like a question mark, fighting to say something. When the bullets came screaming in, his head whipped up, gray hair flying wild. He flopped backward onto his horse's hindquarters while, beyond him, Hosford and Stringer grunted and fell into the road by the motionless Klein and Billheimer.

Pixley felt something pick at his shoulder, tearing a little patch of fabric from his overcoat. He reflexively looked down at it just as Klein's now-riderless horse, panicked, charged into his path. His horse and Klein's screamed as they collided, and Pixley was flipped head over heels out of the saddle.

He landed flat on his back and lay there a moment blinking up at the sky, stunned. Then more shots blasted out of the forest—all of them aimed at him now. Clods of dirt flew up around him as the horses scattered, Featherston's with his lifeless body still in the saddle.

The blur of motion in the road gave Pixley a moment of cover, and he pushed himself to his feet and lurched, hunched, toward the trees. Shots chased after him, coming in individual pops rather than roaring volleys.

Another spray of dirt and grass kicked up beside him. A whistling *whoosh* passed between his feet. A leafy branch brushed his shoulder as it fell, sliced from a bigger branch jutting out directly overhead.

He plunged into the forest and its welcome shadows, and the gunfire tapered off.

Pixley straightened up and quickened to a full sprint, dodging tree trunks and leaping over rotting logs. He didn't stop for nearly a minute. Then he darted behind a big oak to crouch down and catch his breath. And listen.

The birds, startled into silence by the cacophonous noise of human killing, were already singing their morning songs again. A crow cawed. A horse nickered.

A twig snapped.

It wasn't close. Perhaps as much as seventy yards away, to his left. But despite the distance, the sound was clear and unmistakable.

A footstep. A man. A hunter.

Hunters, Pixley knew, though he'd only heard one. Hunting *him*.

He slipped a hand into his coat pocket and pulled out his snub-nosed Bull Dog revolver. In the dense woods, maybe the rifles of the men stalking him would be no advantage. If he popped out at the right moment, maybe he'd catch them by surprise. Maybe the five rounds in his Bull Dog would be enough. Maybe he could kill them before they killed him.

Maybe maybe maybe. Too many maybes to count on. But the odds would do nothing but worsen if he waited until the hunters—the killers—were on top of him.

His grip was growing slick on the Bull Dog's rubber stock. It was probably all of fifty degrees there under the trees, yet it felt like sweat was pouring out of him. He wiped it from his eyes with the sleeve of his coat, then steeled himself for his last stand. Rise, turn, lift, point, fire fire fire fire. And perhaps live.

Pixley started to stand—and suddenly felt himself jerked back and pushed against the tree trunk, a rough hand wrapped tight across his mouth.

He let loose a little cry of surprise, but the palm clamped over his lips muffled it, and the fierce gaze he found himself looking into instantly silenced him.

Shut up, it said. *Be still.*

Keeping her right hand over his mouth, the Indian woman who'd come with Col. Crowe's men—Ogawa? Owana? Owaga?—put the index finger of her free hand to her lips, then tilted her wrist to point to the left. She fanned out all five fingers and shook her head.

Five men were coming.

There'd be no *maybe* if he made a stand. Just certain death.

Pixley nodded, and the woman jerked her head over her right shoulder. When Pixley nodded again, she took her hand from his mouth and crept away. Pixley followed her.

The woman led him deeper into the forest, glancing back from time to time to make sure he was keeping up and staying low. When they crossed a narrow deer path, she veered off onto it, the strip of moist earth at its center deadening the sound of their steps.

After a couple minutes the woman cut to the right and scrambled up to the rocky crest of a low hillock. When they reached the boulders at the top, she crouched behind them and cocked her head. Pixley kneeled beside her, his Bull Dog still gripped in his right hand.

Together, they listened. And listened. And heard nothing. Or at least Pixley did. But then the woman stiffened, and a moment later he heard it, too.

Footsteps. Voices. Coming closer.

"…still heading away from the road," a man was saying. "We must be half a mile from our horses by now, Major."

"I know," another man replied, his voice deep and gruff and firm.

"We might catch up to them," said the first man, "but by the time we do—"

"Even up here in Dade County, a bunch of shot-up bodies in the road are gonna get noticed right quick," yet another man cut in. "And we don't wanna be anywhere around when they are, Major."

"I. Know," the deep-voiced man said.

It sounded like they were only thirty or forty yards off. Almost close enough to see where the footprints along the deer path ended. Another twenty strides, and they'd start looking off the trail.

The men had tracked them this far. Pixley had no doubt they could follow them up the hill.

He looked down at his gun, back to wondering how lucky he could get with five bullets.

The woman noticed his gaze and knew his thoughts. She held up her left hand.

Not yet.

But maybe soon. Maybe in a matter of seconds.

The approaching footsteps stopped.

"All right," said the deep-voiced man. The major. "If Young Duck and Crump did their job, there's just these two left to worry about. Another old Yankee and a woman. We can carry on with the mission."

"Yes, sir," one of the men with him said. He sounded relieved.

The footsteps continued—heading away now.

Pixley sagged, sighing with relief.

The woman kept her hand up.

Once again, the footsteps stopped.

"I know you can hear me!" the major shouted, his hoarse voice cracking.

Pixley jerked his head up.

The woman shook her head, her eyes darting to her raised hand and back. Repeating the message.

Wait.

"Learn a lesson from your friends!" the major went on. "This isn't your place! This isn't your fight! Go home! If you keep following us, you die!"

The sound of movement began yet again. This time it didn't stop until it faded away in the distance.

Still, Pixley and the woman waited, wordless, for another ten minutes. It was the woman who finally peeked out over the rocks, rose to her feet, and spoke.

"It could be a trick," she said. She headed down the hill toward the deer path. "Keep your gun out and stay quiet."

It was a shock to Pixley to hear her flawless English after so long with nothing but glares and curt gestures.

"Thank you," he whispered as he followed her away from the rocks. "You saved my life."

The woman snorted.

"Don't thank me yet," she said.

She reached the path and turned left. Headed west. Back toward the road.

"If my husband or brother are dead," she said, "I'll kill every son of a bitch in this goddamn state."

CHAPTER 11

When Onawa saw Hoop and Eskaminzim galloping up the road with Diehl, she didn't celebrate, despite her relief.

She and Pixley were carrying Stringer's bloody body off the road at the time.

They set the corpse down beside Hosford, Klein, Billheimer, and Featherston. The dead men's horses were also lined up nearby, tied to the lowest branch of a sweetgum tree.

Diehl and Hoop reined up near the bodies.

"Damn," said Diehl.

Hoop looked at Onawa, his eyes saying he was glad to see her upright and unbloodied. But all his mouth said was, "So it was like we thought."

She nodded. "And up there?"

"There were four waiting for us. Indians, but dressed American-style," Hoop said. "Cherokees probably, given where we are."

Eskaminzim had never come to a full stop. Instead he was trotting around in a wide circle, eyes down, riding sign.

"The same here?" he asked his sister.

"The same," she told him. "Indians in white-eye clothes. Five of them."

Eskaminzim slipped off his horse, quickly tied it to the sweetgum tree beside the others, and disappeared into the forest with his Winchester.

"So they *were* Cherokee," Pixley muttered. He turned toward Featherston's body looking on the verge of tears. "That's what John suspected."

"Really?" said Diehl. "Why?"

Pixley faced the others again, blinking, confused. "Why? Well... you know. Dark-skinned men heading southwest across Missouri. Toward the Indian Territories."

"But why Cherokee?" Diehl said. "There are a lot of tribes in the Territories."

Pixley shrugged. "Aren't the Cherokees the biggest? And the closest to Illinois?"

"One of the biggest," said Hoop. "One of the closest."

"Well, there you go," Pixley said quickly. He moved back into the road and busied himself collecting the guns his dead friends had dropped.

Diehl and Hoop locked eyes with each other.

"There are plenty of outlaws striking out from the Territories these days," Diehl said. "Blaze Bad Water's gang, the Wild Bunch. But these men—"

"Too old," Hoop cut in. "Too organized."

"The leader was with the ones here," Onawa said. "They called him 'Major.'"

Diehl's eyes widened.

"*Way* too organized," he said to Hoop.

Hoop grunted in a way that said he agreed.

"So," Onawa said, "what now?"

"That's up to Mr. Pixley," Diehl told her.

"Me?" Pixley said. "Why would it be...? Oh."

He threw another miserable glance at Featherston stretched out in the grass.

Pixley was their client now.

"I see three options," Diehl said. "One, we find the county sheriff and tell him everything that's happened and let the law take it from here. Two, we bury your friends, my associates and I leave, and you head back to Illinois and tell whatever story you think is best. Or three, we bury your friends, then we find the bastards who killed them and make 'em pay."

"There's a hitch to option three, though," said Hoop.

Diehl gave him a small, grim smile.

"A few," he said. "But yes—one we'd have to work out before we got started."

Pixley looked at him quizzically.

"Before we make *them* pay," Diehl explained, "we have to know who's going to pay *us*."

Pixley's confused expression soured into disgust. "You want money."

Diehl shrugged. "Of course, we do. You may be here out of friendship or loyalty or a sense of civic duty, but we came to do a job. And we're still here, ready and willing to work. But not gratis, Mr. Pixley. Not with the…special challenges the task at hand entails."

His gaze flicked over to the bodies and back.

"John and Col. Crowe had everything all arranged," Pixley said. "Crowe's not going to call you off, I assure you. He knows the importance of what we're doing here. But if you're so worried about a payday, telegraph the colonel and ask him about it."

"That's a fine idea," Diehl said pleasantly. "We'll do that."

Pixley kept frowning at him.

"It was friendship *and* loyalty *and* a sense of civic duty that brought me here, by the way," he said. "That's why John and Alvin and Isaac and Peter and Frank were here, too. They were willing to risk their lives for something bigger and more important than themselves."

"Indeed," Diehl said. He took off his hat and pressed it over his heart. "The First Bank of Springfield."

He put his hat back on and swung down from the saddle.

"If we want to carry on without delay—or interference—our first priority has to be cleaning up the road," he said. "We don't know who might come this way next, but if *they* have any sense of civic duty they'll go straight to the law."

As he spoke, he untethered a piece of equipment lashed beneath his saddle bags. Hoop dismounted and did the same.

They'd brought the tools of their trade with them.

Spades. For quick digging of narrow, shallow holes.

Once they'd moved the bodies far enough into the forest, they got started.

———

Eskaminzim didn't return until they were done. He'd had a lot of practice perfecting that kind of good timing.

"I think we're safe for now," he said as he approached. Hoop and Diehl were standing off to one side leaning on their spades while Onawa and Pixley spread more leaves and twigs over the freshly filled pit in the woods. "The men behind the ambush here went south, but not on the road. They scattered into the forest. Split up at different creeks and trails. Hard to follow quickly while watching for another trap."

He glared at a nearby oak.

"These Missouri trees," he said with disgust, as if the oak should be ashamed of itself. "So big and *fat*."

He was used to the prickly-needled, narrow-waisted firs and shrubby junipers of the Southwest.

"They won't stay scattered. They'll come back together," Diehl said. "And soon."

"Around the wagon," said Hoop.

Diehl nodded. "Maybe they didn't look like it today, but they're still an escort. Killing us was important. Whatever's in the wagon—that's more important."

Pixley glanced over at him, then cleared his throat and straightened his back.

"I'd like to say something," he said.

"Yes?" said Diehl, cocking his head expectantly.

Pixley clasped his hands.

"Over the grave," he said.

"Oh," said Diehl.

Pixley took off his hat and bowed his head.

Hoop lowered his head, too. Diehl took a deep breath, then did the same.

Onawa and Eskaminzim just watched.

"Dear Heavenly Father," Pixley said, "we ask you to take unto your bosom these five souls we lay before you. John Jay Featherston, Isaac Klein, Peter Billheimer, Alvin Stringer, and Frank Hosford. They were brave men. Godly men…"

Pixley cleared his throat.

"Well…mostly," he said. "John and Peter and Alvin, definitely. Or usually, anyway. They meant well and tried to do the right thing. In general."

Pixley had started strong, with firm words and a ringing voice. But the more he spoke the more his tone became thin, warbly, uncertain.

"Isaac—he was one of your Hebrew peoples," he went on. "So, you know…I'll let you two sort that out. I'm sure in your infinite wisdom and mercy you'll see fit to…umm. Well. Not to tell you your job. But he was a good man. And Frank…well, you know about Frank. He wasn't so great with the commandments, perhaps. The sixth and ninth in particular. But say what you will about Frank Hosford, he heeded the call. Just like his friends. Thirty-three years ago, when his country needed him, and now, too. So I hate to leave him…hate to leave any of them…out here, like this. They deserve better. But we can't sort that out until we've…somehow…"

Pixley's head drooped so low his chin was practically on his chest.

After a moment, Diehl began to worry he'd passed out standing up.

"Uhh…Mr. Pixley?" Diehl said.

Pixley snapped up his head and opened his eyes and spoke again in a strong, steady, confident voice.

"'We can not dedicate—can not consecrate—can not hallow—this ground. The men lying here have consecrated it far above our poor power to add or detract. It is for us, the living, rather, to be dedicated to the great task remaining before us. That from these honored dead we take increased devotion to that cause for which they gave the last full measure of devotion. That we here highly resolve that these dead shall not have died in vain.'"

And with that Pixley slapped his hat back on and went striding away.

"He likes reciting poetry as much as you," Eskaminzim said to Diehl.

"That wasn't a poem," Diehl said. "It was from a speech. Written by a neighbor of his."

"The Gettysburg Address," said Hoop.

Onawa peeked over at her brother to see if he was following this.

He shrugged.

"I thought they were from a place called 'Springfield,'" Onawa said. She jerked her head at the grave.

"That's right," said Diehl.

"The speech was from the opening of a graveyard in Gettysburg, Pennsylvania," Hoop explained. "By Abraham Lincoln."

"Who's in a tomb in a graveyard in Springfield," Diehl added.

Onawa grimaced. "Oh. Him. I see now."

Diehl looked over at Hoop. "Seems a little highfalutin', doesn't it? Men trying to cover up a bank robbery quoting Lincoln?"

Eskaminzim burst out laughing. "I like that word! 'Highfalutin'. I know 'high,' of course, but what is it to 'falut'?"

The others ignored him.

"His friends are dead. Let him say whatever helps him feel better," Onawa told Diehl. "You're the last one who should criticize anybody for using fancy words."

Eskaminzim laughed again. "That's true! When I die, he'll bury me with lots of long, meaningless words. Only they'll be by Charles Swain…the big *pendejo*!"

Diehl didn't try to defend himself or his favorite poet. Instead he turned to watch Pixley walk away. Hoop did the same.

Pixley wasn't a big or young or particularly strong man. He was a sad, scared, tired one. His purposeful, stiff-backed stride had faded fast into a slump-shouldered trudge. Yet he carried on toward... what? And why?

Onawa and Eskaminzim began to follow him.

Hoop and Diehl looked at each other again. They'd buried lots of men together over the years. Comrades. Friends. Enemies. Diehl had never found the right words to share over the dead—not from Swain or anybody else—so eventually he'd stopped looking for them. And if Hoop knew the right words, he'd kept them to himself like so many others.

They turned from the grave in silence and carried their spades back toward the road.

CHAPTER 12

The boy with the telegram came to the mansion's back door in the middle of the second course—bowls of beef consommé that the old man and his daughter and her husband had been slowly emptying with dainty sips from silver spoons. All three raised their heads at the sound of the knock, watching each other expectantly but silently until a fortyish man entered the dining room with a slip of paper.

"Sorry to interrupt, ma'am," he said to Mrs. Dockery. "Message for your father."

"Thank you, Matthew," the lady said with a smile. "If you please…"

She nodded at the lean, sharp-featured, gray-haired man—elegantly dressed in a black dinner jacket, starched collar, and white tie—who'd been honored with her husband's place at the head of the table.

The butler brought him the telegram.

The old man took it wordlessly. As he read it, the butler bowed and returned to the kitchen.

"Our friends have encountered a complication," the old man said. He began folding the telegram. "Uninvited company. The major is sending for…"

He glanced at the woman standing at attention by the sideboard. Like the butler, she wore the simple but tasteful black-and-white clothes of a house servant. Also like the butler, she was black.

"…extra help," the old man said.

"His own or ours?" asked his son-in-law—the master of the house, Garland Dockery.

The old man went back to folding the telegram until it was a long, thin strip.

"His own. More of his Cherokee brethren from his days in gray," he said. "It's a matter of pride with him."

The old man stretched out his arm to poke the telegram into the flickering flame of a tapered candle. He kept it there while the paper lit up like a little torch.

"And a matter of trust?" Dockery said.

The old man let the telegram burn until the fire almost reached his fingers. Then he dropped it into his consommé.

"Why shouldn't he trust us?" he said. "We want the same thing. The same future. The same revenge. More or less."

"Where did the telegram come from, Daddy?" his daughter asked.

She was a pretty woman, with her father's high cheekbones and fair skin and sky-blue eyes.

"Carthage, Missouri," her father told her. "Despite the interference he's encountered, the major still expects to meet us in Joplin tomorrow…with our guest of honor."

Una Dockery smiled again.

"I'm sure they'll both receive a warm welcome," she said.

"Oh, I'll see to that," the old man replied.

He picked up a crystal wineglass and took a long drink. When he was done, he turned to his son-in-law.

"This is a fine claret, Garland," he said. "I always knew you were a man of good taste."

"How could he not be, Daddy?" Una said, beaming at her husband. "Look who he married."

Garland Dockery beamed back.

The old man grunted at his daughter's little joke, then tilted back his head again and drained his glass.

Una looked over at the female servant and nodded toward her father.

The servant lifted a bottle off the sideboard.

"More," she said, taking a single step forward, "Senator?"

The old man held out his glass.

He didn't say, "please."

CHAPTER 13

The dinner Onawa passed around was brick-like biscuits soaked in creek water and pemmican made from beef fat and blackberries the week before. They couldn't risk a fire, so they'd have to make do with what she'd brought along in her war bag. That also meant they were spared her coffee.

There'd be no relative comfort of a barn and farmyard that night either. Instead Eskaminzim found a clearing sufficiently far from the road to feel secluded. Hoop picketed the horses even deeper in the woods.

He wasn't worried about horse thieves. If the men they were following circled back for them that night, it wouldn't be to take their mounts. It would be to take their lives.

The plan for the morning was to keep going south, head for the next sizable town, and sell the extra horses and gear left over from the five men they'd buried.

"I can send my message to Col. Crowe from there," Diehl told Pixley. "If he gives us the go-ahead like you say he will...well, we go ahead."

Pixley nodded, then looked down glumly at the biscuit in the metal mug Onawa had handed him. His first bite had nearly broken off half his teeth. The biscuit had been soaking for five minutes since then, but he still looked nervous about giving it another try.

"Don't worry—another couple minutes, and it'll be edible," Diehl said. "Kind of."

Pixley threw wary glances this way and that.

Onawa had left to bring dinner to her brother and husband on watch out in the darkness.

"She's not much of a cook, is she?" Pixley whispered.

Diehl shrugged. "It's hard to say. I've never had what you'd call a fresh home-cooked meal from her. And biscuits and beans and pemmican that's supposed to last for weeks can only be so tasty. So who knows? Maybe she makes an excellent quiche Lorraine."

He poked his own soaking biscuit with a finger. It was still hard as a rock.

"But I doubt it," he said.

"I'm surprised you'd bring a woman along at all," Pixley said, still keeping his voice low. "I mean…given what you do."

Diehl pointed up at the dark night sky.

"'The moon will have its waning hour. The dim stars set in gloom,'" he recited. "'The buried seed will spring to flower. The leafless branch may bloom. And each its own allotted task, in season due fulfill. But never, in any season, ask a woman to change her will.'"

"Uhh…all right," Pixley said.

Diehl sighed.

"It's not a matter of bringing Onawa with us," he explained. "It's a matter of stopping her from coming."

He ran his free hand over his face. There weren't any wrinkles there yet, but there were a few scars. It wasn't an old face, but it was far from young.

"I guess I'm not up to it anymore," he said.

"But why would she *want* to come along? This is no business for women."

"It is for Apache women. Wives, anyway. In the old days, the young ones would go with their husbands on raiding parties. They made camp, cooked, cared for the wounded. Onawa's not exactly one of 'the young ones' anymore, but she still sees it as her duty. Plus she brings us luck...or so she says."

"Women are lucky to the Apache?"

Diehl shook his head. "*Four* is lucky to the Apache. And with three—Hoop and Eskaminzim and me—we've taken a lot of battering over the years. Last month we had a job in Arizona Territory that banged Hoop up *really* good. So here she is—for which you should be extremely grateful."

"Oh, I am! If not for her, I would've been shot down like John and the others. I just found her presence puzzling, that's all."

"Sure. I understand," Diehl said. "Which reminds me of something *I* find puzzling."

Diehl tapped his biscuit again, then turned it so the hard top half was dunked in the sulfurous creek water that had been soaking into the bottom.

"Yes?" said Pixley.

Diehl looked up at him. "Why are *you* here?"

"You already know that. The bank. My friends. My community."

"Bullshit," Diehl said.

Pixley blinked once. Twice. Three times.

"That's offensive," he said weakly.

Diehl shook his head. "Descriptive."

"But why should it be bull-...what you say? John *is* the president of the First Bank of Springfield. I'm on the board. Peter, Isaac, Alvin, Frank—we all are." Pixley cleared his throat. "Were. With our money *in* the bank. If it fails, we all fail. Hundreds of people fail."

"So you hire the Pinkertons or the Dickinsons or one of the other big agencies to get it back," Diehl said. "Or you bite the bullet and go to the law. Maybe there'd be a kerfuffle, but your chances of recovering the money would be a hell of a lot better. What you don't do is turn to a tiny new outfit like the AA Western Detective Agency *and* go after the robbers yourselves. It's the reason your friends are dead...and it doesn't make sense."

"Mr. Diehl, I assure you—"

"*Pixley*. It doesn't. Make. Sense," Diehl said. "Whatever your problem *really* is, you can't expect us to solve it unless you tell us the truth."

Pixley blinked one more time. Then he stared into the orange embers of their little fire.

"The truth?" he said.

A shushing rustle in the underbrush turned Diehl's head aside for a moment.

"The truth," he said when he looked at Pixley again. "If you really want this job done and as many of us as possible to go home alive."

Pixley took a deep, shuddering breath.

"All right. The truth. I suppose I have no choice now," he said. "It goes back to the war. Me and John and the others—we were in the same regiment."

"The 7th Illinois Infantry," Diehl said.

Pixley's eyebrows shot up.

"That's right," he said. "How did you know?"

"Featherston said he served with Crowe, and that was Crowe's regiment during the war. Where he made brevet colonel. When I served under him, in the Tenth Cavalry, he was just a runty little major. But I don't mean to interrupt…"

Diehl held out a hand in a "please go on" way.

"I was never more than a first lieutenant," Pixley said. "John made it all the way up to brigadier general by the end. We were at Fort Donelson, Shiloh, Allatoona. The March to the Sea, the Carolinas Campaign. '*Volens et potens*'—that was our regimental motto. 'Willing and able.' Well…we were. We saw a lot of action together. A lot of death."

Pixley went quiet again.

This time Diehl didn't push him to continue. He just waited.

After a long silence, Pixley went on.

"We were in North Carolina when the war was winding down. The rebel leaders were scattering like rats. Nobody knew where Jeff Davis and the rest might scurry to, so we were on the lookout for them. Everybody in Sherman's army wanted to net one of those traitors. And one of our patrols did. Tried to stop a coach outside Roxboro and ended up exchanging fire. All the men with the coach died. And when the sergeant leading the patrol went through the dead men's papers, he realized they'd just killed an assistant secretary of the Confederate Treasury. He brought that to me, and I brought it to a captain who brought it to a major who brought it all the way up the chain of command to a general. And we were all present when one of that dead rebel's trunks was opened, and there before us were thirty bars of gold bullion."

The look on Diehl's face didn't change as he listened to the story, but something in his eyes—glistening with intensity when Pixley started—went dry, flat, dead.

"The captain and the major and the general. The whole chain of command," Diehl said. "Featherston and your other friends we buried today?"

Pixley nodded. "It was the six of us who knew the secret."

"Not seven? Not Colonel Crowe, too?"

"No. We didn't know him well at the time. He started in a different company."

"Ah. So the *six* of you—you never reported the gold."

Pixley nodded again.

"And after the war you went home to Springfield and started a bank."

Pixley kept nodding.

"And now...what?" Diehl said. "Some group of old rebs figured out where the gold went and decided to take it back for the Southland?"

"Yes. Or just for themselves. One of them was called 'Major,' remember. They must be old soldiers who knew about the gold." Pixley finally stopped nodding. "What else could it be?"

Diehl shrugged. "It's hard to say...about so many things. How about Crowe? How'd he get involved?"

"Oh. Well...we all followed his career after the war. The regular army, the Southern Pacific Railroad Police, this new detective agency. So we'd bring him in to consult on security matters from time to time. And naturally when someone stole the gold—"

"Which was still sitting in a vault in Springfield three decades after you got your hands on it?"

"Well, not all of it, of course. But a lot of it."

Pixley puffed himself up and put on an affronted look. It didn't come naturally to him.

"The details don't matter," he said. "What's important is getting that wagon turned back toward Illinois."

Diehl started to reply, but a dull *clink* in the darkness stopped him.

He pulled his biscuit from his mug and gave Pixley a mirthless smile.

"I guess we'll see how much the details matter," he said. "Eat up."

He took a bite of his biscuit.

"Yum," he said as he chewed, though from the way he laboriously worked his jaw it looked like he was trying to eat a mouthful of rope. "Duhwishush."

"What?" said Pixley.

But Diehl looked past him as he swallowed.

"Delicious," he said again. This time to Onawa, who was stepping out of the darkness with the cups she'd brought Eskaminzim and Hoop. She'd politely made some recognizable noise as she approached so as not to startle Diehl and Pixley—and perhaps get shot.

Without a word, she stowed the cups in her bag then crawled under the blanket she'd left spread out for herself.

"Good night, Mrs. Hoop," Diehl said.

She just grunted and turned her back to him.

That was another language she and her husband shared. English, Spanish, Mescalero Apache, and Grunt. They were both fluent.

Diehl and Pixley ate their biscuits in silence after that. When they were done, they put down their mugs and snuggled in under their blankets. Diehl listened to Pixley's breathing for a while—and his occasional sighs—and knew he wasn't sleeping.

The man had buried five friends that day. It would be natural for sleep to come slowly. Yet Diehl wondered if something else was keeping Pixley awake. Something other than sadness or the fear that tomorrow would find him digging another grave…or lying in one.

———

"Halt," Eskaminzim said. "Who goes there?"

He knew exactly who was going there, of course. He wouldn't have said anything otherwise.

"Ahh," Eskaminzim said, peering at the large, shaggy shape coming closer through the woods. "It's just a lone buffalo wandering lost through the forest. Funny—I didn't think they had any in Missouri anymore."

Hoop stepped into the moonlight. He was wrapped in his massive buffalo coat, furry beaver hat on his head.

Hoop hated being cold.

"Oh," Eskaminzim said, feigning surprise. "It's you."

"I was listening to Diehl push Pixley on the bank story," Hoop said. "We got us a new story now."

"Yeah?"

Hoop nodded. "Confederate gold."

Eskaminzim popped his eyes wide and clapped a hand over his mouth.

Hoop waited patiently while the Apache snorted into his palm.

When Eskaminzim lowered his hand it revealed a huge, incredulous grin.

"Did he offer to sell us a map?" he said.

Hoop shook his head. "They got the gold during the war, Pixley says. The men we're chasing took it back, he says."

Eskaminzim nodded gravely, fighting to wipe the grin off his face.

"Right," he said. "What is this…the fifth time we've chased Confederate gold?"

"Sixth."

Eskaminzim began counting on his fingers.

"Texas. Colorado. Texas again. California. *Four*."

"And New Mexico."

"New Mexico?"

"Four years ago."

Eskaminzim stared at Hoop blankly.

"The Biggs brothers," Hoop prompted.

Eskaminzim kept staring.

"The ones you…" Hoop said.

He mimed stuffing one thing into another thing. Then mimed the other thing exploding.

Eskaminzim's grin returned.

"Oh, them! Do they count? I thought that was another lost mine."

"Run by rebels during the war. Or so the Biggs brothers said."

"All right, then. This is six," Eskaminzim said. "At least we've had lots of practice. Maybe this time we'll actually see some gold."

"Yeah. Maybe," said Hoop.

But before he carried on with his rounds, he indulged himself in a short, sharp laugh.

CHAPTER 14

"Now this tree I like," Eskaminzim said. He pointed at a scrawny eastern redbud covered with bright pink blossoms. "It's proud. Bold. But not arrogant and lazy and old like these...these..."

He flapped a hand at the rest of the forest.

"White-eye trees," he said.

Pixley looked around at the big green-leaved elms and oaks surrounding them.

He didn't enjoy making conversation with the Apaches. It made him nervous. But with Hoop and Diehl gone—into a town called Carthage to sell the extra horses and send a telegram to Col. Crowe —it was just him and Eskaminzim and Onawa left behind to hide in the woods. And to Pixley's surprise, Eskaminzim liked to talk.

He thought Indians were supposed to be taciturn, aloof, inscrutable. And Onawa was. But not her brother. He was full of observations. Opinions. Jokes. Farts.

"Aren't you going to ask me why this tree is like a white man?" he asked Pixley, pointing at a particularly large oak.

"Uhh...why?"

"Because it's fat in the middle, and it grows too tall," Eskaminzim explained, grinning. "I think it must be greedy like a White man. It fights to get big so it can steal more sun and water and earth from the other trees." He stretched out his arms, his fingers splayed out like leaves. "More more more. Mine mine mine." He lowered his arms and jerked his head at the redbud. "But he knows his place."

"Not just he," said Onawa. "*Nádleehi.*"

She was walking around the redbud, admiring it.

She plucked off some of the blossoms and popped them into her mouth.

"Really?" said Eskaminzim as his sister chewed thoughtfully, swallowed, then pulled off more blossoms. "Oh."

"What's '*Nádleehi?*'" Pixley asked.

As long as he had to make conversation he may as well learn something—and keep the conversation from going in uncomfortable directions. And he'd found that the more he kept Eskaminzim talking the less inclined the Apache was to fart. Onawa scolded her brother in Apache every time he did it, but that hadn't stopped him yet. In fact, it seemed to encourage him. He was clearly a man who needed stimulation, activity, action, even if it was just annoying his sister and embarrassing a "white-eye."

"It's a Diné thing," Eskaminzim said. "Navajo."

Onawa stuffed a handful of blossoms into the leather pouch on her hip, then began harvesting more.

"This tree is both male and female," she said.

It could be hard to predict when she'd choose to speak in English. An interest in accommodating the members of the group who didn't speak Mescalero Apache—Pixley and Diehl—seemed to come and go.

"Oh. I see," Pixley said. "Yes, I've heard of that. Trees with both…attributes. In English, we call those plants and animals… um…well…"

He turned and drifted off to stare forlornly toward the north, in the direction of the road, though it was far out of sight.

How long were Diehl and Hoop going to be gone? How long

would he be stuck in the woods, making no progress, disaster moving ever further beyond his reach to stop while he chatted with Apaches about hermaphrodites?

"Are you looking for our enemies or our friends?" Eskaminzim asked. "Because Hoop and Diehl won't be back for a long time. And our enemies aren't there. They're that way."

Pixley turned to find Eskaminzim pointing to the south with his left hand.

"And that way," Eskaminzim said, swiveling his hand so the finger was aimed at the southwest.

"They scattered after the ambush yesterday," Pixley said. "Surely they could be anywhere."

Eskaminzim grinned and shook his head. "Oh no. They're to the south and the southwest. My sister saw them."

Onawa stopped gathering blossoms and growled something at her brother in Apache.

"Saw them?" said Pixley, alarmed. His hand went to the Bull Dog revolver in his coat pocket. His rifle was in its scabbard with the horses, hidden deeper in the forest so they couldn't be heard from the road. "When?"

"This morning, before Hoop and Diehl left," Eskaminzim said. "She prayed to Usen, and He showed her."

Onawa snapped at her brother now, obviously snarling the Apache equivalent of "Shut up."

Eskaminzim replied to her mildly in their language, then went back to grinning at Pixley.

"Of course, I already knew we had enemies that way," he said, nodding to the southwest. "That's where the wagon's been headed the whole time. That's where the Cherokee Nation is. And the men we fought yesterday were Cherokee, weren't they? Or from one of the 'civilized tribes' anyway. Cherokee, Choctaw, Chickasaw. Those. The ones penned up in 'the Indian Territories.' The ones who dress like whites and make laws like whites and love money like whites."

Eskaminzim snorted.

"'Civilized,'" he said, shaking his head.

"I didn't get a look at the men who attacked us," said Pixley, relaxing—a little—now that he knew Onawa hadn't *seen* their enemies. More like foreseen them. Or simply imagined. "I can only guess who they were."

"Oh, they were Indians all right," Eskaminzim said.

Something on the ground caught his eye, and he squatted down and snatched up a rock. It was about the size of a crabapple, and he straightened up and began tossing it from hand to hand in a way that made Pixley nervous. More nervous, that is.

Eskaminzim began walking slowly in a circle, eyes down, still tossing the rock back and forth.

"The Confederate soldiers you took the gold from..." he said. "Were they Cherokee?"

"Oh," Pixley said. He had to fight not to have it leave his lips as a groan. This was the very conversation he'd hoped to avoid. "Diehl told you about that, did he?"

"No. But he let Hoop overhear it, and Hoop told me, and I told my sister. It's important that we all know who we're up against... right?"

Eskaminzim stopped and looked up at Pixley and gave him another smile.

"Of course," Pixley said. "Only I don't *know* who we're up against. The soldiers transporting the gold...they weren't Cherokees."

"But these Indians now are led by a man they call 'Major,'" Onawa pointed out. She'd stopped gathering blossoms and was kneeling at the base of the tree eyeing a cluster of mushrooms. "And there *were* Cherokees who fought for the Confederates."

She plucked up one of the mushrooms and sniffed it.

"Slave owners," she said.

She grimaced with disgust and tossed the mushroom aside.

"Yes. I know," said Pixley. "But like I said, I don't think there's any connection to the soldiers who—"

"Apaches killed lots of Confederates during the big war," Eskaminzim cut in cheerfully. He went back to circling, eyes down, the rock flipping from hand to hand. "Texan fools who tried to take over Apacheria and sell us into slavery. Of course, I was too young then to help much with the killing." He sighed wistfully, as if at a happy memory. "But I did what I could."

"Uhh…good," Pixley said.

Eskaminzim laughed with delight and bent down to pick up another rock. It was nearly identical to the first, and when he straightened up again he tossed them both into the air at the same time.

They clunked into each other and ricocheted in different directions.

"I wish someone would teach me to juggle," Eskaminzim sighed. He gave Pixley a hopeful look. "Can you juggle?"

"Uhh…no."

"That's too bad."

Eskaminzim retrieved his rocks.

Onawa said something scornful to him in Apache.

"She's just jealous," Eskaminzim told Pixley without translating. "She's my younger sister, so she missed the big war. Later she was caught by the Mexicans, and they made her a slave down there. She escaped…but she's never forgotten how she feels about slavers."

Onawa repeated a phrase she'd used earlier—the one that seemed to mean "Shut up."

Eskaminzim set his feet and readied his rocks.

"Cheer up, sister. You might get to kill some Confederates yet," he said. "We were told the big war was over a long time ago. But…" Eskaminzim locked eyes on Pixley. "Maybe not?"

Pixley said nothing.

Eskaminzim tossed his rocks into the air. Again they collided violently, flying in opposite directions as they plummeted to the dirt.

––––––

THE WESTERN UNION TELEGRAPH COMPANY INCORPORATED
   SENT TO UNION STATION, OGDEN, UTAH
   9:22 A.M., MARCH 31, 1894
   FROM CARTHAGE, MISSOURI

To C. Kermit Crowe, A.A. Western Detective Agency, Chamber of Commerce Bldg., Rm. 303

Sudden retirement for most Illinois associates. Only Pixley remains in business. Rival operation from the Indian Nations. Competition intense. Profit questionable. Prospectus unsatisfying. Proceed?

Diehl

————

It took Diehl and Hoop an hour to find a horse trader and sell the extra animals and tack after sending the telegram. They swung back by the Western Union office before leaving Carthage just in case by some miracle Col. Crowe had already received the message and sent a reply. Even if the telegram got through the Western Union log jam quickly and was instantly run over to the Chamber of Commerce Building in Ogden, there was no guarantee the colonel would be at his desk or that he'd send the messenger boy straight back with a response.

But that's exactly what happened.

————

The Western Union Telegraph Company Incorporated
    Received at 156 West Central Ave., Carthage, Missouri
    10:19 a.m., March 31, 1894
    From Ogden, Utah
    To Oswin Diehl, general delivery, Carthage

Proceed proceed proceed. All expenses covered by this office. Amlingmeyers, Diana, Burr unavailable but reinforcements

POSSIBLE. CONTINUE LOCATION UPDATES BUT AVOID UNDUE ATTEN-
TION. SECRECY CRUCIAL. IMPOSSIBLE TO OVERSTATE VITAL IMPOR-
TANCE OF ENTERPRISE. PROCEED PROCEED PROCEED.

COL. C. KERMIT CROWE

———

"That's a lot of proceeds," said Hoop.

"Twenty cents worth," said Diehl.

They were standing by their horses in front of the Carthage
Western Union office. Diehl was holding the telegram. Hoop read
over his shoulder.

"'All expenses covered by this office'?" said Hoop.

"That's a new one," said Diehl. "'Impossible to overstate vital
importance of enterprise?'"

He shook his head.

Hoop grunted.

"'Enterprise vital'" would've said the same thing. Though it still
would've been a bit unclear. What was of vital importance? The
endeavor they were engaged in—saving the First Bank of Springfield? Or was it the need for them to be aggressive? Or was it both?

Hoop reached out and tapped one word.

Reinforcements.

"Surprised that slipped in," Hoop said.

"Yeah," said Diehl.

Euphemisms were the norm in their telegrams and letters. Not
"reinforcements." "Supplementary resources." "Additional
colleagues." "Further support."

The alarmed tone, the disregard for expense, the sloppiness—
those weren't Col. Crowe's usual way.

But using the word "reinforcements"—that was *really* telling.

It sounded like the old days. The days of the cavalry.

The days of war.

Diehl turned to look back at Hoop.

Hoop met his gaze but said nothing.

Each knew what the other was thinking—and was thinking it himself.

What the hell are we riding into?

"Well…" Hoop said after a moment.

"Proceed proceed proceed," said Diehl.

They mounted up and started riding.

CHAPTER 15

It didn't take Eskaminzim and Onawa long to pick up the trail again after Hoop and Diehl returned from Carthage. It wasn't a hard trail to find. There was the wagon, after all. That was easy to spot.

As were the new arrivals.

"They regrouped here," said Eskaminzim. "With ten more men."

"Nine," said Onawa.

Eskaminzim gritted his teeth.

"From the west," he said.

He waggled his eyebrows.

They all knew what was directly to the west.

"So they got reinforcements…" said Hoop.

"…from the Cherokee Nation," said Diehl. "Great."

Eskaminzim turned and walked off up the road, eyes down, leading his horse by the reins.

Onawa did the same.

"I don't need your help," Eskaminzim told her in Apache.

"Yes, you do," she replied.

"Ten more of them?" Pixley fretted from atop his horse.

Diehl was on one side of him, Hoop on the other.

"Nine," Hoop said firmly.

"Whichever. It may as well be a hundred," said Pixley. "We can't take on so many men. Not head-on. What are we going to do?"

"We could try to bring in the law," said Diehl. "These *are* thieves and murderers we're trailing, after all. I know we're in Southern Missouri, and the local law might not like Yankees. But they're going to like Cherokees running around shooting the place up even—"

"No!" Pixley cut in. "If the authorities get involved we'll lose the gold even if we get it back from those Indians. There's no way the bank would be allowed to keep it if the truth came out. It *must* remain a secret!"

Pixley was a mild-mannered man, and not a big one. But as he spoke he straightened his spine and hardened his gaze and generally tried to look resolute.

He did a good job of it, too. Diehl didn't argue. Col. Crowe had said something similar in his telegram—"Secrecy crucial"—so he was willing to accept it, if not like it. But he did lean forward in his saddle to look past Pixley, at Hoop.

Well…? the look said. *What the hell are we gonna do then?*

It was a good question.

Hoop had another.

"So we keep doing this on our own. All right," he said. "But it's a funny thing, all them Cherokees being here…"

He lapsed into silence, leaving it to Diehl to go on for their client's benefit. It was a system that usually worked well for both of them. Hoop was spared the exhausting process of talking, while Diehl (who never minded opening his mouth, and who White folks were more inclined to listen to anyway) got to look smart.

"Groups that large—nine men, ten men, men with a wagon who have to stick to the roads—they're going to be noticed," Diehl said. "Probably stopped from time to time, being Cherokees outside of the Territories. They might dress like whites, but they'll get scrutiny. And Indians off their lands, traveling in the States, usually need written permission."

"Usually, but not always. I believe it depends on the individuals, the tribes, the treaties," Pixley said. He nodded at Eskaminzim and Onawa, who were debating in Apache over a pile of horse turds. "Just look at them. They don't have permission to be off their reservation."

Diehl reached under his sheepskin coat and pulled out a folded piece of paper.

"Signed by John S. Bell," he said.

Pixley's jaw dropped.

Up till the year before, John S. Bell had been the chief of the US Secret Service.

Colonel Crowe had friends in high places.

"So you're wondering how the Indians we're following could be traveling so conspicuously," Pixley said slowly.

Diehl gave him a nod as he tucked the letter away again. "Springfield and back is a long way to go for a bunch of Cherokees with an ice cream wagon. If they have paperwork—some kind of safe conduct pass—what does it say?"

"And how did they get it?" Hoop added.

Diehl held out a hand toward Hoop, the gesture saying *Exactly*.

Pixley looked back and forth between the two men then stared off into the trees, shoulders slumping. After a quiet moment he tried to straighten up again, but he couldn't get his head quite so high as before.

"That's just tactics. Methods. For the robbery," he said. "It doesn't matter anymore. What's important is what *we* have to do *now*: get that wagon."

"What those men are capable of—and who's helping them—is going to determine *our* tactics," Diehl countered, "and their chances for success."

"Well, figure it out fast and do it, dammit," Pixley snapped. "That's what you're getting your precious money for, isn't it?"

Hoop and Diehl gave each other a long, unhappy look.

"Hey!" Eskaminzim called out. "Come here!"

It looked like he and his sister were disagreeing about the significance of some milkweed petals by the side of the road. He waved

Hoop, Diehl, and Pixley forward irritably, as if he was going to ask them to vote on who was right.

"Have you discovered something?" Pixley asked as they rode up.

"Two things," Onawa said. "They——"

"They didn't all stay together long," Eskaminzim broke in, speaking over her. "Two of the Cherokees broke off from the rest and left the road here, headed south."

"The rest stayed with the wagon," Onawa managed to get in.

Diehl looked up the road. It wound this way and that through the hills, but all the twists and turns eventually took you in one direction. West—into the Cherokee Nation.

"And the second thing?" Pixley asked.

Onawa opened her mouth to answer.

"Stay still when you hear it," Eskaminzim got out first, speaking to Pixley.

"What do you——?" Pixley began.

"I'm telling you, don't move," Eskaminzim said.

"Is something——?"

"Keep your eyes on me," Eskaminzim said.

"But I don't——"

"We're being watched," Hoop said. He looked at Onawa. "Right?"

She nodded.

Pixley jerked up straight.

"That's what I wanted to avoid!" Eskaminzim said.

"Easy, Pixley," Diehl said. He slowly lifted a hand and pointed at the milkweed Eskaminzim and Onawa had been arguing over. Then he shifted his finger to the trees to the south, pretending to take in the already obvious: that they'd discovered two horses had left the road. "We don't know it's an ambush. We don't even know it's the Cherokees." He looked over at Onawa. "Or do we?"

"No," she said.

"Why are you asking her?" said Eskaminzim. "I'm right here."

"Which side of the road they on?" Hoop asked.

"North," Eskaminzim said quickly, before his sister could.

"About a quarter mile ahead, near where the road bends. Up the slope by another of these fat Missouri trees."

Pixley was still sitting up stiffly, but he successfully resisted the impulse to turn and look.

"You saw them?" he said.

"I saw movement," said Onawa.

"Well, maybe it was…I don't know…a deer or something."

"A deer with a rifle?" said Eskaminzim. "Because *I* saw a rifle."

Diehl heaved a sigh.

"Damn," he said. "We don't have much time. The second they realize we know they're there, they'll either start shooting or run. And I want one of these bastards alive."

"And I don't wanna get shot," said Hoop.

"It's easy," said Onawa. She nodded at the woods to the south. "My brother and my husband and I head in there, like we're following the two who split off. Then we circle back to the east, cross the road where we can't be seen, and come up behind whoever's waiting."

"Ah," said Diehl. "Easy. Right. And meanwhile what are Pixley and I doing?"

He already knew the answer.

"You keep going up the road," Onawa said. "To hold their attention."

"You can speak plain to Diehl, sister," Eskaminzim said. He grinned at Diehl. "You'll be the bait."

Diehl pushed back his hat and rubbed his forehead. "Of course."

"It'd make more sense if three of us stick to the road," Hoop said. "Only two of the Cherokees headed south. Why would we send three of us after them and leave two to trail the rest of the party and the wagon?"

"Because she doesn't want you getting shot with Diehl and Pixley, of course," Eskaminzim said, still smiling.

Onawa glowered at him. "They won't get shot if we do this right."

"But—," Pixley began.

"Fine," Diehl said. "We don't have time to debate it. Hoop, Pixley, and I will continue up the road like we're none the wiser. Onawa, Eskaminzim…please work quickly."

"And be careful," Hoop added, his eyes on his wife.

"We can be fast, or we can be careful," Onawa replied as she and her brother swung up onto their horses. "We can't be both."

"Then be careful," Hoop said.

"Then be fast," Diehl said at the same time.

Eskaminzim laughed.

"For once I'm with Diehl," he said. "I like fast better, too. Careful is boring."

He rode into the forest. Onawa gave him a heavy-lidded, long-suffering look, turned to give Hoop a nod, then followed her brother.

Hoop, Diehl, and Pixley watched them go in grave silence.

After a moment, Pixley finally let himself turn—slowly and seemingly calmly, but with white knuckles on his reins—for a look up the road.

"I don't like the idea of being bait," he said.

"Good," said Diehl. "If you did, you'd be crazy. *I* don't like it, and last time I checked I was still sane."

He glanced over at Hoop as if looking for backup on that.

Hoop withheld his opinion.

"But like it or not," Diehl went on, "it's what we gotta do."

He looked at Pixley and held his hand out toward the west.

Pixley just kept staring at the road without urging his horse toward it.

"You wanted us to do something," Diehl reminded him.

"Riding into a trap on purpose wasn't what I had in mind."

Still Pixley didn't move toward the road.

Diehl lowered his hand.

"So," he said. "The 7th Illinois Infantry."

Pixley turned back toward Diehl, his expression wary. "That was our regiment, yes."

"You know, I've always admired you fellas in the big war," Diehl said, his tone breezy and relaxed, as if he wasn't suddenly changing the subject. "You were the last generation to fight the old way. Thousands of men shoulder to shoulder, marching straight ahead at long rows of rifles, not breaking ranks as you got closer and closer and waited for the shooting to start. Me and Hoop—we've never had to fight like that. Not two straight lines in a field and volleys on 'Fire.' What you did—that sure took nerve."

Pixley searched Diehl's face for insincerity, condescension, smirking irony. He didn't see it.

"You're telling me to be brave," he said.

Hoop shook his head. "He's reminding you that you *are*."

Diehl held out his hand again, making the same "After you" gesture as before.

"That was a long time ago," Pixley said. "I'm a bookkeeper now, for God's sake."

"Yet here you are," said Diehl, his hand still out, palm up.

Pixley considered his words, then gave his horse his heels and headed back onto the road.

Hoop and Pixley did the same, and the three men trotted toward whatever awaited them to the west.

CHAPTER 16

Eskaminzim and Onawa left their horses in the trees on the south side of the road, then darted across to the north side. Once undercover in the forest again, Onawa turned left and began making her way with judicious precision toward the west, avoiding the foliage and underbrush that might make some sound as she passed.

Eskaminzim, meanwhile, hurried on into the woods at an angle, headed not for the bluff where the watchers were but toward the back of the hill they were on. He'd have to cover more ground, but he could do it more quickly, without taking such elaborate care to watch every footstep. And it would bring him up behind the watchers.

Behind was always good. Hopefully he could kill whoever it was, or maim them if he felt like keeping someone alive like Diehl wanted, before he was even noticed. And before Onawa got there.

That wasn't the plan. He and Onawa were supposed to approach in a pincer—him from the back with his Winchester, her from the side with the pump-action Colt Lightning rifle she'd appropriated from one of the Illinois whites they'd buried. They'd close in together…supposedly. But Eskaminzim was rushing to get there first.

He wanted it to be his fight. Alone.

That would keep Onawa out of more danger, yes, but Eskaminzim had another reason for handling this on his own.: There was no way he was going to let his little sister show him up again. He'd agreed to bring her along on jobs for luck, not so she could nitpick his tracking.

He heard a twig snap off to his left, and he was almost pleased. Onawa wasn't perfect.

Slow down even more, sister! he thought as he hurried on. *Slow down, and leave this to me!*

He was proud of her, of course. What Apache wouldn't be? She was a warrior woman like the great Lozen, sister of the Chiricahua chief Victorio. Courageous and deadly as any man. And like Lozen, Onawa was favored by the Creator, Usen, with the power to locate their enemies. At least sometimes. Usen wasn't always in the mood to help.

Eskaminzim had tried praying to Usen once to show him a couple Pima thieves he was tracking. He'd seen nothing, and the Pimas jumped him on the Mimbres River. *They* managed to get behind *him*! He'd only survived because they were stingy with their bullets and foolish enough to think one through his side would kill him. He took care of them later…with no help from the Creator.

Rude, Usen. Rude.

There were no more noises to Eskaminzim's left, but that wasn't because Onawa had stopped, of course. It was because they were both getting close to the watchers now, and his sister was making her way with even more caution. Which was why he was going to beat her to the top of the hill—and make sure the shooting was over by the time she arrived.

He had to hurry not just for his sister's sake but Hoop's and Diehl's and Pixley's, too. How long would the watchers wait before they started firing at the men down on the road? A good brother-in-law is hard to replace, and Hoop had been a good one indeed. And Diehl…well, he was Diehl. He made Eskaminzim laugh, and how many whites can you say that about? And without Pixley they might not get paid. A true tragedy!

Eskaminzim picked up his pace to a sprint...then almost imme-diately slowed again. He smelled horse, and despite his rush he changed course to follow the scent. He found the animal hidden behind a thick patch of blackberry bramble. It was alone, hobbled. A chestnut mare with wary eyes and a McClellan saddle. Eskam-inzim couldn't risk spooking her, so he didn't come close or circle around for a look at the rifle scabbard she was sure to be wearing on her right side. He knew it would be there, and that it would be empty.

Eskaminzim made a quick scan of the woods in all directions. Two men had split off from the Cherokees. If one left his horse here, where was the other?

Eskaminzim saw nothing to his left, nothing to his right. But then a flurry of movement straight ahead—near the top of the hill—caught his eye. It was there and gone in a second. Just a blur in the trees.

A shot rang out from the same direction. Someone was firing from up on the bluff. Not at him, though. No bullet came whistling his way.

Either the ambush had started—and Hoop or Diehl or Pixley were already stretched out on the road dead—or the watcher had spotted Onawa making her way through the forest.

"All right! There!" a man called out. Directing fire for someone else, perhaps. Pointing down at a figure scurrying for cover or already lying bloody and crippled and helpless to escape the coup de grâce shot.

Eskaminzim bolted toward the bluff.

"I believe you!" the man up ahead said.

That was harder to understand. There was no time to pause and ponder it, though. Eskaminzim had to reach the top of the hill before Onawa or one of the others was killed...if he wasn't too late to stop that already.

The incline was steep and thick with trees, but Eskaminzim bounded up fast.

"I believe you," the man said again. Then Eskaminzim came

bursting out into the little clearing around the bluff, Winchester up and ready to fire.

"Whoa there!" the man added, turning toward Eskaminzim with hands already raised. Behind him and a bit to his right, a branch dangled awkwardly from a hickory tree, the wood splintered at the base where a shot had cracked it. A rifle lay on the ground near his feet.

Onawa was on the other side of the clearing, her Lightning aimed at the man's chest.

"He didn't look like he believed I would shoot," she told her brother in Apache. "So I showed him I can pull a trigger. That got him to put his rifle down."

"But you were supposed to wait for me!" Eskaminzim said.

Onawa shrugged. "I decided to hurry up before my husband got shot. I couldn't wait all day for you to catch up."

"Are you two *Apache?*" the man asked, looking them up and down.

Eskaminzim was so mad he was tempted to shoot him.

His sister had done it again!

Fuming, Eskaminzim swiveled to look around the little clearing.

"What if your shooting draws the other one?" he snapped at Onawa.

"There is no other one," she replied. "Look at him. He's not one of them."

Eskaminzim focused on their prisoner.

At first glance he just looked like another Cherokee. A lean, tall man with dark skin and black hair dressed and groomed like a white. He even had facial hair—a neatly trimmed mustache and goatee.

But Onawa was right. There was something different about him. The men Eskaminzim had killed the day before had looked like aging farmers—frayed clothes, drooping hats, leathery skin from years toiling in the sun. And their rifles had been weathered and old —so old they could've been used in the big war decades before. But this man was younger. In his forties, like Eskaminzim, rather than his fifties or sixties. And his Winchester and Smith & Wesson revolver—worn on his left side with the butt across his flat belly, cross-draw style—looked clean, well-oiled, regularly used but pristine.

And there was something about his demeanor that was different, too. The Cherokee Eskaminzim had spoken to (briefly) before he went over the cliff had seemed angry and panicky. But not this one. There was a calm in his eyes despite the two rifles pointed at him. A steadiness that seemed to come both from within and without— from experience and confidence but something external, too.

Eskaminzim laughed when he realized what it was.

"What's so funny?" the man asked. He was still calm, but he certainly wasn't amused.

Eskaminzim pointed at the right breast of the man's brown suit jacket.

"Open your coat," he said.

The Cherokee just glowered at Eskaminzim a moment. Then he reached up and took hold of the lapel and pulled. And there it was pinned to the leather vest beneath.

A badge.

Eskaminzim laughed harder.

"Tribal police!" he said to Onawa.

"I know," she said. Of course.

"What…is…so…funny?" the man asked again.

"I'm just happy I didn't kill you!" Eskaminzim replied. "You're going to explain everything!"

CHAPTER 17

"I don't know anything," Capt. Henry Walkingstick of the Cherokee Lighthorse Mounted Police said for the third time. "Like I told you, I was just investigating suspicious activity on the border."

"A captain. Alone," Diehl said skeptically. "On the *wrong side* of the border."

"Yes," said Walkingstick.

He was by the side of the road with Hoop, Diehl, and Pixley in front of him on their horses, Onawa standing to one side, Eskaminzim behind him. The Apaches' rifles weren't pointed at him anymore, and his revolver was still in its holster. He wasn't a prisoner. But it was clear he wasn't free to go. Not until he provided some answers.

Answers he insisted he didn't have.

"So Col. Crowe didn't send you?" Pixley asked.

"No," Walkingstick said. "Who's Col. Crowe and why would he send someone here?"

"Like *I* told *you*, Captain," Diehl jumped in, simultaneously giving Pixley a look that told him not to ask any more questions. "Hoop, Eskaminzim, and I work for the A.A. Western Detective Agency. Crowe's our boss."

"And mine. I'm here being a detective, too," Onawa said firmly. It was as if she wasn't so much telling Walkingstick as reminding the universe.

"Yes," Diehl sighed. "There are four of us here from the Double-A. You know…for luck?"

Walkingstick nodded. "Four is a good number for the Cherokee, too. I understand…even if not all of you look much like detectives to me."

He glanced over at Onawa.

She scowled back at him.

"I bet my sister doesn't look like good luck to you either," Eskaminzim said. "Because she wasn't…for you."

Walkingstick glanced over his shoulder at him. "You're a long way from your reservation, Apache."

"Oh, I've been wanting to come here for a long time," Eskaminzim replied cheerfully. "I heard Cherokees are easy to sneak up on, and so far it's true!"

Walkingstick frowned.

"Your sister's the one who snuck up on me, remember?" he said. "I heard you coming a mile away."

Now Eskaminzim frowned.

Diehl cleared his throat.

"What 'suspicious activity' were you investigating, Captain?" he asked. "Maybe a large group of armed men riding out of the Cherokee Nation?"

Walkingstick didn't answer.

"No use being tight-lipped," Hoop said. "We already seen 'em."

"*Two* groups of them, in fact," Diehl added. "One coming down from Illinois, one just in from the west. From the Nations. I assume that's the one you were following…?"

Walkingstick eyed Diehl and Hoop a moment before answering.

"Yes," he said. "A couple of my men spotted them last night. I picked up their trail and caught up with them this morning."

Diehl smiled.

"Now we're getting somewhere," he said.

"And you were following the group from Illinois," Walkingstick went on. "Why?"

Pixley stiffened in his saddle.

"We don't have to answer that. Not for a tribal policeman off his reservation," he snapped. Then he sank down again and gave Walkingstick an apologetic look. "No offense."

"I don't come from a reservation," Walkingstick replied stiffly. "It's a sovereign nation."

"For now," Diehl said. He flapped his hand as if waving away an unpleasant odor. "But let's not get into politics. I'm still struck by an officer of your rank, *Captain*, operating by himself miles outside his *nation*. It makes me think one of those riders your men spotted was recognized. Maybe was someone notable…? Someone who'd make this a particularly sensitive situation…?"

"Of course it's a sensitive situation," Walkingstick said. "When we've got outlaws like Blaze Bad Water striking out into the States from the Nations, it's a black eye for all the tribes. Not to get into politics, *Mr.* Diehl, but that gives the whites another excuse to chip away at our sovereignty. So if the Cherokee Lighthorse spots a party of armed men crossing over into Missouri, yes—we're going to investigate. As quietly as we can."

Diehl leaned back in his saddle, nodding. "I see. Very… plausible."

He looked over at Hoop.

Hoop met his gaze.

They'd both noticed the same thing. Walkingstick had sidestepped Diehl's real question.

"Does it ever annoy you how they look at each other like that all the time?" Onawa asked her brother.

"Constantly," Eskaminzim said.

"So…what's in the wagon?" said Walkingstick.

Again, Pixley stiffened, but he managed to stay quiet this time.

"Ah. You saw that," said Diehl. "Well, that means you saw the writing on the side."

Walkingstick scoffed. "You're telling me it's full of ice cream?"

"I hope so!" Eskaminzim said.

"It's private property, Captain," said Diehl. "We're here to retrieve it. As quietly as *we* can. You understand?"

Walkingstick nodded somberly, understanding but not liking it.

"What's going on?" Onawa asked in Mescalero Apache. "What does all this talk mean?"

"It's just the usual," Eskaminzim replied in their language. "He's not telling us everything, and we're not telling him everything, and he knows it, and we know it."

"Quiet," Hoop said—also in their dialect. He jerked his chin at Walkingstick. "How do you know he doesn't speak Mescalero?"

"Good point," said Onawa.

But Eskaminzim looked at Walkingstick and scowled. "I don't know. I bet he can barely speak Cherokee."

He did go quiet after that, though. For a moment.

Walkingstick remained focused on Diehl.

"Remember—if you go into the Indian Territories, you'll be the ones with no authority," he said. "Whatever you're after, I suggest you leave it to the Cherokee Lighthorse."

Diehl leaned to the side to peer past Walkingstick, then looked up and down the road, furrowing his brow in mock confusion when he saw that no one else there.

"Oh," he said, smiling. "You mean *you*. No, I think we'll carry on. But thanks for the offer."

He turned to fix a steady gaze on Eskaminzim.

"You and your sister don't like it when I look at Hoop. Fine," he said, still staring intently. "Now I'm looking at *you*. What does it mean?"

"That's easy," Eskaminzim said. "You're thinking, 'Why am I always looking at Hoop when I could be looking at this amazing Apache? He's the most handsome man I've ever seen. Why was the Creator so kind to him and so cruel to me?'"

"Nope," Diehl said. He shifted his gaze to Onawa. "You wanna try?"

"You want us to find the trail of the two Cherokees who split off," she said. "If they'd sent off one, that might just be a messenger. But two is something different. Someone will have to follow them."

Diehl's eyebrows shot up.

"I should've looked at you first," he said.

"It was obvious," Onawa said dismissively.

She walked off down the road, heading back to the spot where the two riders had entered the woods.

Eskaminzim was grumbling in Mescalero as he followed her.

"Did *you* see the two men who went off on their own?" Diehl asked Walkingstick.

Walkingstick shook his head. "No. I must've just missed them leaving."

"Ah. Unfortunate," Diehl said. "I have a feeling one of them is the leader. A man the others call 'Major.' Any idea who that might be?"

There was a pause before Walkingstick shook his head and said, "No." Not even two full seconds of frozen shock. But Diehl and Hoop saw it.

They resisted the impulse to look at each other.

"That's too bad," Diehl told Walkingstick. "If you want to avoid more black eyes for the Cherokee Nation, I suspect he's the man to find. Who knows? Maybe we'll even find him together."

He gave Walkingstick another smile.

Walkingstick didn't smile back.

CHAPTER 18

United States Senator Samuel Cleburne stepped down onto the platform at the train station, cane in hand, took three steps forward, and planted himself in a pose he had much practice with. His head was high, his back straight, his gaze focused on the horizon as if locking onto a bright future only he could bring about. He was actually looking at the brick buildings and crisscrossing telephone wires and muddy, dung-pocked streets of Joplin, Missouri, which weren't quite as inspiring. But he managed to look like a man facing Destiny all the same.

He waited, unmoving, as if modeling for a portrait or a marble statue, and indeed he had practice posing for both. Then what he was waiting for happened. The inevitable.

He was recognized.

A man who'd stepped off the train further up, toward the engine —second class—turned his way and widened his eyes and smiled. He extended his hand and pivoted toward the old senator.

Cleburne turned to shake the man's hand and graciously accept his words of admiration and thanks.

The man swept past, stepping up instead to the couple exiting the train behind the senator—his daughter Una and her husband, Garland Dockery.

"Mr. Dockery!" the man said. "Why, how are ya?"

Dockery smiled stiffly and accepted the man's hand. "Fine, Bob, fine. And you?"

"Bob" grinned as he pumped Dockery's hand. He was a wiry little man in a checked suit that had seen better days, and hadn't been particularly well made even then.

"Oh, I'm stayin' out of trouble," he said. He released Dockery's hand and jerked his head at Una. "This the missus?"

Dockery nodded. He didn't make introductions, though.

Una smiled politely and didn't encourage conversation either.

Bob didn't seem to mind. He kept grinning as he tipped his dented bowler to Una and gave her a little bow.

"Ma'am, your husband is the best lawyer in Fort Smith. The best in Arkansas. The best in the business! If not for him…well."

Bob chuckled and shrugged.

"Just wanted to shake your hand one more time," he said to Dockery. "Y'all enjoy your visit to Joplin now."

He bowed again and started to turn away. He froze when he saw the senator watching them. Recognition dawned on his face…then quickly faded again.

"Ha!" he blared at the old man. "You look just like somebody famous, grandpa!"

And he carried on into the crowd leaving the platform.

Cleburne looked at Dockery and raised an eyebrow.

"Former client," Dockery said.

"Well, that's obvious," said Una. She leaned closer to her husband and dropped her voice. "What did he do?"

"Murdered his wife," Dockery said blandly.

Una looked shocked but delighted. Then she burst out laughing.

"Oh, you're awful," she said, swatting at her husband's chest.

He didn't deny it. He also didn't seem to be joking.

Someone behind Cleburne cleared his throat, and the senator turned to find a stout man in his midfifties standing behind him. The man's suit was well-tailored, his gaze worshipful.

This was more like it.

"Senator Cleburne...welcome to Joplin," the man said. "Under normal circumstances, I'd have a band here to welcome you. But I know this visit is different."

He reached out his pudgy hand, and as the men shook Cleburne felt a gliding tickle across his wrist.

The secret handshake!

Cleburne had invented it, yet he'd rarely been on the receiving end of one. It was thrilling.

He returned the sign, running the tip of his index finger back and forth over the other man's wrist. Symbol of an oath of loyalty sealed with one's very life blood.

The man nodded grimly as the handshake ended.

"You're Arthur Bewley, then?" Cleburne said.

The man nodded. "We meet face to face at last, Senator. I was so excited I couldn't wait for you at the hotel." He looked past Cleburne at Una and Dockery watching from a few steps away. "You brought guests?"

He looked troubled by the idea.

"My daughter Una and my son-in-law, Garland Dockery," said Cleburne. "Garland's one of us. And Una—"

"Just think of me as a member of the women's auxiliary, Mr. Bewley," Una said cheerfully. "I might not be eligible for membership in the Golden Order of the Knights of Keziah, but surely the daughters of Dixie have the right—indeed the obligation—to serve its cause as much as the sons."

"Hear, hear," her husband said.

Bewley didn't look any less troubled.

"*Now,*" said Cleburne firmly, signaling that the matter was settled, "has our special guest arrived?"

"Not yet," said Bewley.

Cleburne patted him on the shoulder. "Well, don't you fret, Arthur. He's close, I know it. And when he gets here, we'll give him the reception he so richly deserves."

Bewley smiled and nodded, but not with the enthusiasm Cleburne wanted. So the senator patted the man again and gave him some more encouragement: the motto of the Golden Order of the Knights of Keziah. Like the handshake, it had been Cleburne's creation, though it was inspired by an ancient phrase.

"*Ubi jus, ibi remedium.*"

Where there is right, there is a remedy.

There's nothing like a little Latin to make people feel they're a part of something big, Cleburne knew. Sort of like *E pluribus unum*— though that was a sentiment the Knights of Keziah had vowed to prove wrong.

Bewley gave the senator another faint smile.

"Indeed," he said. "I have my surrey waiting if you'd like to have a porter bring your things."

Cleburne nodded and was about to turn to the side to make the familiar train station call—"Boy! *Boy!*"—when another departing passenger stopped to stare at them.

"Well, here's a picture for the papers!" the man said. He'd stepped from first class, like the senator and his party, and his impeccable gray frock coat and glittering diamond stickpin said he belonged there. "Our own Mayor Bewley with Senator Samuel Cleburne of Mississippi. What brings you to Missouri, Senator?"

Bewley looked horrified by the interruption—and the recognition—but Cleburne didn't even blink.

"Oh, a little business, a little pleasure," he replied smoothly.

"Well, it's an honor to have you here," the man told him. "No one's done as much for the Southland as you."

He looked like he was about to go on, perhaps listing Cleburne's accomplishments in the Senate and, prior to that, on the battlefield. But before he could continue, Una slid in front of him and hooked her father with one arm and the mayor of Joplin with the other.

"Thank you, sir—you don't know the half of it!" she called back cheerfully as she steered the men away. "And the best is yet to come!"

———

When Eskaminzim and Onawa returned and reported (Eskaminzim doing most of the reporting before his sister could) that the two Cherokees who'd broken off from the main party were angling off in a more or less straight line southwest through the woods, Diehl turned to Capt. Walkingstick.

"If I'm remembering my map correctly, that'd take them straight to Joplin," he said.

"Could be," Walkingstick replied.

"Definitely," said Hoop.

Pixley had been antsy as they waited for Eskaminzim and Onawa to come back—so fidgety Diehl asked him if he needed to get off his horse and go water the shrubbery. Now he pointed a shaking finger westward.

"It's the wagon that matters," he said. "We're letting it get away."

Diehl gave that a casual shrug. "I think those other two men matter, too. Quite a boom town these days, Joplin. Mining, railroads, and the like. Strange place for a couple Cherokees on the run to go to lay low or get help."

He looked at Walkingstick again.

"Maybe," Walkingstick replied.

"Definitely," said Hoop.

Diehl drummed his fingers on his saddle horn. "Joplin, Joplin, Joplin. You know, I've had a bit of a hankering to see Joplin."

"What are you talking about?" said Pixley.

"Joplin!" Eskaminzim explained helpfully.

"I mean…what are you proposing?" Pixley asked Diehl.

"Joplin," Diehl said. "For me, anyway. The rest of you should stick with the wagon, but I want to see if I can get some answers before we make our next move. Maybe even find out who this 'Major' is and what he's up to. Of course, I can't tell *you* which way to go, Captain. But I have a feeling you'd like to know more on that score, too…?"

Once again, he turned to look at Walkingstick.

So did Hoop, then Eskaminzim, then Onawa, then Pixley.

Walkingstick seemed to be gritting his teeth.

"I'll go with you," he told Diehl.

Diehl smiled.

"I'll be grateful for the company," he said—though he didn't know if Walkingstick wanted the same answers he did or just didn't want Diehl to get them.

CHAPTER 19

The lanky old Cherokee moved out of the trees, his horse moving slow. He stopped in the middle of the road and looked north, then south. He saw no one, though the city was so close now he could smell it.

Chimney smoke and shit. "Civilization."

He turned back toward the woods and nodded.

The major rode out of the shadows to join him.

The old Cherokee in the road—Ned Hatchet was his name—cocked his head, listened, eyed the forest they'd just left, listened some more.

Still nothing. But that didn't mean the Yankees, or whoever they were, weren't behind them.

The major didn't do any looking around himself. His gaze was steady, first on Hatchet, then on the road south.

That's how you get to be the major, Hatchet figured. The leader. That faith and focus. Most men don't have it. They're jumpy, nervous, uncertain. And they'll follow someone who isn't those things no matter where he might go.

"Turkey Creek's a couple miles south," Hatchet said as the major reined up beside him. "Past that, and you're in Joplin."

"Excellent," the major replied in his deep, rumbling voice. "Thank you, Lieutenant."

Hatchet nodded again and tried not to show how pleased he was.

He'd been picked to go with the major because he knew the area well—had spent years sneaking back and forth from Tahlequah to Joplin and back with beer from the Bavarian breweries and bourbon down from Kentucky. Not that he was a bootlegger. He just loved good booze.

He hadn't touched a drop in two weeks, though. Not since the major had called him back to duty after all these years.

It had been a long time since anyone called him "Lieutenant." He'd missed it.

"This is where we part ways," the major said. He patted his saddlebag—the one with the heavy brass plaque he'd brought out of the wagon and wrapped in a blanket. "You know how important it is that this get to Joplin."

"I know, sir. No one's going to stop you. I'll see to that."

Hatchet thought of the future the major was riding toward—the one he himself probably wouldn't see.

"It'll be an honor," he added.

The major eyed him gravely, then slowly lifted his right hand until it touched the brim of his gray fedora.

Hatchet returned the salute, and the two men held the pose a moment, looking into each other's eyes. Then the major lowered his hand and turned his horse and trotted off down the road without another word.

Hatchet watched him go, then went back to scanning the road, the trees, the low hills. Picking his place to die.

It would have to be a good place.

He intended to die with as much company as possible.

CHAPTER 20

"Ambushes ambushes ambushes," Pixley fumed. "Just trotting along waiting for the next ambush. It's intolerable."

He was on his horse with Hoop to his left, Eskaminzim and Onawa to his right.

They were trotting along waiting for the next ambush. Though Hoop was of the opinion there wouldn't be one. Not now anyway. Not while they we were still on the east–west road from Carthage to the Missouri border. They were just past the turnoff south for Joplin, and there were other travelers in sight—a farmer and his boy driving pigs to market behind them, a dinky peddler's wagon and a big dray hauling lumber up ahead.

"You just have to get used to it," Eskaminzim told Pixley. "I grew up always waiting for the next ambush. Mexicans, whites, Comanches, Navajo, Utes—you never knew who was going to jump out and try to kill you."

"Or capture you," Onawa added.

She said it in a seething, snarling way that suggested there was much more she could add if she wanted to. And she didn't want to.

Eskaminzim forced out a laugh.

"Bears, wolves, cougars, jaguars—we had to watch out for

them, too," he said, hurrying the conversation past his sister's memories. "Nobody can ambush like a cougar. You think you're all alone, then…" He slapped his hands together. "She bounces!"

Pixley furrowed his brow in confusion.

"Pounces," Hoop corrected.

"Bounce, pounce, flounce, whatever," Eskaminzim said. "When the cougar does it, you don't have time to figure out the right word for it."

"I'm sorry I brought it up," Pixley muttered.

"Don't be! So you're scared about another ambush. It's good for us to know."

"I didn't say I was *scared*," Pixley objected. "I'm frustrated."

"Eskaminzim…" Hoop growled.

The "shut up" that went with it was implied.

"I know what will help you feel better," Eskaminzim said to Pixley anyway. "I'll check ahead to make sure no more Cherokees have left the road."

He leaned forward, about to give his horse his heels and escape the awkward conversation he was making infinitely worse.

"No!" Hoop snapped. "We stick together for now."

"But why?" Eskaminzim whined, straightening up again.

"You know why."

The looks they'd gotten from some of the whites they'd passed had been less than friendly. Diehl had given Eskaminzim and Onawa's reservation pass to Hoop to hold, but there was no guarantee the right paperwork, even signed by a former head of the Secret Service, would head off trouble.

Armed Apaches on a major Missouri road with a Black man and a Yankee? There was more to worry about than ambushes.

"The time to get off the road and set traps of our own—it'll come," Hoop said. "But when you're outnumbered three to one you gotta be careful about the when, where, and how."

Pixley stifled a sigh and swiveled in his saddle for a long look behind them, at the turn for Joplin.

"He misses *Ba*," Eskaminzim said to his sister, using their

Mescalero nickname for Diehl. The Coyote. "Who is to recite poems and tell reassuring lies now?"

"You could try," Onawa suggested in Apache.

Eskaminzim nodded, then leaned toward Pixley and stretched out his arm.

"Don't worry," he said, patting Pixley's hand as he'd seen whites do. "It will all work out fine in the end. It always does."

He gazed deeply into Pixley's eyes…then burst out laughing.

"No! I can't do it!" he said. "This is why we need Diehl! For bullshit!"

Pixley took a deep breath, then turned for another long, unhappy look back the way they'd come.

He did miss Diehl…even if the man was full of bullshit.

———

"'So here am I,'" Diehl recited. "'Bewildered in the forest, and, what's more, in what wild skirt which bears an evil fame. Yet what care I? Evil can touch me not!'"

He looked over at Capt. Henry Walkingstick expectantly.

This was an important moment. Probably the man's first exposure to the poetry of the great Charles Swain. (This was from "Dramatic Chapters," Chapter VIII.) What would Walkingstick say?

For the moment, the Cherokee lawman said nothing—just kept riding slowly through the woods, eyes fixed on the trail they were following. The ground was still moist from the melting of the winter snows, so it had been easy to follow the path. The men up ahead hadn't tried any tricks to thwart their pursuers. Yet.

Walkingstick and Diehl parted as they rounded a particularly large oak.

When they came back together on the other side, Diehl went back to watching Walkingstick.

"What is that from…the Bible?" men often asked after their first dose of Swain.

Or, "That something outta Shakespeare?"

Or, most frequently, "You sure do talk weird, Diehl."

Yet Walkingstick seemed content to go on saying nothing at all. He just grunted out an "Mm-hmm," as if Diehl had merely made an obvious comment about the weather, and continued to watch the forest floor glide by.

Well, his loss if he didn't want to discuss poetry. Diehl would make the man talk business.

"I really am bewildered in the forest," Diehl said. "I'm still trying to figure out why you'd head deeper into Missouri trailing who-knows-who when the rest of that gang is headed right back into your jurisdiction."

Walkingstick finally met Diehl's gaze.

"That wagon can only move so fast," he said. "I can catch up with it later. In the Indian Territories. For now, it's like you said to your friends. I want to know how Joplin plays into this. If someone there is messing around with Cherokees, stirring something up that'll cause trouble for the Cherokee Nation, it's my job to find out. And stop it."

Diehl nodded, impressed.

"That," he said, "was actually an excellent response. Totally logical. And here I thought maybe I couldn't trust you."

Walkingstick let his surprise show on his face. Not at the idea that Diehl wouldn't trust him. More that Diehl was saying it out loud.

"Only," Diehl went on, "there's still the matter of 'the major.'"

"I told you I don't know him," Walkingstick said sharply.

"But do you know *of* him?"

"I have no idea without a name. There are lots of old Cherokee 'majors.' And whoever it is might not be a Cherokee at all—just a man working with some. Or your friends misheard them. Maybe they said 'Frazier.' Or 'Baker.' Or 'Mayer.'"

Diehl shook his head. "Two of us heard it. Onawa and Pixley. They agree. 'Major.'" He cocked his head and narrowed his eyes. "Are there really that many old Cherokee majors still running around? I wouldn't think so. Old privates, corporals, sergeants— maybe. But officers? Up that high…?"

Walkingstick shrugged. "There were Cherokees on both sides of the rebellion. That means twice as many officers. And like I said—you don't know this 'major' is a Cherokee at all."

"No, I suppose not. He was just leading a bunch of Cherokees. Headed to the Cherokee Nation. I shouldn't jump to the wild conclusion that he's a Cherokee, too. Maybe he's Choctaw. Maybe he's from Rhode Island. Maybe he's French."

"Maybe," Walkingstick growled, his gaze returning to the trail through the forest.

Diehl let out a rueful little chuckle.

"'How, like a broken reed, all worldly trust departs!'" he said. "'There is no hope for earthly need, no rest for weary hearts...'"

"What the hell does that mean?" Walkingstick muttered.

"That I'm *trying* to trust you, Captain. But you're still making it hard."

"And *I* should trust *you*?"

"Touché!" Diehl laughed. "Absolutely not!"

Walkingstick looked over at Diehl in surprise again. And confusion.

He was trying to figure Diehl out. And not succeeding.

"So you work for a detective agency, huh?" Walkingstick said.

Diehl nodded. "The A.A. Western Detective Agency out of Ogden, Utah."

"Never heard of it."

"We're new. And not big. What you might call a boutique operation. Specialized."

Walkingstick threw Diehl a little frown at the words "boutique operation." "Boutiques" of any kind didn't come up much—or ever —in his line of work.

"Specializing in what?" he asked.

"It depends on the operative. A couple of our men are building a reputation for...oh...untangling webs of deceit, you could say. Uncovering skullduggery. Consulting detective stuff. But me and Hoop and Eskaminzim, we—"

Diehl stopped himself, chagrined.

"And Onawa," he added. "Our line is...trouble."

Walkingstick waited for more explanation. It didn't come.

"That doesn't sound very specialized," he said.

"Our way of dealing with it is," said Diehl.

And once again he offered no further explanation beyond a tight smile.

"How about men with bounties on their heads?" Walkingstick asked him. "That the kind of trouble you're talking about?"

"Sometimes. You heard about the Give-'em-Hell Boys getting busted up out in California, didn't you?"

"Yeah, I saw that in the papers," Walkingstick said.

Diehl shook his head in mock disappointment. "And you say you've never heard of the A.A. Western Detective Agency."

"My, my...that is impressive," Walkingstick said, though he didn't look like he entirely believed it. "I don't know what you're getting paid for the wild goose chase with that wagon, but if you can take down the Give-'em-Hell Boys, there's something a lot more rewarding you could be doing around here."

"Let me guess. We should peel off and hunt Blaze Bad Water and his gang. Or maybe Bill Doolin and the Wild Bunch...?"

"Right the first time. Doolin and his boys are way over in the panhandle. No-man's-land. Not a Cherokee problem. But Blaze Bad Water—he's a pain in *my* ass. Add up all the bounties on him, and he's worth nearly five-thousand dollars. And when you throw in his pals—Gerty Wormwood, Nathaniel Pumpkin, and the rest—the payday's nearly ten."

Diehl rubbed his jaw. "Tempting. But if we go after Bad Water aren't we just trading one wild goose chase for another?"

"I've got names," Walkingstick said. "Farmers who let the gang hide out on their land for a cut. Some of 'em are just over the northern border, so I can't touch 'em. Kansas whites, you know? But you could...apply more pressure. Get one to help you set a trap. Bad Water's a nasty piece of work, but I get the feeling you and your friends could handle him."

"We're nasty pieces of work ourselves," Diehl said. "All right—you talked me into it."

Walkingstick's eyebrows shot up. "Really?"

"Absolutely," Diehl said. "We'll head out after Blaze Bad Water and his gang...*after* I figure out who 'the major' is and we get Pixley's property back."

Walkingstick's eyebrows dived downward into a glower.

"Now, who would these farmers be that we should look up," Diehl went on, "and how come you haven't told the US marshals about them?"

"I'll tell you later," Walkingstick grumbled.

He jerked his chin forward.

A gap in the forest was visible about a hundred yards ahead—a long clearing that stretched from north to south. They were too far off to see the ruts and manure that would run along it, but it was clear what it was.

The road to Joplin.

Diehl reined up. Walkingstick did the same.

"We keep following this straight to the road," Diehl said, pointing down at the trail through the woods, "we may as well put bull's-eyes on our chests when we ride out into the open."

Walkingstick nodded. "So we don't go straight to the road. We know which way they'll turn." He swiveled in his saddle to look southward. "We can turn that way now and—"

A shot rang out, the bullet slicing leaves and twigs from half a dozen trees as it tore through the forest.

Both Walkingstick and Diehl flew from their saddles—but only Diehl was screaming when he hit the ground.

The screaming didn't last long.

CHAPTER 21

Ned Hatchet cursed under his breath as he squinted down the smoking barrel of his Spencer carbine.

He was close. *So close!* But not close enough for this to be easy.

He knew the men who'd been trailing him and the major wouldn't just ride out onto the road when they reached it. The bastards had ambushed the Cherokees' ambush yesterday. Killed four of Hatchet's old comrades. Old men, yes. But old *soldiers*. Tough old bastards. Like Ned Hatchet.

Back in the day, Hatchet and his friends had killed Yankee soldiers and Jayhawkers and unionist Cherokees, Choctaws, and Creeks by the score. Their bodies might weaken with age, but their skills would remain. Their experience and instincts. So whoever had slaughtered Young Duck, Jesse Crump, Falling Pot, and Mink Winkleside atop that ravine, they weren't idiots.

Which is why Hatchet had picked a spot for his ambush *before* the trail through the trees reached the road. Where he figured the men would stop and pivot due south and keep on toward Joplin in what they'd think was the safety of the woods.

Only the spot he'd chosen—a dip in the forest floor by the trunk of a tilting elm—was too close to the road. He wanted the men to ride up another fifty yards before turning south, then move past his hiding spot. Show him their backs long enough for him to spring up and put two shots in them from his Spencer, if his aging knees could still manage a spring.

Instead the men had stopped a hundred yards from the road—well within range of the carbine, but far enough away to remain blurs to his myopic sixty-year-old eyes. And with so many trees in the way, Hatchet was as likely to shoot a branch or a passing squirrel as one of his targets. If he let them turn south, though, he'd have to hurry off and collect his horse from the other side of the road and try to catch up or even get past the men without being noticed. Perhaps not impossible, but certainly not likely.

So Ned Hatchet's moment had come, yet—as was so often the case in war—it was far from perfect. So be it. He'd make the most of it.

He'd sighted carefully down the barrel, aiming at the blur that somehow said to him "Cherokee Lighthorse," and pulled the trigger. But it was the other figure—the one that somehow said "white"—that had pitched sideways from the saddle screaming.

The Cherokee policeman, if that's actually what he was, had gone rolling off his horse, as well. Too quickly for Hatchet to lever in another round and get off a careful shot. So he kneeled there waiting, aiming, cursing. Hoping the Cherokee would be fool enough to pop his head up for a look as the horses trotted off and the White's screams quickly faded to choking gurgles then silence.

But no. The Cherokee wasn't a fool. He stayed down.

Hatchet cursed one more time, then lowered the Spencer and began sliding to his left, away from the telltale rifle smoke drifting off through the trees.

The Cherokee would expect that. Assume Hatchet would shift position and try for another shot from a different angle. So Hatchet left the heavy carbine propped against the elm tree and pulled out another weapon—the one tucked in his belt.

"Hatchet" was an old family name, not one he'd earned. But you spend four years fighting alongside rebel Cherokees, Choctaws, and Seminoles with a name like "Ned Hatchet," and you're going to encounter a lot of presumptions and expectations. So Hatchet had learned to live up to them.

He'd never gotten out of practice either, though for the last thirty years the most he'd done with his hatchet—his Cherokee tomahawk with its gleaming steel blade and long, intricately carved hickory handle—was show off for his children and grandchildren.

"You wanna see what ol' Pap would do during the war when he caught him a Pin Indian or a Kansas Red Leg?" he'd say. And when the kids nodded he'd turn and send his hatchet whirling end over end until—*thunk*—the blade buried itself square in the center of a fence post not five inches wide. And the children would cheer.

There was no one to cheer now when that blade thunked into a Cherokee lawman. Hatchet certainly wouldn't. He *liked* the Cherokee Lighthorse. They were symbols of his people's independence.

But what he liked and didn't like didn't matter. This was war. There would be casualties.

Hunched, silent, Hatchet crept through the underbrush, his tomahawk ready to make one more.

———

Walkingstick crawled to Diehl's side, trying to see where the man had been shot. It sounded like it was too late to do anything about the wound, though. Diehl had been very loud, then very quiet.

"Diehl...where were you hit?" Walkingstick said.

Diehl was lying flat on his back, eyes pointed up at the little window of white clouds visible through the treetops above.

"Shh. Don't talk to me," he said. "I'm dead."

He lifted up the left side of his sheepskin coat. There were two holes in it where a bullet had punched in then out.

There were no bloodstains.

Walkingstick let his head droop with both relief and exasperation.

Diehl rolled over.

"Give me half a minute to put some distance between us," he whispered. "Then start talking to *him*."

Walkingstick lifted his head. There was a scowl on his face.

"You want me to talk to whoever's trying to kill us?" he said. "So you've got a distraction while you get away?"

"Something like that," Diehl said.

He reached down to the gun belt at his side, flicked back the thumb break on the holster, and slid out his Colt forty-five.

He and Walkingstick locked eyes.

Walkingstick nodded.

Diehl began slithering away.

It fit, Walkingstick thought as he watched the other man leave. Diehl gliding along the ground on his belly like that. The man was a snake.

Would he keep his silent promise—the one he'd made by pulling out his gun? Or would he wriggle off to a safe distance, collect one of the horses, and flee?

Walkingstick was about to find out.

He pulled out his own gun—a Smith & Wesson Model No. 3—and gave Diehl the time he'd asked for. Then he spoke.

"This is Captain Henry Walkingstick of the Cherokee Lighthorse Mounted Police," he said, "and you are in a *lot* of trouble, mister!"

———

Diehl listened to Walkingstick's words echo through the forest. They got no response, of course. The man who'd shot at them still had the advantage: rifle versus sidearms. He'd be looking to pick Walkingstick off from a distance.

It was Walkingstick's job to let him think he could. He was doing it well, too.

There was a rustle back where Walkingstick and Diehl had come off their horses—what would seem like sloppy, panicked movement in the underbrush. And when Walkingstick spoke again, he sounded breathy and blustery, like a trapped man bluffing for all he was worth.

"Are you a Cherokee? An Indian? Well, you've just killed a White man in the state of Missouri! That doesn't have to mean your neck, though! Surrender to me, and I'll do what I can for you, I promise!"

Diehl slithered on, hoping the man with the rifle would pop off another shot and reveal exactly where he was now.

It didn't happen. Still, Diehl figured he could get close enough. The man would have shifted north or south, parallel to the road, but probably wouldn't risk getting any nearer to Walkingstick. Why give up his advantage?

Diehl wriggled around a fallen tree—and suddenly found himself facing something other than the fern fronds and leaves he'd been moving through.

He was facing a face. Not just facing it but practically nose to nose with it.

A copper-skinned man in sun-faded but tidy clothes, bent over double, was creeping around the same log. He was older than Diehl —maybe sixty to Diehl's forty—but he looked fit enough, with a lean strength showing in his flat belly and sinewy neck and large hands.

Diehl's eyes went wide…then went wider when he saw what one of those hands held.

A tomahawk.

Diehl had served in the Tenth Cavalry for years. Had fought Apache, Comanche, Cheyenne, Nez Percé, and Ute. Come close to death from rifles, pistols, arrows, knives, lances, clubs, and even slingshots. Yet never—not once—had he seen an Indian brandishing a tomahawk.

He said what one says when encountering someone or something new.

"Hello."

"Hello," said the Cherokee, who looked as surprised as Diehl.

Then the man set his jaw and tightened his grip on his tomahawk, and Diehl knew what was coming next.

Diehl's Colt had been angled off to the side as he crawled through the woods, but now he tried to swivel it straight, toward the Cherokee. The other man saw the move and—rather than split Diehl's head open, which had seemed to be his first impulse—instinctively swept his tomahawk down in an arc that knocked the gun away.

The edge of the blade caught the gun on the barrel, just in front of the cylinder. As it swooped up, it not only sent the Colt cartwheeling away, it sliced through the edge of Diehl's hand.

Diehl yelped but didn't let the shock and pain keep him from rolling hard to his right. He hoped to stop with the gun in his hand again, but there was no time to flail around for it. The Cherokee was bringing up his tomahawk as if he meant to throw it, and Diehl felt the forty-five go under his back as he frantically rolled on through the forest scrub.

"Damn it!" Diehl spat, and rather than his gun, he snatched up the only thing he could—a chunk of crumbly, moss-covered wood from a rotting branch on the ground nearby. Diehl hurled it at the Cherokee, then reversed course, rolling to his left now. Back toward the gun.

The hunk of wood bounced harmlessly off the Cherokee's left shoulder. But it caused him to flinch and lower his tomahawk.

This was Diehl's chance. His last one.

He groped wildly for his Colt, smearing the leaves around him with blood. By the time he felt the smooth walnut grip of the gun, it was too late. The Cherokee had reset his stance and raised his tomahawk.

Diehl brought up his left hand to ward off the axe, though he knew it was useless. Either it would spin right past into his forehead, or his hand would indeed stop it—and he'd find himself with a steel blade buried in his hand up to the wrist.

"Wait!" Diehl cried.

It was just one of those things someone about to die says, though. He had no idea what he might say next. Maybe "Please!" That was pretty standard for these situations.

The Cherokee didn't wait. He whipped his arm forward—then stumbled mid throw as a gunshot roared out behind him.

The tomahawk *kachunk*ed into the earth a foot from Diehl's face.

The Cherokee dropped to his knees, stared into Diehl's eyes mournfully, then pitched forward.

Twenty yards beyond him, Diehl could see now, was Walkingstick, his Smith & Wesson smoking in his hand.

"You all right?" Walkingstick said.

"I don't know," said Diehl. "Ask me again in a minute."

He wasn't joking. He'd been in enough fights to the death to know a man can receive a mortal wound and go on fighting like a wildcat without even feeling it. By the time he noticed, all he could do was say, "Oh no," then he'd swoon, and it would all be over.

Diehl sat up, Colt pointed at the fallen Cherokee, and quickly examined himself as he replayed the fight in his mind.

A cut on his hand, mud, leaves, scrapes, more mud—that was all he saw.

Diehl took a deep breath. He was fine.

The other man wasn't. He wasn't dead, though. Not yet. Diehl could see his bloodied back—with its new hole dead center—heaving up and down as he struggled for his last breaths.

"Who are you?" Diehl asked as Walkingstick came toward them.

"Who?" the man wheezed. "Me?"

"Yes. You," said Diehl. "You'll want us to get you to your people, won't you? So you can be buried on your land?"

The Cherokee grunted, then coughed.

He'd been trying to laugh.

He turned his head and lifted it up, wincing in pain, to look at Diehl.

"My land?" he said. "Like you care."

He slowly shifted his gaze to the man stepping up beside him—the man who'd killed him.

"*You* should care," he told Walkingstick. "If you did…you wouldn't have…shot me."

"I care different," Walkingstick said.

The dying man's lips trembled then strained forward, and a little blob of bloody froth dropped onto his chin.

He was trying to spit at Walkingstick's feet.

"Tell me about the major," Diehl said.

"I can't...feel my legs," the man said, his voice fading.

"Tell me about the major! Who is he? What is he doing?"

The man turned his head and let it sink down into the moist earth again, his eyes wide open. For a moment there was a muffled, whispery warbling. He was singing through his final ragged breaths.

Diehl assumed it was a Cherokee death song. Then he recognized the melody.

"Nearer, My God, to Thee."

Soon the singing stopped. Then the breathing.

Diehl sighed and looked up at Walkingstick. "Well? Know him?"

Walkingstick nodded. "I think so. Name of Hatchet."

Diehl raised his eyebrows and gaped at the tomahawk sticking out of the ground between him and the dead man.

"You're kidding," he said.

"No. There are a lot of Hatchets in the Delaware District."

"This one some kind of outlaw?"

Walkingstick shook his head. "Farmer."

"Farmer?" Diehl poked his gun at the tomahawk. "Funny-looking plow."

Walkingstick ignored that.

"It's been a minute," he said. "Are you all right?"

"Yeah, I'm fine," Diehl said. "Thanks."

Walkingstick holstered his Smith & Wesson.

Diehl pushed himself to his feet and turned to peer toward the road. There was no one there.

"Hopefully no one curious was close enough to hear that gunfire," he said. "We don't have time for explanations to the local sheriff."

He gave the Cherokee sprawled face down on the ground a rueful look.

"Hell, we don't have explanations at all." He shifted his gaze to Walkingstick. "Do we?"

Walkingstick held his gaze steadily.

"Nope," he said.

"All right, then." Diehl slid his Colt into its holster and began brushing the bark chips and dirt from his hands. "Let's see about getting some, shall we? This was just a rearguard action. What's important is up ahead. The other one...the major maybe...and whatever his business is in Joplin. Don't you think?"

"We'll see."

"That we shall."

Diehl moved to Hatchet's side and started going through the dead man's pockets. It didn't take long. There weren't many pockets, and there was nothing in them but a gnawed-on plug of tobacco and a dirty handkerchief.

"Well, that doesn't help us," Diehl said. He offered the tobacco to Walkingstick. "Unless you chew."

Walkingstick shook his head.

Diehl tossed the tobacco aside.

"No time to bury grandpa here," he said as he stood up again.

He peeked over at Walkingstick to see what he'd think of that.

"The forest will take care of it," Walkingstick said. "It's a shame about the tomahawk, though. It's beautiful."

And he turned and went striding off to catch the horses.

CHAPTER 22

The further west the Cherokees with the wagon went, the more traffic thinned out, until at last it was just them up ahead and Hoop, Onawa, Eskaminzim, and Pixley a mile behind. Around three o'clock, the Cherokees left the main east–west road for a narrower side lane that angled southwest into the forest.

"*Now* can I move ahead for a better look?" Eskaminzim asked.

It had been half an hour since they last passed a farm or mill or railroad tracks. There was no one around to ask unwanted questions. And no one to see what might happen next.

"Go ahead," said Hoop. "But remember—you're just looking. Don't engage."

"'Don't engage,'" Eskaminzim repeated, shaking his head. "You sound like Diehl."

He looked over at his sister.

"'Don't engage' means don't kill any of them even if they make it easy and we'll regret not doing it later," he explained.

"*Is* that what it means?" Onawa asked Hoop.

"Pretty much," he said.

Onawa nodded. "Fine. We won't 'engage' then."

She sent her horse bolting ahead before either Eskaminzim or Hoop could say, "We?"

"You know, just because four is a lucky number doesn't mean we have to bring *her* along next time," Eskaminzim said.

"'Next time?' 'After this is over'?" said Hoop. "I like your optimism."

Eskaminzim grinned. "It's what I'm famous for…among other things."

He shot off after Onawa. Within half a minute, they'd both disappeared around the next bend in the road.

Pixley swiveled for a long look behind him and Hoop. There was no one there.

It was the fiftieth time Pixley had looked back that day. Or maybe the sixtieth.

Hoop was tired of it. Tired enough, even, to keep talking.

"If you're worrying Diehl and Walkingstick won't know we headed this way, don't," he said. "That wagon leaves ruts a quarter inch deep. They'll see it. And anyway, if they're doing the same as us—hanging back and seeing where the trail leads before doing anything—they won't be back today anyway."

"Is that supposed to be comforting?" Pixley said. "Another day we'll do nothing? Another day we'll give those men to get away?"

Hoop grimaced.

This is what he got for talking.

"We'll see," he said.

"So we're going to camp out in the forest again tonight?" Pixley went on. "On the edge of Indian Territory? With a dozen enemies aware that we're here?"

Hoop took a quick look up, judging the color of the sky and the position of the sun. They still had three hours of good light left.

"We'll see," he said.

Pixley scowled at him.

Hoop braced himself for more.

"But what about—?" Pixley began.

The sound of gunfire cut him off.

It wasn't a booming blast. It was a single distant *pop*. From up ahead.

It was quickly followed by more. *Pop-pop…pop-pop…pop.*

"They must have sent some of their men back after us!" Pixley said. "Onawa and Eskaminzim ran into them!"

Hoop cocked his head, listening intently.

The gunfire was already over.

"Well?" Pixley said. He was sitting up straight, gripping his reins, feet out a bit to the sides, heels poised to jab into his horse's belly. "Aren't we going to go up and help?"

"Naw," said Hoop.

"No?"

Hoop shook his head. "No need. Too distant. A mile, I bet. Onawa and Eskaminzim wouldn't be up that far yet."

"What could it be then?"

"Ain't no fight," Hoop said. "More likely a celebration."

"A celebration? Of what?"

Hoop lifted his left hand and circled it in the air.

Pixley looked around. There was nothing notable about where they were. The terrain—low, rolling hills, green-leafed trees, flowering bushes, distant bluffs—was the same they'd been riding through for days.

Hoop saw that the confusion wasn't leaving Pixley's face. He'd have to use more words.

It was getting exhausting.

"This ain't the edge of Indian Territory anymore," he said. "This is it."

"Really? So they've left Missouri? *We're* leaving Missouri?"

Pixley looked around again as if he expected to see a sign reading "WELCOME TO THE CHEROKEE NATION."

"There won't be no big black line dividing this from that. This ain't no map," Hoop told him. "And we ain't in the United States anymore, strictly speaking. That's why they're so happy up there."

Pixley settled back in his saddle. The bewilderment and alarm faded from his face.

Apprehension and aggravation returned.

"Because now we're on Indian ground," he said.

Hoop didn't reply. He was tired of talking. And Pixley was right anyway.

Onawa and Eskaminzim had ridden separately for a time—her scouting the woods on one side of the road, him on the other—but when they heard the gunfire they came back together in the middle.

Onawa jerked her chin at the road ahead.

"They're home," she said. "The Indian Territories."

"I knew we were close," said Eskaminzim. He sucked in two big sniffs. "It doesn't smell like White man's land anymore, and the Earth here is happy."

Onawa turned toward her brother. She'd known him her whole life, of course, yet she'd learned a lot about him lately. Like that he hadn't been joking when he talked about how much he loved risk and conflict. And that he *had* been joking about almost everything else.

Like most Mescalero Apache women, Onawa prided herself on her chasteness, propriety, and dignity. But spending so much time around her brother and her husband and Diehl, it was hard not to pick up bad habits.

She used an English phrase she'd heard Eskaminzim bandying about earlier that day.

"Bullshit."

"You mean you can't smell it?" Eskaminzim said. "The difference in the air?"

Onawa took a tentative, testing whiff.

The air *was* different. Cleaner. Earthier. Without the undertone of smoke and chemicals and feces that had swirled around them as they'd moved past Joplin.

"All right. I see what you mean about the smell," she said. "But as for the Earth here being happy—"

"Wherever I go, the Earth is happy," Eskaminzim cut in. "I always plant fresh new men in it. Such rich soil they make. After dark, I'll make some new land for the Cherokees." Eskaminzim smiled. "*With* some Cherokees."

"You'll have to talk Hoop into that."

"No, I won't. The fight isn't going to wait until Diehl thinks the time is right. Not now that we're here, on their land. Whether it's them coming after us or—if we're smart—us going after them, it's going to happen. Tonight."

Onawa eyed her brother silently for a moment. He was still smiling, amused, excited. But this was no joke. No bullshit. He believed it.

So Onawa did, too—though she knew it was nothing to smile about.

CHAPTER 23

Diehl and Walkingstick were in a hurry, but they took the time to look for Ned Hatchet's horse. They found it hidden two hundred yards east, on the other side of the road. They searched it quickly for anything useful—instructions, maps, a safe conduct pass for a Cherokee outside the Territories—but there was nothing. If Hatchet had been carrying anything informative, he'd gotten rid of it before settling in to kill them. He'd known what his chances were.

They set the horse loose rather than take it with them. There was no time to deal with it.

They had a man to find in Joplin.

After half an hour's ride on the road—south out of the woods, over a little bridge beside a railroad trestle, past fields full of workers preparing the soil for spring planting—they came trotting into the outskirts of town. Now they passed brick houses and picket fences and telephone poles, then stores of every variety and men and women and children dressed for city living. In the distance, beyond the skyline of steeples and buildings as staggeringly high as half a dozen stories, the smokestacks of smelting plants belched black into the dimming late afternoon sky. A young couple zipped past on bicycles, and the bell of a trolley car clanged as it rumbled along its route.

The horses didn't like it. Diehl looked over to judge Walkingstick's reaction. If he was having one, he hid it, which was probably wise. He hadn't drawn much attention, looking from a distance like any sun-darkened man in the saddle. But a blue-coated policeman strolling up the sidewalk had given him a long, probing, mistrustful look—one he and Diehl had studiously ignored.

Diehl steered his horse to the side of the street and reined up in front of a bowling alley.

"I don't think he went in there," Walkingstick said as he stopped beside him.

"How would we know if he did?" Diehl jerked his head back at the street and its crisscrossing wheel ruts and hundreds of hoof prints. "It's not like we're following a trail anymore. Not through that mess. We just hope he's here somewhere, so here we are. But what good does that do us if we don't know what he looks like?"

Walkingstick started to answer. Diehl repeated himself before the man could get out whatever he was going to say.

"*If* we don't know what he looks like."

Walkingstick ignored the implication.

"Your friends should've gotten a look at him while they could," he said dismissively.

"Don't blame them. If they'd tried it, they probably wouldn't be alive now. And anyway—they didn't need to. *You* know what he looks like."

Walkingstick shrugged, still acting blasé. "Sure. And so do you. If he's anything like Hatchet, he's an older Cherokee man, maybe in his sixties, maybe a little older than that."

Diehl shook his head slowly. "Captain, Captain, Captain...we both made it. I'm still alive, you're still alive. There's no use waiting any longer to see how things play out. Either we lay our cards on the table and truly work together to figure this thing out, or we may as well split up now and be no help to each other at all. Maybe worse than no help. I vote for the former."

"I don't know what you're talking about, Diehl. I've told you I—"

"I'll go first," Diehl said. "Pixley claims the Cherokees we were following stole gold from a bank in Springfield, Illinois. Gold that he and his pals took from the Confederates at the end of the war. I and *my* pals do not believe him. We don't know what's really in that ice cream wagon, and I want to find out. Not because I'm such a naturally curious fellow, but because we have a job to do—get whatever it is back—and we can't do that if we don't know what the hell it is and who'd want it and why."

Walkingstick gaped at Diehl in surprise.

Diehl went on to surprise him even more.

"The Cherokees tried to kill us, by the way. We killed four of them. All older men, like Hatchet. The right age to have fought in the rebellion. Under 'the major,' maybe. Pixley's friends served in the war, too. For the union. We buried them in the woods north of Carthage."

Walkingstick was too surprised to respond at first. Diehl gave him a moment to take it all in, then held out a hand, palm up.

"Your turn," he said.

Walkingstick rubbed his jaw, then blew out a breath. "I assume you know our political situation in the Indian Nations is… complicated?"

"So complicated I barely understand it," Diehl admitted.

"Most whites don't understand it all. Or care," Walkingstick said. "The bottom line is we're supposed to be sovereign. Separate. Self-governing, with our own laws, courts, elections. That was the deal when we got shoved off our old lands back east and marched off into nowhere. But now it's looking more and more like the Indian Nations are going to lose their independence *again* and get sucked up into a state of 'Oklahoma' one of these days. And that's got a lot of Indians pretty damn mad. Mad enough maybe to do something stupid and speed the whole thing up. So when a couple of my men spotted Cherokees heading into Missouri looking like the damn cavalry—we knew that wasn't good. I was sent to find them and watch them and learn what they're up to."

"All that I more or less knew already," Diehl said.

"Yeah, well…here's what you don't know. When I heard you'd run up against a Cherokee they were calling 'Major,' I realized whatever trouble was getting brewed up is way, way bigger than I'd thought. So big I can't even imagine what's really going on."

"Because you *do* know who he is."

"Yeah," Walkingstick sighed, drawing out the word, chagrined to find himself admitting to a lie. "There were plenty of majors to come out of the Nations during the war. That's true. But only one mattered. Only one is still '*the* major.' Solomon Hosmer."

"Jesus," Diehl whispered.

He didn't know much about Cherokee politics, but like a lot of American boys who'd been alive during the rebellion—and he'd been almost ten when Lee surrendered—he knew Major Solomon Hosmer. There'd been a time he'd read about him in the newspaper every day. His tin soldiers must have killed the man a hundred times.

"Of the 1st Cherokee Mounted Rifles," Diehl said, "last Confederate regiment to surrender."

"That's right."

"Commander, Company E."

"You have a good memory."

"How could I forget 'The Butcher of Big Bat Creek?'"

Walkingstick didn't wince, but it looked like he wanted to.

"Yeah, that's what the newspapers called him," he said. "The pro-union newspapers, anyway."

"Those were the newspapers in my house," Diehl said. "My god…*him*. I'd have thought the old bastard was dead."

"No such luck."

"He still a troublemaker after all these years?"

"Not exactly. Not like back then. He has strong opinions. And he's rich, and he's a war hero. So a lot of people listen to him."

Diehl snorted in disgust.

"A war hero *to some*," Walkingstick added. "We were pro-union in my house, too. I bet that made things a lot tougher for us than wherever you were."

"Chagrin Falls, Ohio. And I'm sure you're right," Diehl said. He leaned back in his saddle and shook his head. "Well, well, well. Major Solomon Hosmer. Christ. It's like finding out you're tracking the Boogeyman. And you say he's rich?"

Walkingstick nodded. "Big slave owner before the war. Lots of tenant farmers after. In the end, emancipation didn't really change much for him."

"Well, then. That settles it. Thank you, Captain."

"Settles what?"

Diehl raised a finger in a "Give me a moment" way, then turned toward a pair of women strolling past the bowling alley.

"I do hope you will pardon me, ladies," he said, sweeping off his Stetson. "But could you direct me to the nicest hotel in town? The one best-suited for the traditionally-minded gentleman?"

The women—fiftyish and prim and proper (but not so prim and proper that one of them couldn't give Diehl an inviting smile) — stopped to look at the two men on horseback.

"Well..." one of them (the unsmiling one) said skeptically.

"I might appear a little rough from the road, but I'm here on business," Diehl said. "Negotiating mining rights in the Indian Territories. My guide here'll be headed home to his teepee tonight, but I'd like to check in somewhere a weary man of means can get a hot bath and a decent *pâté de foie gras*."

"Oh, that's easy," the smiling woman said. "You'll want to go to the Joplin Hotel. That's where the visiting businessmen of the best sort stay. The corner of Fourth and Main. The Keystone Hotel is newer and more modern, if that appeals." She wrinkled her nose. "Electric lights and steam heat and telephones in the big suites. The Joplin's kept up in certain ways—they have an *elevator* now—but the main focus is on maintaining their traditional elegance for those who appreciate the fine old ways. And the *foie gras* in the restaurant is *très magnifique*, I might add."

"*Parfait, Madame*," Diehl said. "Sounds like the place for me."

He returned the woman's smile.

The woman's friend glowered at her.

Walkingstick had been glowering at Diehl ever since his "teepee" remark.

"Thank you," Diehl said with a little bow. "I hope you lovely ladies have a most excellent evening."

The women moved on (the smiling one reluctantly).

"I live in a two-story house with an indoor pump in the kitchen," Walkingstick grumbled.

"But do you have an elevator?" Diehl said.

Before Walkingstick could reply, Diehl raised his finger again.

"Solmon Hosmer is old and rich and is here on business," he said. He slapped his hat back on. "We have a new trail."

CHAPTER 24

The "new trail" led Walkingstick and Diehl up the street and around a corner and around another corner. Then there it was: the Joplin Hotel.

It didn't look particularly swanky from the outside, but it did look big. Four stories of sun-faded brick and clouded windows, with a few stubby balconies jutting out from what must have been penthouse suites.

While Walkingstick headed around to the stables in the back to strike up a friendly conversation with the grooms and farriers there, Diehl kept an eye on the entrance. The men he saw going in and out—and they were *all* men—appeared plump and prosperous and middle-aged. There were many hail-fellow-well-met greetings and long, lingering handshakes among the guests, while the doormen posted out front in black top hats and long, gray overcoats stood at attention so stiff and serious they looked more like sentries.

After a while, Diehl turned to face the cigar store across from the hotel and pretended to be torn between the Romeo y Julieta and Hoyo de Monterrey cigars in the display window. Walkingstick joined him a minute later—pausing as he did so to give the wooden Indian by the shop door an unfriendly look.

"A gentleman arrived a little while ago," he said. "Fine horse, but seen a lot of miles lately. Stirred up some conversation in the stables." Walkingstick looked over at Diehl. "The Joplin Hotel usually doesn't accept guests who look like they came from the Indian Nations."

Diehl smiled. His guesses didn't always pan out.

The smile faded quickly.

So what now?

"All right," he said. "We go in and pretend that we're——"

"There's a complication," Walkingstick cut in. "One I didn't tell you about."

Diehl didn't try to hide his irritation. "Oh?"

"The major and I know each other. Well," Walkingstick said. "We're in the same clan."

Diehl let his jaw drop. He could've stopped it, but he wanted Walkingstick to know how he felt about this.

"So not only have you known who the major is all along," he said slowly, "he's a relative of yours?"

"Not exactly. Not as a White would reckon it. It's not by blood for him and me. More like...family affiliation. Ours are both in the Bird clan. But the how of it doesn't matter. He knows me, that's the thing. So if he is in that hotel, and he's in town to meet someone, and he spots me——"

"That'll be that, and we won't learn a thing."

Walkingstick nodded.

"Damn," said Diehl. "When you complicate things, you do a good job."

He thought about it a moment, then put his hand to his forehead and slowly dragged it down his face.

"Fine," he said, resigned.

"You're going in alone?" Walkingstick guessed.

"I'm going in alone."

Diehl threw a glance back at the Joplin Hotel.

"They serve *pâté de foie gras,*" he said. "How dangerous could it be?"

Walkingstick didn't answer. Which was all right with Diehl. He knew it wouldn't be what he wanted to hear anyway.

————

Onawa and Eskaminzim rejoined Hoop and Pixley at dusk. The four of them dismounted and led their horses off the road. When they were a safe distance into the darkening forest—though there was no truly safe place for them here, just somewhere they could be a little harder to find—they began weighing their options.

The Cherokees had pulled into a clearing to make camp. Either their final destination was deeper in the Indian Territories, or they were waiting for the men who'd split off to return from Joplin. Pixley and the others could cross back over into Missouri for the night and hope the border stopped the Cherokees from sneaking back and trying to kill them. But even if it did—and it didn't seem likely—they ran the risk of losing the Cherokees if they cleared out in the night. Perhaps one member of the party could stay behind to keep an eye on the road, but whoever it was would be taking a big risk going it alone on land the Cherokees knew well.

There were no good options. Which is why Eskaminzim proposed a *really* bad one.

"These are all the things they expect—move off, camp far away, try to watch from a distance," he said. "I say do what they *don't* expect."

"You'll be killed," said Onawa.

"You haven't even heard my idea."

"I know what it is."

Eskaminzim folded his arms and glared at his sister. "You might be wrong."

Onawa folded *her* arms and glared at her brother. "I'm not."

"What's your idea?" Pixley asked.

Eskaminzim and Onawa answered at the same time.

"Steal the wagon tonight," they both said.

"Your sister's right," Hoop told Eskaminzim. "It's too risky."

"Everything's risky!" Eskaminzim said. "So let's make the most of our risk. No one is better at stealing than an Apache, and no Apache is better at stealing than me. You know that. A wagon? Ha! I could steal a thousand wagons. I could steal a mountain from the Earth!"

Hoop made a non-committal noise—half grunt, half growl.

"They'll send men out looking for us tonight. You know it," Eskaminzim went on. "The ones left behind won't be expecting me to come for them."

"Because you'd be killed," Onawa said.

"But I won't be!" Eskaminzim turned to Pixley. "You're with me, right? It's about time we did something, yes?"

"Well..." Pixley said.

"Listen," Eskaminzim said. "Diehl wants us to wait while he goes off to *maybe* learn something. But we have the chance to learn something right here tonight. If I go into their camp, I can steal the wagon if I get a chance. But if not...if it's too *risky*..." He rolled his eyes to show what he thought of the concept of "risk." "...I can still listen. Learn. If I can find out where they're going, we won't have to keep following them like we have been. We can get ahead of them and lay a trap. You know they'll be all chatty around their cozy campfire, not watching for *me*." Eskaminzim thumped his chest. "I bet I can find out more than Diehl does!"

"You keep saying 'I' and 'me,'" Onawa said. "Not 'we.'"

Eskaminzim looked offended. "Who needs 'we' when you've got me?"

"Let him try it," Pixley said. "He's right. They won't expect it, and it's better than just cowering in the dark waiting to see if they find us."

Eskaminzim grinned.

"I like this White man," he said.

Hoop let out another grunt-growl. It sounded the same as the first, but Onawa knew it meant something different.

"You're actually considering it," she said.

Hoop said nothing.

"If you say yes, I'm going, too," Onawa said.

Hoop frowned.

"If I say yes," he said, "*I'm* going, too."

"Say yes," said Eskaminzim. "Say yes!"

"I say yes, if that counts for anything," said Pixley. "But only if you're sure you can do it without getting the wagon shot to pieces."

Hoop shook his head. "Wouldn't be no guarantees. It ain't so much a matter of *stealing* the wagon. Not with horses to hitch up and men all around. You understand?"

Pixley nodded.

It wouldn't be about stealing. It would be killing and taking.

"Yes. I understand," Pixley said. "Just like I understand that every day we let them get deeper into Indian Territory, the worse off we are. Better to see if we can do something now than waste a night hiding."

"Diehl won't like it," Hoop said.

Eskaminzim laughed. "Another reason to say yes!"

Hoop and Onawa looked at each other.

Hoop growled again.

"It's settled then," said Onawa.

"It is?" said Pixley.

Eskaminzim clenched his fists and leaned back looking like he was about to howl at the moon.

"It's yes!" he said.

"All right, then." Pixley straightened up as if snapping to attention for a superior officer. "When do we go?"

"*We* go," Hoop said, "after we've laid a false trail back toward Missouri, and it's pitch black, and we've got *you* hidden as deep in these woods as we can manage."

"But the more of us who go on the offensive, the more the odds will be in our favor," Pixley protested.

"We ain't necessarily going on the offensive," Hoop said. "We're going to scout and listen, close as we can get. There'll be more than that only if there's opportunity."

Onawa shook her head.

"'Odds in our favor,'" she snorted.

She nodded at her brother, who'd started singing and dancing in circles.

"If there was any chance of that," she told Pixley, "he wouldn't be so excited."

CHAPTER 25

THE WESTERN UNION TELEGRAPH COMPANY INCORPORATED
    SENT TO UNION STATION, OGDEN, UTAH
    6:34 P.M., MARCH 31, 1894
    FROM JOPLIN, MISSOURI
    TO C. KERMIT CROWE, A.A. WESTERN DETECTIVE AGENCY,
CHAMBER OF COMMERCE BLDG., RM. 303

COMPETITORS SPLIT SO HAVE DONE LIKEWISE. YOURS TRULY TO
JOPLIN WITH INTERESTED PARTY REPRESENTING CHEROKEE NATION.
GATHERING AT THE JOPLIN HOTEL. NO INVITATION BUT HOPE TO
ATTEND DISCRETELY. MAJOR S HOSMER IN ATTENDANCE. OTHER
NOTABLES POSSIBLE. WISH ME LUCK. YOU DO NOT PAY ME ENOUGH.

DIEHL

CHAPTER 26

After Diehl returned from the telegraph office, he and Walkingstick watched the Joplin Hotel a little longer, waiting to see if they'd get lucky and spot Major Solomon Hosmer coming or going. All they saw, though, were more middle-aged businessmen giving each other smiles and long handshakes and slaps on the back. In fact, every arriving guest enthusiastically greeted every other one, with only the bustling porters and grave, hulking doormen exempted from the hearty salutations and general good cheer.

"Do all rich White men know each other?" Walkingstick asked.

"It is a chummy club," said Diehl. "But no. Not usually."

"I wonder how they will greet you."

Walkingstick looked Diehl up and down. He didn't appear particularly rich. Or particularly clean. But there wasn't time for a shave, a bath, and a trip to the nearest tailor shop.

"It's getting dark," Diehl said. "Hopefully they won't notice I look like a cowboy fresh from the stockyard."

"They'd be sure to notice *that*, though," Walkingstick said, glancing down again. "Not something a respectable businessman straps on."

He was looking at Diehl's gun belt.

Diehl knew he was right. Dammit.

He was just walking into a fancy hotel to find out if an old man was around. He'd probably be in and out, learning nothing, in three minutes. What would he need his Colt for? Yet his nerves were on edge, and he didn't want to give up the comforting weight at his side.

He unbuckled the gun belt anyway.

"Wish me luck," he muttered as he handed it over.

Walkingstick said something in Cherokee that sounded like "Dough naw talo saw ee."

"Until we meet again," he translated.

Diehl nodded, then turned and started toward the hotel. He tried to time his arrival at the door so as to sweep inside with two of the well-dressed guests who'd just finished greeting each other on the sidewalk out front. Yet though he was right on their heels, the doormen managed to cut him off, swinging into his path from either side like iron gates clanging shut.

"Do you need something?" one of them said.

He was the smaller of the two—which didn't make him small. He just didn't tower over Diehl quite as much.

"Yes, I do," said Diehl. "To go inside."

Neither doorman stepped aside.

"Do you have a reservation?" the other one asked.

"Of course," Diehl said.

Three prosperous-looking business types breezed past them without getting a glance from the doormen.

"...so excitin' to finally be meetin' y'all face to face..." one of them was saying in a thick Southern accent.

Diehl took a chance.

"I'm here for the convention," he said.

"Oh, you are?" the first doorman said.

"*Ubi jus...*" said the other.

The two of them stared at Diehl suspiciously.

A response was expected. One they didn't think Diehl could give.

It took a moment for the sounds that had come from the second doorman's mouth to coalesce into words in Diehl's mind.

Ubi jus…

It wasn't English, but it was familiar, dredging up an old, not very happy memory.

Captain Miles Tipple. Humorless New Englander. Contemptuous martinet.

West Point instructor of Latin.

Diehl had never been as good at memorizing Latin as he was at poetry. It was just a bunch of dissonant, ungraceful sounds to him— nothing he could hang meaning on. But fear of Captain Tipple had helped him chisel the phrases into his brain. Enough to pass Latin anyway. Barely.

Diehl smiled.

"…*ibi remedium*," he said.

The doormen looked at each other, trying to conceal their surprise.

Then they stepped aside.

All these years later, Diehl had managed to pass another Latin test. Captain Tipple would be proud. Or at least slightly less scornful.

"Sorry, sir," the first doorman said.

"You know the importance of privacy for the proceedings," said the second.

"Of course," Diehl said as he walked between them. "Keep up the good work."

He was trying to remember what *Ubi jus, ibi remedium* actually meant as he went through the door into the lobby.

Know thyself?

Fortune favors the bold?

Nothing comes from nothing?

Love conquers all?

Definitely not.

Oh well. It was just a passphrase. It didn't have to *mean* anything.

Diehl walked across the thick, fraying carpet, weaving around chattering clusters of middle-aged men. He heard more Deep South accents and more expressions of delight to be meeting at last, but no more Latin.

It was a strange destination for a man like Major Solomon Hosmer. An old Cherokee rebel mounts up for one last offensive—against an Illinois bank this time—then winds up at a convention of doughy merchants in Joplin, Missouri? One that had taken over an entire hotel and required a password just to get in the door? How did that make any sense?

Diehl found himself headed toward the front desk…and locking eyes with a chipmunk-cheeked, mustachioed man wearing a pince-nez and an ascot. He was on the other side of the desk, beside the registry book, and his position and expectant look made it clear who he was.

A clerk or, to judge by the gray streaking his hair, the manager eager to sign in the latest guest. Who had no actual reservation, of course.

Diehl turned away quickly and held his hand out to the first man within reach.

"My goodness! Can it really be?" he drawled, grinning. "Mr. White? From Tallahassee?"

The man returned Diehl's smile as they clasped hands.

"I'm afraid not, sir," he drawled back. "I'm Hettle. From Mobile."

Hettle from Mobile's smile wilted a bit, and Diehl felt a light yet stinging stroke just under his right palm. The man was running a finger across Diehl's wrist, touching the edge of the scabbed-over cut left there by Ned Hatchet's tomahawk.

Diehl cursed himself but kept his grin as big as before.

It was a goddamn secret handshake. He should've guessed they'd have one. For all he knew he'd just crashed a convention of the Shriners.

Diehl lowered his index finger and ran it over the other man's wrist hoping that was the right response.

"Sorry," he laughed. "I haven't had many chances to practice." He cleared his throat and lowered his voice. "*Ubi jus…*"

"*…ibi remedium,*" Hettle replied, looking relieved as the handshake ended. "None of us have had many chances to practice, have we, Mr. ...?"

"Lilly. From Memphis. And you're right. It's inspiring to see so many of us fellows here together."

Hettle—a stout, bearded man in a frock coat and paisley waist-coat—nodded happily. "All the Knights together under one roof. All that's missing are Guinevere and the Round Table...though come to think of it I might have seen Guinevere come in with the senator."

Hettle laughed, so Diehl joined in.

The senator? Diehl was thinking.

"So—?" Hettle began.

Whatever question was coming from the man—and it was probably "Who's this Mr. White from Tallahassee I look so much like?" —Diehl didn't want to answer it. So he interrupted with his own question first.

"Have you seen old Major Hosmer, by any chance? I'm in a hurry to get an important message to him."

"I have seen him. He's in the dining room right now. Went striding in not five minutes ago. Parted the crowd here in the lobby like it was the Red Sea. I'd been thinking I'd ask him for his auto-graph, but I didn't dare. Fiercest eyes I've ever seen. You feel your blood freeze in your veins when you look into them." Hettle simulta-neously shivered and chuckled. "I'm glad he's on our side."

"I know what you mean," Diehl said, though he didn't. "Thanks, Hettle. Nice meeting you."

"Likewise, Lilly. Always a pleasure to meet a fellow patriot."

Diehl gave that an, "Indeed," and a frozen smile.

What the hell kind of Shriners were these?

It was easy enough to spot the dining room—it was just off to the right, through a pair of opened double doors with the words "The Fontainebleau Room" above them in slanted cursive script. Diehl tried to hurry through the doors without looking like he was hurrying.

The Fontainebleau Room was typical for the restaurant in a large but past-its-prime hotel—wide, with dingy-white pillars and low lighting and scattered ferns and palms. Tuxedoed waiters glided past prosperous-looking men in cherrywood chairs with green padded seats. The smell of roast duck and oyster stew was in the air. Diehl couldn't smell pâté de foie gras, but he knew it was around somewhere.

His stomach rumbled. All he'd had for days was Onawa's camp cooking. It was a wonder he didn't swoon.

He had to stay focused, though. Resist the urge to snatch a roll off the nearest table and stuff it into his mouth. Food later. Right now he had to find—

And there he was. Walkingstick had described him to Diehl, but even if he hadn't Major Solomon Hosmer would've been easy to spot. A barrel-chested, broad-faced man with thick white hair flowing down over his shoulders. He was seated at the far end of the dining room at a table with three other men—one young, one middle-aged, one old—and an attractive, elegantly dressed blond in her midthirties. The oldest man had his back to the entrance, but Diehl assumed he was probably "the senator" Hettle had mentioned, and the young lady his "Guinnevere." The middle-aged man had the look of a politician about him, too—well-dressed and well-padded—but somehow even from a distance Diehl could tell he lacked the gravitas of a US Senator. A city councilman or state representative or simply a "pillar-of-the-community"—that would be more his speed.

"Can I help you?" a man to Diehl's right said. He sounded skeptical, as if he thought Diehl beyond help.

Diehl turned toward the voice, smiling apologetically. He knew what he'd see, and he saw it, for of course The Fontainebleau Room would have one of these to go with the tuxedos and ferns and *foie gras*.

A maître d'. One who looked less than thrilled to have Diehl come through his door looking very much like a man who'd been spending his nights camped out in the woods.

"Oh, I hope so," Diehl told him in his best Southern accent. Which was pretty good thanks to all the Southerners he'd known at West Point and in the Army. "I imagine I'm violatin' your dress code comin' in like this, without a tie or a clean white collar, and for that I do apologize. But it has been *such* an arduous journey you would not believe it, and then when I get here I find that my room is not ready. The gentleman at the front desk suggested I revive myself here with a bowl of your excellent oyster stew while the help finishes preparin' my lodgin'. Could you see your way clear to accommodatin' a famished traveler who has journeyed many a mile over hill and dale to join his fellow patriots for this most momentous occasion?"

The maître d' gave Diehl a tight little smile—the only kind he looked capable of—and picked up a pencil from his host stand by the doors.

"Of course, sir. I'm terribly sorry you've been inconvenienced," he said. He moved the pencil to a sheet of paper on his little podium. "Your name is…?"

"Hettle," Diehl said. "From Mobile."

The maître d' wrote that down, then picked up a menu and held his free hand out toward the tables.

"This way."

"Bless you. You are too kind."

There was a ring of empty tables all around the major and his party, perfectly positioned for eavesdropping on their conversation.

The maître d' led Diehl in the opposite direction, to a tiny table in the corner.

Diehl didn't argue. Maybe the Cherokees they'd been following had gotten a good look at him at some point, who could say? The major hadn't glanced his way yet there in the restaurant—his eyes were fixed on the old gentleman seated across from him—and if he did it would be better if Diehl were as far off as possible.

"In case you'd like to consider something other than the oyster stew," the maître d' said once Diehl was seated. He handed Diehl the menu. It was just one page, but it would be better than nothing. Diehl promptly lifted it up and tried to hide himself behind it.

A moment later, once the maître d' was well on his way back to his post by the entrance, Diehl lowered the menu just enough to peep over the top. He was too far away to hear anything the major and the others at his table were saying, but it didn't seem to be the jovial, celebratory talk of partners toasting success. The young lady and the slick dude seated beside her—a handsome, fortyish gentleman with oiled hair and a pencil mustache—were staring at Hosmer with obvious unease, and "the senator" jabbed a pointed finger at the Cherokee and shook it accusingly while the pudgy middle-aged town councilman-type watched aghast.

"Have you decided what you'd like, sir?"

Diehl nearly jumped out of his chair. He'd been so focused on the table across the room he hadn't noticed the waiter sliding up beside him.

"You know, I thought I had, but every time I settle on somethin' I go and change my mind," Diehl told him. "You have altogether too many delicious-lookin' options. If I could just have another few minutes to wrestle with my choices…?"

"Of course, sir."

The waiter gave him a little bow and went away, *almost* managing to hide his annoyance.

Diehl went back to watching Hosmer and the others. The senator wasn't pointing a finger at the major anymore. He'd curled his hand into a fist, and he thumped it on the table hard enough to draw looks from all around the restaurant.

The young lady leaned forward, a phony smile on her lovely face, and said something to the old man. Almost certainly "Calm yourself. People are watching."

Hosmer said something to the man, too, his expression calm and cold. He picked up an object from the table that Diehl hadn't noticed before—a flat rectangle wrapped in muslin or canvas—and handed it to the senator. The others at the table watched with widened eyes as the old man unwrapped it.

Damn! All the answers Diehl was looking for were right there, he was sure of it. The real motive for the robbery. The reason an old Confederate Cherokee was behind it. An explanation for the presence of a senator and a hotel full of "knights" and "patriots" with passwords and secret handshakes.

As the senator looked at whatever he'd just uncovered, part of it caught the light and gleamed dully.

It was metal or metal-plated. Probably brass.

Diehl had to see it. Quickly, before the old man wrapped it up again or Hosmer took it back and turned it over.

Diehl put down the menu and stood up and started walking across the restaurant. He knew this was the kind of thing you have to make yourself do right away, the moment the impulse hits you. If you stop and think about all the risks, you'll *stay* stopped.

Hosmer's table was at one end of the dining room, not far from the door to the kitchen. Diehl could sweep past, get a quick look down at the whatever-it-was, then carry on through the door and into the kitchen and out the exit that would no doubt lead to a trash-strewn alley. It would mean he was done as a spy in the hotel, but that was all right. Hopefully, he'd have the information he'd come for. And how much longer could he last in there anyway without being unmasked as an impostor?

That was the answer Diehl got first. The answer being *Not any longer at all*.

As Diehl moved past tables of murmuring men, most of them also watching the major and the senator, a flurry of movement pulled his eyes to the left. One of the hulking doormen who'd let him inside a few minutes before—the one who was big but not huge —was moving to cut him off. Just beyond him, watching grimly from the entrance, were the maître d' and the chubby-cheeked man Diehl had seen behind the hotel registry desk. Just beyond *them*, staring straight into Diehl's eyes, slack-jawed, was the *real* Hettle from Mobile.

Damn damn damn!

But maybe it wouldn't matter. Diehl's plan could still work— he'd just have to go through all the steps a hell of a lot faster. Starting *now*.

Diehl broke into a sprint.

He could hear the heavy footfalls and gasps of surprise around the restaurant as the doorman did the same. Diehl didn't look over at the man chasing him, though. His gaze was locked on the copper-colored rectangle in the senator's hands. A brass plaque, he could see now. There was writing engraved on it—writing it would be impossible to read in the split second he'd have as he ran past.

The senator turned toward the commotion behind him, and Diehl instantly recognized his face. He'd been seeing drawings of it in newspapers and magazines for years. The senior US Senator from Mississippi, Samuel Cleburne. Another rich old rebel who hadn't let a little thing like a civil war and its hundreds of thousands of deaths inconvenience him in the long run. And now here he was meeting with a murderer and thief.

If Diehl had the time, he'd have scooped up the soup before the man and dumped it over his head. Instead he just snatched the plaque from his hands and kept running toward the door to the kitchen.

Hosmer still had quick reflexes—quicker than anyone else at his table. He sprang to his feet as Diehl zipped past, but he was too late to stop him. Diehl rushed on toward the door to the kitchen, just a few strides away from escape.

The door opened, and a man stepped into the dining room. A man who filled the doorway so completely he may as well have been a brick wall.

The other doorman.

Diehl spun around and zagged to his right, hoping he could skirt along the wall back to the entrance and squirm through the men standing there. But the other diners were overcoming their surprise and catching the gist of things now, and a dozen got to their feet and moved to block his path. They didn't look like fighters—they were lumbering, soft-bellied men wearing tailored suits and spats— but that didn't matter. They made excellent roadblocks.

Diehl was trapped. In about three seconds he was going to be grabbed, beaten, dragged off for questioning, beaten some more, questioned some more, then probably killed.

Fine. He'd been through it all before, except for the killed part. At least he could still get what he came for. Answers.

He slowed and looked down at the plaque. The damn thing was heavy, and once he'd absorbed the words carved into it he'd try to brain one of his pursuers with it.

Instead he froze.

"No," he said.

"Yes," said Hosmer.

Diehl started to look up at him. But then one of the doormen was on him, and he was thrown to the floor.

The major walked over and picked up the plaque as the other doorman hustled up and kneeled down next to Diehl.

"Where are the others?" Hosmer asked Diehl.

But the beating had already started by then, and Diehl didn't hear him.

CHAPTER 27

It was agreed.

Hoop would go up high with his Sharps rifle, to a bluff over-looking the little valley where the Cherokees were camped. He wouldn't have a clear shot down at the wagon—the Cherokees wouldn't have picked a spot where there was any chance of that—but he would be able to see both the eastern edge of the encampment and parts of the path that wound out to the road. It was the best place to watch for comings and goings...and maybe pick off anyone careless enough to make himself an easy target, if it came to that.

Onawa and Eskaminzim, meanwhile, would go in close enough to learn what they could and look for opportunities *but absolutely positively not do anything unless the others knew about it and were ready*. (The emphasis was for Eskaminzim's sake.) The signal for action would be two calls of a whip-poor-will followed by the croak of a bullfrog.

Or maybe not.

"Your whip-poor-will is all right," Eskaminzim said to his sister. "But your bullfrog...?"

He shook his head.

"What's wrong with my bullfrog?" Onawa snapped.

"It needs more belch," Eskaminzim said. "From the belly. Yours is all in the throat."

"Her bullfrog is fine," Hoop said.

Eskaminzim looked skeptical.

"Maybe the problem is your bullfrog," Onawa said to him. She jabbed him in the stomach. "*Too much* belly."

Eskaminzim jumped back a step.

"My bullfrog has the perfect amount of belly," he said.

"I'm going," said Hoop. He looked at his wife, then Eskaminzim. "Please be careful."

He turned and moved off into the woods. It was a dark night, without much moonlight, and within seconds he was gone from sight.

"'Please be careful,'" Eskaminzim repeated mockingly. "He never says that when it's just him and me."

"Because he knows you won't listen," said Onawa.

Eskaminzim nodded. "True."

"So," said Onawa, "I'll come around from the west and see who's guarding their horses. You—"

"Will sneak in so close I can count the hairs in their noses," Eskaminzim said. He switched from speaking to singing as he hurried away. "'Please be carrrrefulllllll!'"

Before Onawa could reply, he'd disappeared into the darkness, too.

Onawa gritted her teeth and stared after him. How he and Hoop and Diehl had managed to stay alive so long without her was a mystery. And now here they were without even Pixley, who they'd left hidden at the center of a briar patch a mile away. So they were reduced to three again, not the lucky four.

Onawa would have to make luck for them in other ways, if she could.

She headed through the forest toward the Cherokee camp, one hand on the sheathed knife at her side, the other carrying her rifle.

———

After all these years, it still felt strange to Hoop to be married to an Apache woman sometimes. Like when he was letting her go risk her life. That was a strange enough thing for a husband to do right there. But "please be careful" was the most he could say to her as he did it if anyone else was around, even just her brother. If Hoop had said something as unspeakably, mortifyingly private as "I love you," Onawa would never forgive him. And having Onawa mad at you—that would be a serious problem for anyone, her husband included.

He did say those words sometimes, though. When it was just him and her. He meant them, too, though theirs hadn't been a love match. Onawa needed a husband, and Hoop…well, he hadn't *needed* a wife. Not that he knew of. He'd gotten by just fine without one for forty years, he said when Eskaminzim first suggested the idea. But it would solve certain problems for Onawa and Eskaminzim and their family, so why not give it a try? Marriage might have its advantages for Hoop, too…so long as Onawa didn't expect him to talk much.

And she didn't. In fact, one of her favorite jokes was to wait until he finally said something—"Goin' huntin'" or "Gonna check that pony" or whatever after hours of silence—then tell him, "You talk too much," with a straight face.

Of course, it took Hoop about two years to figure out it *was* a joke. Nobody could keep a straight face like Onawa…

Hoop thought the words he couldn't say to her minutes before. Then he pushed those soft thoughts out of his head. He was nearing the bluff overlooking the edge of the Cherokee camp. He couldn't be distracted by worries about his wife now. He had work to do—work that might help keep her alive, if he did it right and something happened.

He could see where the earth dropped away up ahead. There were two trees close together at the summit. Hunkered down beside one or the other would be the best position. He'd have height and a clear view and cover. Perfect.

Hoop started to step around the first tree—then staggered back from the blow that came smashing into his forehead out of the darkness. He grunted and dropped his rifle and tried to turn away before

he was hit again. But he was already falling even as the second blow
came, catching him on the back of the head this time.

The world kept spinning even after he hit the ground face down.

Stupid, Hoop thought. *Stupid stupid stupid!*

If he could recognize the perfect spot to set up with his rifle, so
could someone else. And someone else had. Someone who'd used
the butt of their rifle to nearly split open Hoop's skull.

He expected to feel the bite of steel running across his throat
now, followed by the gushing of blood and the final swooning spiral
down into death.

Instead, he heard voices. Though he could make out the words,
he couldn't understand what they meant.

"Who the hell is he?" said one.

"I got no idea," said the other.

Then Hoop heard—and felt—no more.

Onawa knew she was near the Cherokees' horses before she could
say *how* she knew. She didn't see or hear them yet, and if she smelled
them she wasn't consciously aware of it. She just had a sense of
where they'd be, so she went that way.

She moved slowly, knowing that one misplaced step—onto a
twig, onto loose rock, into a gloppy mud puddle—could make the
noise that drew gunshots into the darkness and got her killed. She
was used to moving silently across deserts and high, dry mountains,
past trees (when there were trees) with thin branches studded with
needles. This Cherokee land, with its thick trees and loamy soil
covered with rotting leaves, didn't suit her.

Maybe it didn't suit the Cherokees either—that was something
to hope for. Maybe they wouldn't know it and feel it the way she
knew and felt the old range of the Mescalero. So well it almost
seemed she could walk across it with her eyes closed. The Cherokee
had only been here a couple generations, after all. Their real home-
land was somewhere to the east, Onawa knew. Land the whites had
wanted, of course. Like the whites wanted Apacheria, though she

had yet to meet a single one who seemed truly suited to the desert. Maybe when the land had been sucked dry—leached by over-farming in the east, hollowed out by mines in the west—the whites would give the Cherokee and the Apache both their old homes back. But she doubted it.

She heard a snort straight ahead and slowed even more. She could smell the horses now, which meant they could smell her. If her approach made them nervous, even the sleepiest, laziest Cherokee on night watch would notice.

She began sliding to the right. Not closing in on the horses anymore. Searching for a clear view of them through the trees.

And there they were. Large, dark shapes lined up in a row. The horses picketed for the night. And near them, a smaller shape. One that was suddenly more than just a shape as a flickering flare of orange light revealed the weathered face and hands of a man.

A man lighting his pipe. The fool!

Onawa lifted her rifle and put the Cherokee in her sights. Maybe she'd get lucky, even without Diehl or Pixley around to bring their number back up to the charmed four, and she'd hear the whip-poor-will calls and bullfrog croak that meant it was time to act.

"Don't," someone behind her whispered. "Or *we* shoot *you*."

Onawa froze.

"'We'?" she said.

She didn't believe it. It was stunning enough that she'd missed one man in the dark. More than one? Impossible.

He was bluffing. Trying to convince her not to do what she was considering: diving, rolling, coming up firing.

The man behind her cocked his gun.

"That's right, bitch," another voice whispered. A woman's voice.

She came out of the darkness and took hold of Onawa's rifle and ripped it from her hands.

"'We.'"

———

Eskaminzim smiled. Everything was going perfectly.

There were only five men by the wagon, two of them on the eastern edge of the camp, where Hoop would be able to see them (and pick them off) from the ridge. If there was one more guarding the horses—probably already in Onawa's sights—that meant the Cherokees had split their party in two. Half were out looking for *them* somewhere. The half left behind would be easy to deal with.

Two for Hoop, one for Onawa, three for him.

Eskaminzim liked the way the numbers broke down.

The wagon—and whatever was really inside it—would be theirs in minutes.

It was parked in a clearing not far from a narrow, winding creek. The trickling of water helped cover any sound Eskaminzim might make as he slithered closer. The Cherokees, overconfident and comfortable on their land, had chosen convenience over safety. Soon they'd pay for it.

Eskaminzim stopped thirty yards from the wagon and the three men hunkered down near it. His three. The other two—Hoop's, another thirty yards beyond—were talking, but they were keeping their voices low, and it was hard to make out the words.

"I still *something something* grabbed Mary *something something* when we had the chance," said one.

"Yeah, but *something something* want her back?" said the other.

Apparently, that was a joke. The two men laughed.

"It was hard enough getting one of them down here," one of the men closer to Eskaminzim said. Like all the Cherokees, he was in his fifties or early sixties and looked grizzled and disheveled from days on the trail. He was huddled under an old blanket that looked like it had once been a colorful checkerboard but had now faded to a patchwork of dingy grays. "Is it gonna be worth it in the end? That's what worries me."

"The major knows what he's doing," said the Cherokee sitting to his left. They had a small fire going, and he stretched out long arms to warm his hands over the glowing embers.

"Tell that to Young Duck and Jesse Crump," said the blanketed man. "Or better still, tell their wives. I'm the one who has to let 'em know they ain't coming home. And you're gonna have to do the same for Falling Pot and Mink Winkleside's people."

"There'll be good news, too," said the third man by the fire. His hands were wrapped around a chipped mug filled with rotgut so strong Eskaminzim could smell it on the cold nighttime breeze. "We're gonna be heroes when they hear we got *him*."

All three men glanced at the wagon parked behind them. The first—the grumbler under the blanket—just grunted. The other two grinned.

Eskaminzim was still smiling, too. He congratulated himself on his most excellent skulking and eavesdropping skills.

Of course! he was thinking.

It wasn't a *whatever* the Cherokees had taken from Illinois. It was a *whoever*.

They had a prisoner. A hostage.

Which gave him and Hoop and Onawa all the more reason to act now. Strike while the odds were as good as they were likely to get. A bigger battle, without complete surprise on their side, would probably get the hostage killed.

Eskaminzim lifted his head, about to show his sister what a proper whip-poor-will and bullfrog croak sounded like.

A coyote yipped in the distance. A coyote that wasn't a coyote.

Eskaminzim froze, now thinking, *We* did *say two whip-poor-wills and a croak, right?*

"Bowlegs…that you?" said one of the Cherokees further from the wagon. "You get those bastards trailing us already?"

Whoever "Bowlegs" was, he didn't answer. Instead the "coyote" yipped again.

"Who goes there?" said the other Cherokee at the edge of the camp.

Eskaminzim had heard White men say that, but this was the first time he'd heard it from an Indian. He stayed utterly still, worried at first that he'd been spotted. But the Cherokee who'd said "Who goes there?"—along with all the Cherokees now—was peering in the opposite direction, toward the path back to the road.

A man stepped into the moonlight there.

"Evening, fellas," he said. "Where's the major?"

The pair standing at the far end of the clearing threw a quick glance at each other before answering simultaneously.

"We don't know any 'Major,'" said one.

"How do you know about the major?" said the other.

The first glared at the second.

The man in the distance moved closer to them. It was too dark to make out his features, but Eskaminzim could see that he was tall and wore a big, flat-brimmed hat.

"Got word from some of the major's friends that he was headed to Joplin with a special gift from up north," the man said. "Had the dickens of a time finding you all when you swung west into the Nations instead."

"How's he know where we was supposed to go?" the blanket-wearing Cherokee whispered.

"Shut up," said the one with the whiskey.

The two men at the edge of camp looked at each other again, then took a nervous step backward as the stranger drew close.

"You one of them Knights of Whatever?" one of them said.

The man was fully in the clearing now, far enough from the forest shadows to reveal a broad, smiling face and large, expressive eyes and a red handkerchief knotted around a thick neck.

"Do I look like one of those White assholes?" he said.

"Jesus Christ," whispered the Cherokee with hooch in his mug. There was shocked recognition in his voice.

The man heard him, and his smile grew wider.

"Not quite," he said.

Then he drew his gun and shot the Cherokee closest to him in the chest. As the man toppled backward, there were more gunshots in the distance—some from the ridge to the south, some from the east, by the horses. The other Cherokee who'd been standing further from the fire grunted and spun, hit in the side. Another shot from the ridge plowed square into his spine, and he hit the ground spread-eagled.

The three men around the fire scattered. The one who'd been sipping liquor hadn't gone five steps before he was cut down by a blast from the forest. The one with the blanket over his shoulders was hit from the trees, too, the slug passing through his left upper arm. He yelped and kept going as more shots tore through his flapping blanket until one-two-three they tore into *him,* and he went down.

The third man had spun around and run for the creek, hunched low and fumbling for the clunky old Colt Dragoon revolver stuffed under his belt. Just as he managed to get out his gun his right toe slammed into something hard, and he stumbled and turned and saw what he'd tripped over.

A man lying on the ground. A man with long dark hair and a calico shirt and his hand pressed to his bloodied forehead.

Eskaminzim.

There was no time for questions. No time for thought. No time even for surprise.

The Cherokee just shot him, then turned and kept running.

He'd almost reached the stream when the shots came that killed him. They exploded out of the forest and caught him in the thigh and the back of the head. He collapsed in a heap six feet from the water.

For a moment, the only sound was the burbling of the creek. Then men in the darkness began to whoop triumphantly.

"Good job, boys!" Blaze Bad Water told his gang. "Now hitch up that wagon—we've got who we came for!"

CHAPTER 28

They only beat Diehl in the hotel restaurant for a minute or so. Then they dragged him up to the senator's suite and tied him to a chair and got serious.

"Where are the others?" one of the doormen would say, repeating the question Major Hosmer had asked down in The Fontainebleau Room.

"What others?" Diehl would say.

Then he'd get punched in the stomach and get asked again.

His "What others?" were growing quieter and more mush-mouthed as his head sagged closer and closer to his chest.

The doorman started slapping him between punches to keep him conscious.

"This wouldn't have happened if you'd stuck to the plan," Senator Cleburne growled at the major.

"Yes, it would've," Hosmer said.

He was staring at the senator's daughter and son-in-law, Dockery, with even more distaste than he showed when he looked at the torture going on a few steps away. This was work for hardened men of war, not women and dilettantes. Bewley, the soft-bellied mayor who'd been dining with them when the ruckus started in the dining room—there to toast the success of the senator's plan, though the old Cherokee had complicated that—had done the sensible thing and excused himself, leaving the dirty work to others in the manner befitting a politician of his stripe. So what the hell were a lady and her lawyer husband still doing here?

Mrs. Una Cleburne Dockery met Hosmer's disdainful gaze with cheerful indifference. She didn't seem to be relishing what she was seeing, but she wasn't the least bothered by it either. She was too young to have witnessed the whippings on her family plantation before the end of the war, but she knew of them and had seen men broken for transgressions and intransigence in other ways. Usually Black men, of course—Black women, too, occasionally. But the principal still applied. Those who disobeyed paid.

Her husband, on the other hand, looked away, clearly disturbed by the violence and blood. Those things were sometimes part of his business as a defense attorney, but that was all talk. This was the real thing right in front of him, and he didn't like it.

He drifted to the far side of the room—to the table where Major Hosmer had left the plaque he'd brought to prove he'd completed his mission though he was changing the terms of his deal with the senator. Dockery ran his fingers over its cool, smooth surface and tried to force himself to smile. Things had gotten complicated and unpleasant, but the first part of the plan—the hardest part—was over.

They had what they wanted. *Who* they wanted. Someone a shocked nation would pay millions to get back.

"With Malice toward None, with Charity for All," read the words on the plaque—the one that had been removed from a crypt in Springfield, Illinois, along with the body interred there. "ABRAHAM LINCOLN. February 12, 1809–April 15, 1865."

PART TWO

EVERYBODY VS. EVERYBODY

CHAPTER 29

The old man stepped up to the podium in The Fontainebleau Room of the Joplin Hotel and said, "Good morning."

"Good morning," two hundred well-dressed middle-aged men replied from the large, round tables that had been brought in for the plenary session.

Some of the men said, "Good morning, Senator."

Senator Samuel Cleburne of Mississippi smiled.

"*Ubi jus…*" he said.

"*…ibi remedium,*" his audience intoned.

The senator nodded.

"Where there is a right, there is a remedy," he said. "The White South has the right. To its autonomy. Its restoration. Its revenge. And *we* are the remedy."

There was a smattering of applause, and one halfhearted, "Hear, hear."

The senator turned to the nearest of the white-coated men weaving through the tables with gleaming silver pots.

"You need to work faster, son," the senator told him. "These gentlemen obviously need more coffee, and I prefer my audiences awake."

There were sleepy chuckles throughout the room.

The server—white, like all the others on duty that morning—smiled and stopped to offer a refill to a grim-faced, stiff-backed man with a flowing mane of thick, snowy hair. The man glared up into his eyes with a scowl that seemed to say not just, "No thank you," but, "Get the hell away from me if you value your life."

The server quickly pivoted and headed for the next table.

Major Solomon Hosmer turned his scowl back toward the podium.

"I want to apologize for the disruption last night," Senator Cleburne told the crowd. "I cannot tell you how disappointed I was to cancel the midnight ceremony." He swept his gaze over Hosmer without letting it linger. "It will be rescheduled."

There was a sharp *clank* of porcelain on porcelain to the senator's left, and he glanced over at the long table being prepared there by more white-coated workers.

Cleburne turned back to his audience.

"Right now, though, I'm sure it's the first item on our morning schedule that is very much on your minds, as it is on mine," he said. "While it's being readied, I cannot resist the urge to say a few preliminary words. I suppose it's the price you must pay for being here with a politician in your midst."

There were more chuckles, a little louder this time.

"Of course, I'm hardly the only politician here, am I?" the senator went on. "Looking out over our distinguished membership, I see our gracious host, the mayor of Joplin. I see other mayors from Mississippi and Louisiana and Alabama and Georgia. I see councilmen and commissioners and chiefs of police. I see the *crème de la crème* of Dixie. Pure and white...and ready to take back what's ours. What the Klan fought to preserve through the torch and the rope we are resurrecting through the city hall and the statehouse."

There was another, "Hear, hear," and many murmurs of agreement and nodding heads.

"Now, you know your Bible as well as I," the senator said. "After his many long sufferings, including the deaths of all his children—the snuffing out of his very future—Job was granted three new daughters by God. And the fairest of these—the symbol of life and renewal and hope—was...?"

Cleburne paused and looked out over his audience expectantly.

The word he was waiting for rose up on a hundred voices like a rumble of distant thunder.

"Keziah."

The senator grinned. "Indeed. My friends, the dream of a free Southland is *our* Keziah. And we...?"

The pause was shorter this time, and when he supplied the missing words himself he was suddenly forceful, passionate, almost frenzied.

"We are her knights! Her champions! Covered in the scars of old battles and unending afflictions yet full of the strength to throw off the bootheel of oppression!"

There were dozens of clinks as men put down their coffee cups and sat up straight and balled their fists.

"When that bootheel came down upon our necks at the end of the war," Cleburne raged on, "there were some who suggested that we flee! Go further south and recreate our great society there, in Mexico or Honduras or Nicaragua!" The old man's mouth puckered with disgust as he pronounced these foreign names. "But I said no! Dixie is our home! Our cradle! Our birthright, won for us through the sweat and blood of our fathers and their fathers and theirs!"

The senator leaned forward onto the podium and looked around the room with satisfaction as the audience erupted with shouts of "That's right!" and "You tell 'em!" that had all the fervor of "Amen!" and "Hallelujah!" He noted but didn't acknowledge the one darkened, glowering face so near to him—on Major Solomon Hosmer—that had turned all the more scornful at talk of birthrights won by forefathers without mentioning the fathers and mothers who'd died while giving theirs up.

"Does the South belong to the Yankees?" Cleburne asked.

"No!" most of his audience roared back.

"Does the South belong to the darkies?"

The "No!" this time was even louder.

"Does the South belong to the agitators and miscegenators and the arrogant, meddling busybodies in Washington, DC?"

The "No!" shook the glass in the chandeliers.

"Who does it belong to?"

"Us!"

Cleburne cupped a hand to his ear. "Who?"

"Us!"

"I said, '*Who?*'"

Half the men in the room were on their feet now, their usually pasty faces flushed red as they screamed their answer.

"US!"

"Yes! Usssssss!" the senator howled triumphantly. "The South is ours, and the day we pretend otherwise is coming to an end!"

Major Hosmer watched stone-faced as the men all around him cheered and clapped and stamped their feet and pounded the tables.

Cleburne basked for a moment in the cacophony he'd created, then glanced to his left and saw that all was in readiness. The moment his audience had been waiting for had at long last arrived.

"Now, my friends, my comrades, my brave and true Knights of Keziah...!" the senator boomed. He swept an arm out toward the long table against the wall and the steaming steel serving dishes lined up upon it. "Who wants pancakes?"

CHAPTER 30

George Pixley woke up hungry and cold and sore and scared. Yet he felt grateful. He'd spent most of the night convinced he wouldn't see the morning at all.

He'd listened, curled at the heart of a huge tangle of blackberry vines, as quiet, careful footsteps moved past not once, but twice. Some of the Cherokees were out looking for the men trailing them —and coming within a few feet of finding *him*.

Fortunately, the hiding spot Onawa had shown him had worked. But where was Onawa now? And Eskaminzim and Hoop?

If they'd succeeded—scouted out the Cherokees' camp and grabbed the wagon if the opportunity presented itself—they would've come back for him...right? Or would they have hightailed it out of the Indian Territories thinking they had a wagonload of gold for themselves?

No. That wouldn't be their way. They were mercenaries, but they weren't cutthroats.

Well, they *were* cutthroats, but they were professional cutthroats. His cutthroats, so long as they thought they'd be paid for it.

Which circled him back to the question—where were they?— and the most likely answer. The one he didn't want to face. Because it would mean he was alone in the Cherokee Nation with a sacred mission he couldn't possibly complete. But he had to try.

Pixley pulled off his thin blanket and rolled it up and, carrying it and his rifle in front of him, began wriggling his way out of the briar patch. It was slow going. Damp soil smeared the front of his suit, and thorns snagged on his sleeves and raked his hands and face. But after a couple minutes he slithered out into the open and pushed himself to his feet and looked around for the sun. When he found it peeping through the trees of the forest, he warmed himself in its rays for a moment, then turned his back to it and headed in the opposite direction.

Into the west. That's where Onawa and Hoop and Eskaminzim had gone, so it's where he went now. To find them. Or what was left of them.

The road was about a hundred yards to his left, and he threw glances that way every few steps, looking for either heaps abandoned to rot there or men on horseback looking for *him*. He saw neither. He didn't hear anything either, beyond the whistling songs of cardinals and robins and the occasional squawk of a blackbird and cooing of doves. It might've been a cheerful sound if Pixley hadn't half-expected death to step out from behind a tree any moment.

It stirred up old memories, this walking and aching and bird song and death. Thirty years before, he'd walked across half the South with the 7th Illinois Infantry. And why? In the beginning, it had been, "The Union forever! Hurrah, boys, hurrah!" But as it had gone on, and they walked away from more and more of those boys' graves, thoughts of the Union and glory faded, until Pixley was still marching simply because the friends beside him were still marching, too.

Now the last of those friends were gone, and here he was marching alone. Not even a soldier anymore. He was an accountant for the Illinois Coal and Iron Company, for Christ's sake. One with a wife waiting for him to come home from his last-minute "camping trip" with his old comrades. *He* was supposed to save the nation's honor from a bunch of Cherokee thieves? Utterly and completely alone?

"Wake up, Pixley," someone said.

Pixley whipped around. He'd walked right past two men watching him from behind a black walnut tree. The one who'd spoken—Eskaminzim—was leaning against the trunk, while the other—Hoop—sat on the ground nearby.

"I've heard of sleepwalking, but this is the first time I've seen it," Eskaminzim said to Hoop.

Hoop just grunted.

Both men looked awful.

There were bloody bandages—made from someone's torn shirt —wrapped around Eskaminzim's right shoulder, and the arm beneath was bound up in a sling of the same material. His back was hunched, his face beaded with sweat. Without the tree to lean against it looked like he'd fall down.

Hoop sat with one hand against the ground as if he were on the verge of toppling over, too. There were no bandages on him, but a purple lump the size of a silver dollar had swollen up over his left eye.

Pixley took the two of them in with alarm...then grew even more alarmed when he remembered he should be seeing three of them.

"Where's Onawa?"

"We were hoping she was with you," Eskaminzim said.

"You ain't seen her?" said Hoop.

Pixley shook his head. "Not since the three of you left last night."

Eskaminzim and Hoop looked at each other grimly.

"What happened?" Pixley asked.

"Someone else ambushed the Cherokee camp before we could," Eskaminzim said. "Hoop and me got caught in the middle. My sister, too, I guess."

"We can't find no trace of her. These new fellas—they must've taken her with 'em," added Hoop. He cocked his head and stared hard into Pixley's eyes. "Eskaminzim heard some of what they said.

Sounded like they knew better than we do what's in that wagon. Or *who's* in it, more like."

Pixley blinked and said nothing. He wasn't ready for this conversation.

Hoop and Eskaminzim saw that. And didn't care.

"My sister is out there somewhere with men who came to take what? A person? A *body*?" Eskaminzim snapped.

"It's time you dropped the bullshit, Pixley," said Hoop, "and told us what's really going on."

"I…"

"I swore an oath of secrecy," Pixley had been about to say. But what difference did that make now that the men he'd sworn it with were dead?

Like it or not, these were his comrades now.

"I'm sorry. You're right," Pixley said. "I shouldn't have tried to carry on without you knowing the truth."

He drew in a deep breath, then told them the whole story.

CHAPTER 31

First was the sting on his cheek and the feeling of something moist pressing against raw flesh there. Then came the pain in his neck— a byproduct of the head that sagged down toward his chest—followed by the aching in his sides where he'd been punched over and over. The tingling in his hands faded in next, as well as the bite of the ropes wrapped around the wrists tied behind his back. Then finally, least welcome of all, came the memory of where he was and why.

Diehl opened his eyes and lifted his head and saw Una Dockery leaning in toward him with a wet rag in her hand. She smiled at him, then reached up and gave his cheek another wipe.

"Ow," Diehl said.

Una stepped back, still smiling. The rag in her hand was streaked red.

"I'm sorry, Mr. Vatefairefoutre," she said. "But I just couldn't stand talking to you when you looked such a mess. It truly breaks my heart to find you in this condition."

"Yeah, well…it breaks my heart, too."

Diehl probed his teeth with his tongue. By a miracle, none were missing.

At least he'd go to his grave with all his teeth.

He blinked once, twice, three times, and the world around the lady came into focus.

He was still tied to a chair in a large, well-furnished room in the Joplin Hotel—the bedroom of a suite. To the left was the door out to the sitting room and the exit. It was closed.

"You know, if you're so upset about it," Diehl said, "you could always let me go."

Diehl expected the woman to grow flustered. To protest that she'd love to release him but her hands were tied. To which he'd reply that she wasn't the one with tied hands.

Instead her smile widened.

"That's the plan," she said. "But first we need to come to an understanding."

"Ah. I tell you everything, and you just let me walk out of here, right?"

"Why, that's it exactly, Mr. Vatefairefoutre! Or perhaps I should say, 'Monsieur Vatefairefoutre?'"

Una reached out again and wiped crusted blood from the corner of Diehl's mouth.

"I speak a little French, too," she said. "Such an interesting name you gave last night while being questioned. I once got my mouth washed out with soap for saying it at boarding school."

"I'm sorry, ma'am. Obviously, that was a lie," Diehl said. "My real name is Embrassemoncul."

Una stepped back and laughed.

"I see! Would that be the Kiss-My-Asses of Paris or the Kiss-My-Asses of Marseilles?" The lady shook her head and swiped at Diehl with the bloody rag. "Oh, I do like you, whoever you are. You are a *scamp*."

Diehl had nothing to say to that. Compliments from pretty ladies were usually very much to his liking, but he couldn't take any pleasure from these.

Una walked over to the bed and sat on one corner, facing him.

"I understand your reluctance to trust me," she said. "How could you trust any of us here, given what you've gone through? So I will demonstrate my goodwill. Before you take me into your confidence, I will take you into mine. Please, sir—ask me what you wish to know. Upon my honor, I will answer to the best of my ability."

Diehl squinted at her skeptically. But what did he have to lose?

"All right," he said. "Who are you?"

"I am Mrs. Una Cleburne Dockery," the woman replied without the slightest hesitation, "daughter of Senator Samuel Cleburne of Mississippi and wife of Mr. Garland Dockery, esquire, of Fort Smith, Arkansas."

"What are you doing here?"

Una gave Diehl another of her sunny smiles. "Now that *is* a complicated question. And I will answer it, as promised. But perhaps first, to sort of lay the groundwork, there's something else you'd like to ask…?"

"Fine," said Diehl.

He struggled for a moment to boil all his other questions down into one. And he failed. The best he could do was, "Stealing Lincoln's body? What the hell?" Which is what he asked.

Una kept on smiling.

"It is audacious, isn't it?" she said. "But yes. Abraham Lincoln's body has been taken from its tomb in Springfield, Illinois. Or from beneath its tomb, more like. There was an earlier attempt to steal it, I'm sure you'll recall. A gang of counterfeiters, in 1876. Quite the kerfuffle. After that, a small group of local men—'the Lincoln Guard of Honor,' they call themselves, all veterans of the war— took on protection of the body as their sacred mission. I believe you've made these men's acquaintance. Perhaps even been hired to work for them…? They thought it would be safer if the body were secretly moved to a chamber underneath the official monument. Basically, they stuck him in the basement. Only such things never stay secret forever, do they? Especially not when the cemetery sextons who did the actual work are drunkard loudmouths. Word filtered out into various unsavory circles until it reached my husband's ears—him not being unsavory, of course, but a defense attorney whose clients are often so. He mentioned it to my father, and…well, here we are."

"My god…"

Diehl dropped his gaze to the floor and shook his head in disbelief though the woman was merely filling in the details of a conspiracy he already suspected.

He lifted his head and looked her in the eye again.

"And your father recruited Major Solmon Hosmer to do it?"

"That's right. Old Hosmer had been in touch many a time to air his grievances about the treatment of the Cherokee Nation and his opposition to any state of 'Oklahoma' subsuming the Indian Territories. And of course Father remembered well the skill and, shall we say, *vigor* with which Hosmer and his men fought for the Cause during the war. 'The Butcher of Big Bat Creek,' etc. If you needed a true believer to carry out a dangerous mission behind enemy lines —or in this case up into Illinois and back, which Father still sees as the same thing—you couldn't do better than Major Hosmer."

"Only he could've done better, maybe. Because it sure looked to me like the senator wasn't very happy with Hosmer in the restaurant last night."

Una chuckled and shook her head. "My my my—you are the sharp-eyed rascal, aren't you? Yes, indeed. My father *was* displeased. Major Hosmer was supposed to bring the body here, you see. But he grew concerned when there were complications along the way. Complications I believe we can thank you for. So he sent his men into the Indian Territories instead."

"But brought the plaque from Lincoln's tomb as proof they had him."

Una nodded. "Correct again. Any other questions? Or are you ready to start answering mine?"

"Oh, I've got more questions. Like *why* steal Lincoln's body, and what's this secret club meeting here, and where are the senator and the major now?"

"Well, to begin with the simplest of those, my father and Major Hosmer are downstairs enjoying a pancake breakfast and fellowship session with the Knights of Keziah. Which brings us to question #2. The 'secret club' is an association of community leaders from throughout the South who believe it's time to throw off the yoke of Northern oppression and sweep away the last vestiges of Reconstruction. You know—voting and property rights for coloreds and the like. And as for the why, there are various reasons—simple revenge and the symbolism of the thing, of course—but mostly it's about money. They plan to ask for two million dollars to give the body back. Half would go to the Knights of Keziah and their efforts to liberate the South, and the other half would go to Major Hosmer and *his* efforts to maintain the sovereignty of the Cherokee Nation. Now is *that* enough information for you?"

Diehl shifted in his seat as he took all this in. He'd been conscious long enough now for simple discomfort—like the aching of his ass after sitting in the same wooden chair all night—to penetrate through the pain of his wounds.

"Just two more things," he said. "You told me you'd explain why *you're* here. And I'm wondering why you would explain. Why you'd tell me any of this at all."

Una beamed at him.

"I'm here," she said proudly, "because this was my idea. Not every aspect of it. Not the stupid parts, like involving the Knights of Keziah in such a blatant way. My father insisted on that. But having the major borrow Mr. Lincoln so we could bill the federal government some reasonable amount for his return…? That was me. Yet as a female I'm not welcome in the Knights of Keziah an organization with a woman in its very name! I am forced to procure my pancakes elsewhere. To make myself useful elsewhere. Such as here…obtaining the services of a go-between."

Diehl cocked his head at that.

It hurt his sore neck, and he winced.

Una laughed.

"You didn't foresee that?" she said. "I'm surprised, wily a fox as you are. I mean, you *must* have some connection to the Lincoln Guard of Honor. And clearly they wish to keep this affair secret, sparing the United States of America a grievous stain to *its* honor. Otherwise all Illinois and Missouri would be aswarm with US deputy marshals searching high and low for 'Honest Abe.' So despite the little wrinkle of your involvement along with your rather persistent friends, there's still a chance to conclude this matter

discretely. *You* can take the ransom demand to the government…
leaving out the details that would prove embarrassing to both the
Guard of Honor and the Senator. I don't see why you couldn't even
make the ransom two-point-two million dollars. A ten percent finder's fee seems reasonable to me for the man who helps us secure
what we want while ensuring that poor Mr. Lincoln returns to his
rightful resting place in Springfield."

"That seems…generous," Diehl said.

"Oh, it certainly is that, Mr. Kiss-My-Ass. Yet completely
sincere. If you and I can come to an agreement, there's no reason
you couldn't leave Joplin not only alive but *rich*. I only ask that you
be as forthcoming with me as I have been with you. Tell me who
you are and who's been working with you, and we can put the
wheels in motion that will send both you and Mr. Lincoln home
only a little the worse for wear."

The lady was still holding the moist rag she'd used to wipe
Diehl's bloodied face. She put it on the bed beside her and folded
her hands in her lap and awaited Diehl's response with a look of
patient, wry anticipation.

"All right," Diehl said. "I'll tell you everything."

He took in a deep breath (and suppressed another wince at the
ache it brought to his bruised ribs).

"My name," he said, "is Rufus Featherston. My father is J.J.
Featherston, president of the First Bank of Springfield and execu-
tive chairman of the Lincoln Guard of Honor. When the theft of
the president's body was discovered, my father sent me to find it
along with some of his old friends and a couple guides and a cook
we hired along the way…"

———

Una Dockery stepped out into the suite's front room, closing the
bedroom door behind her. Her husband Garland was sprawled on a
settee nearby with a newspaper in his hands he hadn't been able to
focus his eyes or thoughts on to read.

"Progress?" he asked, sitting up straight.

Una shook her head.

"He fed me some codswallop about being a dutiful son trying to get back the body with the help of old friends and hired hands," she said. "As if it wouldn't be clear as can be to the major that he'd run afoul of something more than amateurs out there. Or that I wouldn't remember his surprise when he saw that plaque last night."

Una walked over and plopped down onto the settee beside her husband.

"I *told* Father to just kill him and be done with it," she sighed. "Oh, well. He'll have to kill him now. I told him everything."

"What? Why?"

Una gave her husband a playful shove. "Because I'm proud of it, you big silly! And Father did say I could try working my charms on the man. When you're trying to get someone to open up, I find the truth—or something close to it—to be so much more persuasive."

"But...but...now he *knows*."

Una shrugged. "And soon he'll be dead."

She reached beneath the newspaper Dockery was holding and began stroking his thigh. Slowly, languidly, her hand moved higher, gliding in swirls up to the bulge in his suit jacket.

"Maybe we should just take care of it now." She squeezed the gun in her husband's pocket. "We could say he got loose and tried to escape."

She gazed deeply, longingly into Dockery's eyes.

"But Una...darling..." he said. "Do we really want to do something so bold now? With everything in flux?"

Una batted her eyelashes. "What's wrong with a little boldness?"

"Nothing...when the moment is right." Dockery gave his wife a small, quivering smile. "You'll see."

She squeezed the gun again.

"I'd better," she said.

CHAPTER 32

When daylight came, Onawa could finally get a good look at the people who'd taken her prisoner. The infamous Blaze Bad Water Gang. In the night, it had all been harsh voices and dark shapes and sharp blows and the possibility of sudden death. But now, with the sun in the sky and her captors on their horses all around her, she could see them for what they were.

A bunch of kids. Scruffy, surly-looking ones, but kids all the same. None was older than twenty. One—the meanest of them, the girl—looked a lot younger than that. They were like the packs of dogs you'd sometimes see near abandoned settlements. Every size and shape and breed, but all hungry and ready to bite.

The girl noticed Onawa watching them. She moved her pony closer to the big, plodding Bay they'd put Onawa on—the one they'd taken from the Cherokee men they'd killed in the night.

"What are you looking at, old woman?" the girl said.

She was a runty little thing—wiry and short, with angry eyes that said she was ready to fight if you dared to notice. Like most of the others, she had black hair and light brown skin. Her clothes were the same as everyone else's, too—weathered, broad-brimmed hat, dingy shirt, baggy pants, and jacket. The one thing on her that looked new was her gun belt. It was too large for her—so much so that an extra hole had to be punched into it so she could cinch it around her waist. Obviously, it used to belong to someone else. Someone far larger who no longer had the need for guns or holsters or drawing breath.

"I don't know," Onawa said, gazing calmly into the girl's dark eyes. "What *am* I looking at?"

The girl put a hand to the butt of her gun.

"Cherokee?" Onawa went on. "Choctaw? Osage? Quapaw?"

"Wormwood's like my momma's stew," said one of the other riders—a husky, round-faced boy of perhaps eighteen who was trotting along beside the ice cream wagon. "Got a little bit of everything in her."

"Shut up, Nathaniel," the girl said. "This is between me and the squaw."

She thumbed back the fastening strap on her revolver.

There was only one thing Onawa could do. Her hands were tied together in front of her, useless. If the girl brought up the gun, Onawa would have to throw herself off the horse and make a run for the woods. She'd need to cover about twenty yards without getting shot in the back by either the girl or one of her friends.

Impossible. But better than a bullet to the face.

"Leave her alone, Wormwood," said the young man riding ahead of the rest.

"She's asking questions, Blaze," said the girl—Wormwood, apparently. "She's *looking* at me."

"Leave her alone."

"I don't even know why we brought her with us."

"You'll see."

Wormwood's expression brightened. She liked the sound of that.

"Oh, yeah?" she said.

"You'll see," Blaze Bad Water said again. "Soon."

The girl slipped the retention strap back in place over the hammer of her gun.

"Don't look at me, old woman," she growled at Onawa.

Onawa dropped her gaze to her bound hands.

Wormwood remained beside her a moment, glaring. Then she sped up to rejoin the burly one she'd called "Nathaniel" alongside the wagon.

That left two members of the gang still behind Onawa. If she tried to turn the Bay and gallop off—assuming she could even get the big, slow horse up to a gallop—she'd be dead in seconds.

She had no choice. Like Wormwood, she had to wait and see what Blaze Bad Water had in mind for her.

Onawa wore her long hair loose—no braids—and she reached up and stroked it from time to time as if soothing herself. It was awkward with her hands tied, but not impossible. Not like the days she was remembering.

Hands not just tied together but tied to more bound hands— more captured Mescalero and Lipan Apaches—with a long rope that pulled pulled pulled them deep into Chihuahua. Into slavery.

Onawa tugged and twirled her hair as she thought of those days. Then she lowered her hands and let the breeze carry off the few stray black-gray strands that had come away in her fingers.

"There's Gootch!" the burly young man named Nathaniel said, and he straightened up in his stirrups and waved.

Ahead about two hundred yards, a buckboard was parked near the turnoff for a narrow side lane. The figure standing beside it waved back at Nathaniel. As they drew closer Onawa could see that the new man fit right in with the rest of the gang. He was young, dark-skinned and dark-haired, shabbily dressed, skinny. He grinned as the little procession drew up before him—a wide smile that showed off black gums.

His front teeth had been knocked out at some point, and the brown dribble stains on the front of his shirt said he loved chewing tobacco.

"You got him!" he said, pointing at the ice cream wagon.

"You ever doubt we would?" asked Blaze Bad Water.

Gootch shook his head, still grinning. "Hell no, Blaze! But I'm still glad to see you." He glanced at Onawa, but seemed to decide against asking about her. Instead he nodded back at the buckboard. "Got everything all set just like you told me to."

"Good."

Bad Water swiveled in his saddle to peer back up the road behind them. It gave Onawa her best look at him yet.

He had a square face and a thick neck, and the black hair under his flat-brimmed hat was neatly trimmed. Though he was young like the others—just nineteen—there was a calm somberness in his eyes you usually didn't see in one his age.

Onawa had taken a sort of professional interest in the country's most wanted outlaws, knowing there was a chance the A.A. Western Detective Agency might set its sights on one or another. So she was aware of this Blaze Bad Water and the horrible things he'd supposedly done in the Indian Territories and Kansas. But if she'd passed him on the reservation back in New Mexico Territory she wouldn't have looked at him twice, except perhaps to note that he didn't dress like most Mescalero men and there was something about his expression that suggested both cunning and intelligence—not always the same thing.

When Bad Water noticed Onawa watching him, he turned to Wormwood.

"Keep your gun on her," he said. "And don't hide it."

The girl unholstered her revolver—a gleaming pearl-handled Remington that seemed far too big for her little hand—and rode back and pointed it at Onawa. She looked happy and excited, like a child anticipating a cookie.

"The rest of you get to it," Bad Water said.

The gang already had its instructions, apparently. They got down from their horses, and some hurried over to the buckboard while others went to the back of the ice cream wagon.

Bad Water turned his horse and slowly rode back to join Wormwood and Onawa.

"Who was the Black fella with the Sharps rifle up on the ridge last night?" he asked.

A chill went through Onawa.

"That sounds like my husband," she said. "He went out hunting."

Wormwood snorted. "I bet he did."

"Did you hurt him?" Onawa asked.

"Nathaniel did," Bad Water said. He said it flatly, matter of fact, as if answering a question about the weather. "Didn't kill him, though. Left him for me to talk to—then he managed to slip away in the dark. I'm wondering how big a problem that is for us."

"It doesn't have to be any problem. He will come looking for me, so let me go."

Wormwood snorted again.

"What do you know about *him?*" Bad Water asked Onawa, jerking his head at the ice cream wagon. The back door was open, and Nathaniel and another young man were pushing out a long, low pinewood box.

"That's a 'him?'" said Onawa.

Bad Water nodded.

"I don't know anything," Onawa said, "except that it is very bad luck to disturb the dead."

Wormwood wiggled the fingers of her left hand.

"Oooooooo," she moaned. "The ghost of Abe Lincoln's gonna get us."

Bad Water shot her a frown. It was the first time Onawa had seen anything like emotion on his face.

"Abe Lincoln?" she said. "The old president? From the big white-eye war?"

"It ain't Abe Lincoln the barber," said Wormwood. She gave Bad Water a look of mock contrition. "Uh oh...now she knows too much."

She aimed her Remington at Onawa's heart.

"*No*," Bad Water said.

Wormwood didn't lower her gun. "Oh, come on, Blaze..."

Onawa wondered if she should start singing a death song—and if doing so would *ensure* that Wormwood shot her.

"There's still too much we don't know," Bad Water said. "And she might be useful."

He turned and looked up the road again. There was no one there.

Some of the gang members, meanwhile, were moving the box to the buckboard while a couple others stood by with cut branches they'd taken out of its bed.

"Anyway," Bad Water said, turning back toward Wormwood and Onawa, "we don't have time for this. We gotta get moving again."

"Aww," Wormwood said. "You just have a thing for old women."

She lowered her gun...a little.

"Put her in the buckboard and tie her horse behind Hosmer's wagon," Bad Water told her. "We'll get the truth out of her when we hit the river."

Wormwood smiled. She liked the sound of that.

Bad Water rode off to supervise as Nathaniel and two other young men slid the pine box onto the buckboard. A couple minutes later — after Wormwood had roughly dragged her down from her horse and pushed her that way—Onawa was sitting miserably beside it. The skinny one called Gootch was in the driver's seat of the Cherokees' ice cream wagon now, and he snapped the reins and rolled off fast with two of the other gang members riding alongside.

"See ya at the church!" Gootch called out.

Nathaniel gave him a grin and a wave. Wormwood a nod.

Bad Water said nothing. He just sent his horse trotting up the other road—the narrower one that angled off at the intersection. The driver of the buckboard sent the wagon after him, and Wormwood and Nathaniel followed, too. The men holding branches stepped out and started sweeping the dirt behind them.

They were literally covering their tracks. Trying to hide any signs that they'd split off.

Hoop and Eskaminzim wouldn't be fooled—especially not if she could give them a little help. They'd be along eventually, perhaps with Pixley, to try to get her back...assuming she was still alive when Blaze Bad Water and Wormwood were done with her at whatever river they were heading toward. Some of the old Cherokee Confederates were still out there somewhere, as well. They hadn't *all* died in the attack on their camp.

Onawa stroked her hair and watched this new road wind away behind her and wondered which of the men following she might see first.

CHAPTER 33

"Damn," Eli Lizzenbe said as he took in the campsite and the bodies strewn around it.

He'd lost a lot of friends fighting under the major as a sergeant in the 1st Cherokee Mounted Rifles. He hadn't expected to lose so many more—not in the same way, from bullets, not old age—all these years after the end of the war.

"They hit our camp while we wasted the night looking for theirs," said the man on horseback beside him, shaking his head. "We shoulda been ready for that. Now we got more bodies to bury *and* we lost the wagon."

"No time for burying. We gotta get that wagon back," Lizzenbe said. He nodded down at the ruts leading off to the road. "Interesting that they took it west not east. Deeper into the Nations, not back to Missouri. Mighty damn interesting."

He looked over at a tall, thin, grizzled man wearing a beaten top hat and a shabby old-fashioned greatcoat with a flowing cape around the shoulders. His legs seemed too long for his saddle, the knees pointing off sharply to the sides, his thighs splayed.

"Bowlegs," Lizzenbe said, "someone's gotta go to Joplin and tell the major."

The one called Bowlegs nodded unhappily. No one wanted to give Major Solomon Hosmer bad news, and riding into a White town to do it wouldn't make it any easier. But he knew when he was being volunteered for something. He wheeled his horse around and left.

Lizzenbe and the other remaining Cherokee men—they were down to five now—didn't linger long over their fallen comrades. No one said any earnest words, no one sang a song, no one even removed his hat or offered a salute. They just stared in solemn silence at the dead men splayed in the grass and thought of the hundreds more they'd once seen lying like this in fields and roads and gullies.

Then, still wordless, they rode off determined to make more.

CHAPTER 34

Capt. Henry Walkingstick knew how to creep up on cattle rustlers and whiskey runners and killers in the Indian Nations. He could slip through forests, up stream beds, around villages and farms and road houses.

But brick and mortar? That he couldn't sneak through. So there was no way into the Joplin Hotel that didn't involve a door—and no door that didn't have a burly doorman in front of it.

Walkingstick's badge wouldn't get him past them. He hadn't even flashed it at the occasional Joplin cop who'd spotted him lingering and given him the evil eye. Telling them who he was would have been worse than useless. He wasn't just out of his jurisdiction, he was an Indian out of his jurisdiction. One who wouldn't want to explain why he was really there.

A single step out of the Cherokee Nation—over a line that existed only on maps—and all his authority disappeared. So whenever he saw a policeman rounding the corner, he just moved on... then circled back a little later to keep watching and waiting and wondering all through the night.

Obviously, something had gone wrong in the hotel. Obviously,

Diehl was in trouble…or dead. But what to do about it? That wasn't obvious at all.

He was going to give it until ten in the morning. If he hadn't spotted something that changed things by then—Solomon Hosmer leaving, perhaps, or the doormen carrying out a Diehl-shaped bag of trash—he was going to head back into the Nations and look for Diehl's friends and the ice cream wagon. Start all over again. *After* he found a soft, safe spot in the woods to get some sleep.

For years, his wife had been telling him he should take up carpentry. He was good with his hands. And when a carpenter does his job right, nobody shoots at him, and he can spend every night in his own bed.

Not for the first time, Walkingstick asked himself why he didn't listen to her.

He pulled out his pocket watch—a gift from his wife on their tenth anniversary—and checked the time.

Nine forty-five. Diehl had fifteen more minutes. Then Walking-stick was giving up on him.

He didn't like it. It would be risky, but maybe he should at least try to bluff his way inside before leaving…though he had no idea what he'd do next even if he made it. Go door to door through the hotel looking for Diehl? Tip a bellhop to tell him where they keep the prisoners and bodies? Try to blend in with the ferns in the lobby and keep waiting for something to—?

Walkingstick felt a tap on his shoulder. He put away his watch and fixed a fake smile to his face and turned expecting to find a policeman standing behind him with a billy club and questions.

Instead, Walkingstick saw nothing—until he looked down.

The tap had come from a man just a little more than five feet tall. He looked to be in his midfifties and seemed to be a gentleman judging by his fine Ulster coat and Homburg hat and white starched collar and necktie. He had an intense expression on his round, slightly jowly face, and there were dark circles under his eyes that indicated his night hadn't been any more restful than Walkingstick's.

"Uhh…can I help you?" Walkingstick asked.

"I certainly hope so," the little man replied, his words coming out clipped and quick. "I'm looking for an employee of mine. He informed me that he'd be here with an associate." He paused and cocked an eyebrow. "'An interested party from the Cherokee Nation?'"

It took Walkingstick a moment to get over his surprise.

"You're looking for Diehl?" he said, keeping his voice low.

"I am." The little man jerked his head at the hotel. "Did he manage to get himself lost in there?"

Walkingstick nodded slowly. "Went in last night and never came back out. Look…before we go any further, why don't you tell me who you are?"

The man straightened up to his full height—which was only about an eighth of an inch taller than he'd been before.

"I am Colonel C. Kermit Crowe, managing director of the A.A. Western Detective Agency. And you are…?" He looked Walking-stick up and down. "A tribal policeman?"

"That's right. Captain Henry Walkingstick of the Cherokee Lighthorse Mounted Police."

"Ah. Excellent. I require your assistance, Captain, and hope I can depend on your discretion. There are powerful forces at play here. A conspiracy at work. That's why I couldn't entrust this to the normal authorities and had to dispatch instead the agency's keenest mind to crack it open."

"Oh. All right," said Walkingstick.

He looked around, searching the sidewalk for the "keenest mind" who'd accompanied Colonel Crowe to Joplin…hopefully with the agency's biggest muscles and best shots along as well.

He saw only oblivious men and women strolling past on their way elsewhere as part of their usual mundane morning.

Colonel Crowe cleared his throat.

Walkingstick looked at him again.

"So," the little man said, "here I am."

CHAPTER 35

With his good arm, Eskaminzim broke a low branch on a hickory tree near the road. He didn't snap it all the way off, though. Just wrenched it enough so that it angled downward but still pointed in the same direction. The direction of the road. Southwest.

It was a message to Diehl. One Eskaminzim had been repeating every mile, first on one side of the road, then the other.

Keep coming. This way. Catch up.

What's taking you so damn long?

Slowly, not groaning but wanting to, Eskaminzim hauled himself back up onto his horse. The pain in his right shoulder, where the fleeing Cherokee had shot him the night before, was excruciating. Yet he'd refused to let Hoop leave the trail sign for Diehl.

"This little scratch?" he'd said dismissively when Hoop suggested it. "It's nothing. Bullet passed clean through. I've hurt myself worse stubbing my toe."

Hoop had looked skeptical, but he didn't argue. He knew it was useless.

Tracking and leaving trail sign were Eskaminzim's job. He'd still insist on doing it if the Cherokee had shot him twice in the chest and left a knife in his belly. Especially when getting his job done now meant more than ever.

The trotting of his horse sent even more pain stabbing through Eskaminzim's shoulder, but he forced himself not to wince as he caught up to Hoop and Pixley on the road.

Hoop was still trying to work out what they were up against.

"So they steal Lincoln's body so they can ransom it back. It's crazy, but I can see it," he was saying to Pixley. "But why risk hauling it all the way down here before asking for the money?"

"I have no idea," Pixley said. "Maybe it's symbolic." He looked over at Eskaminzim. "Do the Cherokees have some special grudge against Abraham Lincoln?"

Eskaminzim cocked his head quizzically. (Which hurt, but he hoped it didn't show.)

"How should I know?" he said. "Until two days ago, I'd never met a Cherokee before. And the only one I got to talk to was dead within a minute."

"Oh. Right," said Pixley. "Sorry."

"It's not like we have a newsletter," Eskaminzim went on. "Or picnics and quilting bees where all the Indians get together to gossip."

"Of course. I shouldn't have assumed."

"Do you know what all the White men think in Canada?" Eskaminzim continued. "What they're all up to in England? Do you all share your secrets with each other? I wouldn't have thought so from the way you're always squabbling among yourselves."

"I said I'm sorry! I shouldn't have said that!"

Eskaminzim gave Pixley a little smile. Without Diehl around, it was nice to have *someone* he could needle.

"Actually, it's a good question," Eskaminzim said. He jerked his chin at Hoop. "I was about to ask him the same thing. He'd know better than me."

Pixley looked at Hoop in confusion.

"I was born in Georgia, not far from the old Cherokee lands," Hoop explained. "Not all of 'em got marched off to this place sixty years ago. Still a few Cherokees back east. But no—I don't know of any special grudge they got against Lincoln, beyond some of 'em owning slaves and fighting to keep 'em. Andrew Jackson, yes. They hate him. But Lincoln?" Hoop shrugged. "Depends. Maybe the Cherokees who brought his body down from Illinois were thinking 'symbolic'-like. But the ones who stole the body from *them*? I don't think so."

Eskaminzim shook his head in mock disgust. (That hurt, too, but again he refused to show it.)

"Indians fighting Indians," he said. "Disgusting."

Pixley obviously didn't know what to say to that.

Hoop took mercy on him.

"He's joking," he said.

"I've fought every kind of Indian in the West! Every kind of Apache!" Eskaminzim proclaimed. "Mescaleros are the best, of course."

"Of course," said Pixley.

Hoop gave him a (painful) nod. He'd said the right thing.

"Although there was this one Coyotero," Eskaminzim said wistfully. "Now he knew how to…"

Without explanation, he suddenly veered left, toward a narrow lane that angled off southward. When he reached the point where the two roads met, he began riding in a slow circle, gazing downward. He leaned far out from his saddle for a closer look at the ground, finding it impossible to keep the pain from showing on his face this time. But that didn't matter now. Not when he didn't have to keep distracting himself from the worry churning in his gut or his inability to do anything about it.

He climbed down from his horse, still grimacing in pain, and began walking up the side lane, back hunched, eyes down.

Hoop sent his horse galloping forty yards up the main road, squinted at the dirt a moment, then turned and rode back.

"Wagon tracks carry on the way they been going," he said. "But don't look to be as many horses with it now, and one ain't got nobody on it."

Eskaminzim nodded. "They have another wagon. Smaller and

NO HALLOWED GROUND   201

lighter. It came up from the south, then went back that way again. With riders when it left."

"Damn," Hoop said.

He looked back and forth from the main road to the side path.

Which wagon to follow? One group was a decoy. The other had the body.

But which had Onawa?

Eskaminzim crouched down and stretched out his good hand and plucked something up with two fingers. He held it before his face and let it flutter for a moment in the gentle breeze.

A single strand of long, gray-black hair.

Hoop was too far away to see it himself, but he could guess what it was from the way Eskaminzim held it.

Eskaminzim let it go, and it drifted away toward the trees.

His gaze met Hoop's, and without a sound or a gesture it was agreed.

They knew which way they were going.

CHAPTER 36

Onawa awkwardly stroked her hair with her bound hands and watched the forest slide past and tried not to think about what was in the box beside her.

The little lane was rougher than the road they'd been on before —uneven and overgrown with grass—and the buckboard rattled and creaked. One hard jolt as they bumped over a big rock, and who knew? The box didn't look very sturdy. A side panel could pop off, and Onawa would have president all over her. Wasn't Abraham Lincoln supposed to be a tall man? There might be a lot of him.

Onawa glanced back, past Wormwood glowering at her from atop her pony to the narrow, winding lane making its way north. She wanted to look anywhere *but* back. Why remind these bandit brats that Hoop and Eskaminzim might be coming up behind them? But she didn't want to look at the box either, and you can't keep your eyes from turning to hope occasionally.

Wormwood seemed to read her mind.

"You better pray your husband *ain't* coming for you," the girl sneered. "He gets too close, and I'll make sure the first one dead is you."

A reply came quick to Onawa's lips, but she held it back.

Then the second one dead, she wanted to say, *will be* you.

But she'd seen enough people killed because they couldn't keep their mouths shut. One moment of defiance, one curse, one mocking laugh—it was enough to bring death if you were with someone who welcomed the excuse. Like Wormwood.

"Go on! Say something!" the girl taunted. Her hand moved to the pearly-white grip of her big Remington. "I can see you want to. Tell me off, bitch!"

Other members of the gang—doughy Nathaniel riding just ahead of the buckboard, the dark-skinned, pock-faced young man beside him, the gap-toothed teen in the driver's seat—turned to watch with wide eyes and leering grins. Enjoying the show. Expecting it to end with a bang.

"Wormwood!" Blaze Bad Water snapped. He was about twenty yards ahead of the rest, leading the little procession through the forest. "Leave her alone."

"I don't like riding with a spy," Wormwood said.

Her hand didn't move from her gun.

"I told you," Bad Water said. "At the river."

He'd only barely turned to look back over his shoulder. Now he faced forward again, confident that Wormwood would listen to him.

Onawa wasn't so sure.

Wormwood kept glaring at her hatefully.

"Keep your eyes down, squaw," the girl said. "And stop playing with your hair. It's annoying."

Onawa did as she was told, lowering her eyes and resting her hands in her lap. There was nothing she could do now but watch the box in front of her for signs it was shaking apart and wait for the sound of gunfire or approaching horses…or water.

———

It was the birds Onawa heard first. Kingfishers, with their high-pitched, chirping warble. Then the chittering squeak of swallows. Then the honking of geese.

All sounds that said they were getting close to a lake, a stream. A river.

When she heard the flowing water, the sound told her which it was. It wasn't small, wasn't big, wasn't shallow, wasn't deep, wasn't lazy and stagnant, wasn't running fast. Just another river in the spring far from the big mountains and their melting snows.

"Water the horses," Blaze Bad Water said. "But not too much. We're almost there anyway. And we might still need 'em to run."

"What about her?" Wormwood asked.

Onawa heard the creak of saddle leather that said someone was getting down from a horse. Then footsteps, approaching fast.

They couldn't expect her to keep staring down at that damn box now.

She looked up just as Bad Water grabbed her by the hair and yanked her backward out of the wagon bed.

Her cry of surprise and pain didn't last long. Her back slammed hard into the ground, knocking the wind out of her. By the time Bad Water was pulling her to her feet—he never lost his grip on the hair at the top of her head—she was gritting her teeth, ready for it, silent.

The gang hooted and laughed as Bad Water guided her from the sandy-silty strip near the riverbank toward the trees.

"Don't be greedy, Blaze!" Nathaniel said. "Leave some for the rest of us!"

"Or don't!" Wormwood added.

So it would be this. Now.

All right. Fine. Onawa had been here before. Not the place but the situation.

Bad Water was about to make himself vulnerable. At the right moment, she could kick, she could scratch, she could bite, she could get his gun, she could run. She just had to stay alive long enough for him to be stupid.

He forced her into the woods with one hand tight in her hair and the other on her back, pushing. They walked over moist leaves and downed trees until they were out of sight of the others.

So Bad Water was shy. Good. That improved Onawa's chances. A little. She just had to hope he didn't—

Bad Water let go of her hair and gave her a shove that sent her sprawling to the forest floor. She rolled over as quickly as she could, her tied hands up, ready to gouge and scrape and flail.

Bad Water was already sitting on a log six feet away, smiling at her. It was a different smile than the others wore. Not mocking. Reassuring. Perhaps even kind.

"It's all right. I just wanted to talk," he said. He nodded back the way they'd just come. "Away from them."

Onawa sat up slowly, wary, and said nothing.

Bad Water let her get comfortable—or as comfortable as she could be sitting cross-legged on leaves and twigs with her hands roped together—still smiling. Then he asked his first question.

It wasn't any of the ones Onawa expected. *Who are you? What are you doing here? Do I really need to keep you alive?*

It was such a surprise Onawa could only blink silently when she heard it.

"Do you have kids?" Bad Water asked her.

When she didn't answer, he added, "You have a husband, and you're the right age, so…"

"I did have a child," Onawa said. "Once."

She thought maybe she should say, "Yes. Four. Waiting for me on the reservation. I don't know what will happen to them if I don't come back." But the truth had popped out instead.

"Oh," Bad Water said. His smile faded away, but the gentleness remained in his eyes. "Was it a long time ago?"

"Yes."

Bad Water nodded. "I thought you were a mother. I could just tell…even if it was once, a long time ago. What nation are you from?"

"I am Mescalero Apache," said Onawa.

"Mescalero? I didn't think we had any of them in the Territories."

"You do now."

Bad Water chuckled. "I guess every tribe'll end up corralled here sooner or later." He waved a hand at the cedars and sycamores and cottonwoods around them. "Then the whites will take this away, too."

"Probably."

"That's why we're leaving," Bad Water said. "Me and my friends. That box of bones is going to carry us far, far away, with pockets full of cash. It's going to save us from the rope. So I can't lose it. I can't let anything stop us. You understand?"

"Yes."

"I figured you would. You're a smart woman. So tell me. Who was that Black man, and what was he doing up on the ridge last night with a Sharps rifle?"

"I told you already. He is my husband. He was out hunting."

Bad Water shook his head sadly.

"Momma Mescalero…please don't lie to me," he said.

"I'm not lying. His name is Hoop. If he is alive, he will come for me. But you don't need to worry about him. Just give me to him, and we'll go. We don't want any part of your stolen bones."

Bad Water kept shaking his head. "You're making this harder. I understand, though. You have to protect yourself. I could try to beat the truth out of you, but I think you're a pretty tough woman, too."

Raucous laughter echoed through the woods.

"Blaze! What's taking you so long?" Wormwood yelled. "Nathaniel wouldn't have been in there thirty seconds!"

There was more laughter and unintelligible shouts.

The gang was done watering the horses. Now they were getting antsy.

"And there's no time," Bad Water sighed. "It's hard to keep that bunch in line long. And if someone's gonna catch up to us from behind, I don't want them to do it while we're still on the road."

He held out his right hand, the palm up, and gestured for Onawa to stand. When she was on her feet again, he waved her forward.

"Back we go," he said.

He stayed still as she moved toward him, apparently waiting for

her to step ahead of him before following her back to the river
bank.

When she drew even with him, he reached out and gripped her
by the upper arm, jerking her to a stop.

"But you know," he said, "they'll be expecting you to come out
looking a certain way. It wouldn't be good to disappoint them."

Bad Water gave Onawa a long, wistful look. Then he brought up
his free hand and slapped her across the face. He held her tight as
she jerked to the side, then he backhanded her, sending her sagging
the other way.

"Sorry, Momma," he said.

He slapped her again.

"Sorry, Momma."

He slapped her again.

"Can you give me some tears, Momma?"

Onawa brought up her bound hands to protect her face.

Bad Water slammed a fist into her stomach.

Onawa doubled over.

"Tears would be good," Bad Water said. "Do we have any yet?"

He grabbed Onawa by the hair again and jerked her head up.

She wasn't crying but her eyes were watering, and her face was
splotched red.

"That's better," Bad Water said.

He let go of her hair and punched her in the nose.

"But blood would be good, too," he said.

Onawa staggered backward, then sagged to the side.

Bad Water held her up.

"It's all right now," he whispered as she steadied herself. "All
done."

He leaned in and kissed her tenderly on the forehead—then let
her go and hopped back quickly before she could make a grab for
his holstered Colt.

He pulled it out himself and jabbed it forward.

"Back to the wagon," he said. "And remember to keep your eyes
down."

As Onawa slowly turned to go, blood streaming through the

fingers she now pressed over her nose, he gave her another reassuring smile that didn't reassure her one bit.

"You'll be able to get a good look around soon enough, Momma," Bad Water told her. "We're almost home."

CHAPTER 37

"How was your little breakfast talk?" Una Dockery asked her father when he and Major Hosmer returned to the senator's suite on the fourth floor of the Joplin Hotel. "Got the next rebellion all ready to go?"

Senator Cleburne shot a frown at her, and her husband huddled together on a settee in the sitting room.

"It was fine, fine," he said, irritated by the sarcasm in his daughter's voice and the sweetly condescending smile on her angelic face. She usually directed those at others, not him. "Encouraging. Stirring. Productive."

"Pancakes," Hosmer rumbled behind him. "With a bunch of bureaucrats. While the plan unravels."

He closed the door to the hallway, then turned and stood there, stiff and scowling.

"Those 'bureaucrats' hold seats of power throughout the South, Major," Cleburne told him. "They're already winning 'the next rebellion' just by being who and where they are. Why, with the resources to keep them in power, *expand* that power, they'll have the war won for us before the Yankees even know it's started…and either Dixie will be free again or the whole of America will *be* Dixie. I'd hoped you'd find meeting them inspiring."

Hosmer said nothing, and his expression didn't change. But it was clear he was *not* feeling inspired.

"And anyway, Major," the senator went on, "you'd have better things to do this morning than complain about our bureaucrats and pancakes if you'd stuck to the plan and *kept* it from unraveling. Which it's not doing, by the way!" He jerked his head at the bedroom door—and the prisoner on the other side of it. "That's just a little wrinkle."

"About that——" Una began, eyes widening with mock chagrin.

The major spoke over her, his gaze still locked on her father.

"I deviated from the plan, yes. One of the parts that never made sense to me," he said. "Why risk bringing Lincoln here? To a city so far from Springfield? My men and I could have hidden him in Illinois and slipped back to the Nations without having to drag a wagon along with us. And then I find all these 'knights' of yours having a club meeting at the hotel you wanted the body delivered to…? You never told me about that. What else aren't you telling me?"

"Not telling you…?" Cleburne said.

He scoffed because the unheard of had happened, and for the moment it was the only sound he could make.

Senator Samuel Cleburne was at a loss for words.

There was a pitcher of water on a table nearby, and he walked over and poured himself a glass.

"Darned syrup," he muttered. "Got my mouth all sticky."

"Oh, Daddy," Una said, swiping a hand at her father.

Her husband swiveled on the settee to give her a look of warning she ignored.

"Just tell him," she went on. "We're all on the same side, aren't we? There shouldn't be any secrets between us."

Cleburne glared at her over the glass he was guzzling from.

"Secrets?" Hosmer said, still staring at the senator.

The old man held up a finger while he drained the glass and collected his thoughts.

"Yes, well…" he said when all the water was gone. He set the glass back down beside the pitcher and took hold of the lapels of his frock coat. "All the great fraternal organizations are built on rites and rituals that bond its members to each other and reinforce their shared values and purpose. So it is with the Knights of Keziah. I've gathered them here not just to make plans with them but to strengthen their sense of unity and devotion to the cause. And in our little joint venture, Major, I saw an extraordinary opportunity to do that. So I thought I'd just…"

He brought down one hand then the other and joined them, the fingers interlacing.

"…combine one with the other for a moment."

He gave Hosmer a smile that said he was done explaining.

Hosmer looked over at Una.

"What is he talking about?" he said.

"A ceremony that was supposed to be held last night for the inner circle of the Knights of Keziah," she replied without hesitation.

"Una!" her husband and father said at the same time.

She giggled and continued.

"He was going to have them tinkle on Abraham Lincoln!"

"*What?*" Hosmer said.

He faced the senator again, his perpetual scowl deepening and darkening.

"It would have been a powerful symbolic gesture!" Cleburne said.

"Oh, fiddlesticks." Una laughed. "You just wanted to do it."

Hosmer was so enraged he was trembling. He clenched his fists as if fighting to keep his fingers from wrapping around the old man's throat.

"Men died on the road to Joplin," he said, "just so you could desecrate the dead?"

"Says the graverobber!" Cleburne shot back.

Hosmer shook his head in disgust. "Now I'm *truly* glad I didn't listen to you and bring the body here."

Cleburne reared up as if Hosmer had spat in his face.

"But you *will* adhere to the plan from here on out," he said slowly. "Do not forget, Major. *I'm* the one with contacts inside the federal government. *I'm* the one who knows how to get the ransom demand through the right channels quietly. And *I'm* the one who knows where the money will come from and how to collect it without getting caught."

"And you shouldn't forget, Senator," Hosmer replied just as slowly, his already deep, rumbling voice seeming to drop another half-octave, "that *I'm* the one with Abraham Lincoln."

For a silent moment, the two old men just stood there glaring, each daring the other to speak next.

"Oh, my goodness—such a fuss between friends," Una said. "And when we have something so important to deal with together, too."

Cleburne and Hosmer turned toward the couch.

"Him. The spy," Dockery said with a jerk of the head toward the bedroom. "While you were gone, Una tried to get him to talk."

"A woman's wiles, and all that," Una said. "Only I wasn't so wily perhaps. I think he ended up learning more from me than I did from him. And now that he's had the chance to listen to *this* conversation through the door..." She shook her head and lowered her voice. "I don't think it would be wise to put off the inevitable any longer, do you?"

"Fine," said Hosmer. "Kill him."

Una gave him a smile, then focused on her father. "Daddy? Shall we?"

"I suppose we must," the senator grated out. "I swear, Una... sometimes I don't know how you got this way."

"Practical, you mean? Why, I get that from you." Una patted her husband on the knee. "Garland here will take care of our guest. Won't you, darling?"

Dockery cleared his throat and said, "Certainly." But then he just sat there.

"Well...?" Una said to him. "Don't keep the man waiting."

"Right."

Slowly, knees trembling, Dockery rose from the settee. He took one unsteady step forward, then froze and cocked his head.

"*Garland…*" Una crooned, shooing him toward the bedroom door.

Then she heard it, too. The noise that had stopped her husband.

Footsteps in the hall. Quick, heavy ones, from more than one pair of feet.

They stopped at the door to the suite, and there was a sharp *rap-rap-rap* that made Dockery and the senator jump.

"Yes? Who is it?" Cleburne said.

"It's Stowers, sir. The manager," a voice replied.

"And Arthur Bewley," another added. "We need to speak to you immediately."

Cleburne took a reluctant step toward the door.

"The hotel's on fire, sir!" the first man said.

Cleburne moved faster after that. When he jerked the door open, the smell of smoke swirled into the room.

Two men stood side by side in the hallway: Bewley, the plump mayor of Joplin, and the smaller but equally chubby-cheeked hotel manager, Stowers.

Stowers began spewing words.

"It looks like it started in the alley out back, and it's already spread into the kitchen and up to the second floor, and I don't know if—"

"You should leave," Bewley told the senator. Cleburne hadn't opened the door all the way, and the big man leaned to the side to peer in at the others inside the room. "All of you."

Already the smell of smoke was growing stronger.

"*Damnation*," the senator spat.

Una reached out and patted her husband on the back.

"It looks like you won't have to deal with that little nuisance after all," she said. "We can just toddle off and let the fire take care of it."

Hosmer stepped up behind Cleburne in the doorway.

"*How* did the fire start?" he asked the men in the hall.

"I don't know!" Stowers cried. He wiped his sweaty face with a wadded-up handkerchief, knocking the pince-nez on his nose askew.

"We can figure that out later," said Bewley. "Right now you *really* need to—"

The sound of rushing footsteps rose up again. Stowers looked to his right, Bewley looked to his left.

"What are *you* doing up here?" Stowers said.

"Who are you?" said Bewley.

Cleburne and Hosmer both squeezed into the doorway and leaned out to see who they were talking to.

Cleburne peered to his left, the way Stowers was looking, and saw an almost comically short middle-aged man marching up the hall from the elevator.

"Who is that?" the senator asked.

"The man who came in to tell us there was a fire out back," Stowers said.

When the little man saw Senator Cleburne peeping at him, his already grim expression grew even grimmer. He'd appeared determined before. Now he appeared determined and furious.

Hosmer, meanwhile, had looked to the right, following Bewley's gaze to take in a figure coming out of the service stairwell that way. It was a tall, dark-haired, goateed man dressed for riding the trail.

By the time the man took his second step their way, Hosmer had recognized him.

"*You*," the major growled.

"*You*," the other man growled back. He pulled a Smith & Wesson forty-five from the holster at his side.

"Captain!" the little man snapped as they stalked toward each other, closing in on the senator's suite from opposite directions. "First things first!"

He reached into his coat pocket, hauled out a stubby-barreled Bull Dog revolver, and aimed it at a spot directly between the senator's widened eyes.

"You! Traitor!" the little man barked. "Take me to Oswin Diehl, or I'll blow out your blasted traitor brains!"

CHAPTER 38

A little confused conversation was required—"Who?" the senator responded when asked about Oswin Diehl—but it went quickly. There was only one man being held prisoner after all. Soon Walkingstick was keeping his forty-five on the group he and the colonel had corralled in the suite's front room—Major Solomon Hosmer, three well-dressed White men in various states of panic, and a beautiful, strangely amused-looking lady—while Crowe forced the man he contemptuously addressed as either "Traitor" or "Senator Judas" to untie Diehl in the bedroom.

"You shouldn't have inserted yourself into this, Henry," Hosmer said to Walkingstick. "You're out of your depth."

"I'm not inserting myself into anything," Walkingstick replied. "I'm doing my job...which includes bringing Cherokee thieves and murderers to justice."

Hosmer rejected the insults with a shake of the head. "Everything I've done, I've done for the Cherokee Nation."

"Yeah, right. Just like during the war," Walkingstick said. "You pledged allegiance to the Cherokees. Fought the federals for the Cherokees. Slaughtered black prisoners for the Cherokees. Drove families from their homes for the Cherokees—even when they were

Cherokee themselves." He brought up his free hand and rubbed his jaw as if deep in thought, then snapped his fingers. "Oh. Wait. That was all for Jefferson goddamn Davis."

"I was supposed to fight for Abraham Lincoln?" Hosmer replied, unruffled. "The side that sought to strip us of our rights and property?"

"Your rights and property?" Walkingstick shook his head. "Your hypocrisy makes me want to puke."

"Then you know how I feel about your sanctimony."

"My oh my, but this is a fascinating historical debate," the White lady interjected from her spot on the couch. "But I must confess that at the moment I have current events much more on my mind. Such as the fact that the building is on fire…"

She took a dainty whiff of the air.

The smoky smell was growing ever stronger, and hotel guests— frightened Knights of Keziah—could be heard shouting and rushing up and down the hallway.

"Far be it for a woman to offer suggestions in a time of crisis," the lady said, "but if we want to rehash the past perhaps it could be done somewhere that is *not* about to burst into flame…?"

"A good dose of hellfire is exactly what you deserve!" Colonel Crowe snapped.

He was walking back into the sitting room with Senator Cleburne and, held up between them dragging his feet, Oswin Diehl.

Walkingstick grimaced when he saw Diehl's puffy, pummeled face and blood-stained shirt.

Diehl greeted him with a slow, wincing nod.

"So," Diehl said, "what's this about a fire?"

"Just a little diversion," Col. Crowe said. "And a reason for this one—" He jerked his chin at the hotel manager, who was wiping his face with his handkerchief and reproaching himself under his breath for not staying home today. "—to lead us to whoever was really in charge around here. I was expecting to see Major Hosmer. Little did I know how illustrious this nest of vipers would prove to be. Traitors of the highest stripe!"

At the far end of the hallway, men screamed.

"Don't get in the elevator! Don't get in the elevator!" another man yelled as he ran past the door.

"Your little diversion seems to have gotten out of hand," the lady said, alarm finally beginning to dispel her languid, detached air. "Now that you've collected your friend perhaps you would allow us to leave…?"

"Ha! Just let you snakes go?" Col. Crowe said.

The hotel manager screeched out a short, sharp shriek.

Everyone else looked at him, then followed his goggle-eyed stare.

Curling wisps of smoke were pushing in under the bottom of the door.

"My stomach was bothering me this morning," the manager moaned, clutching his handkerchief in both hands. "I could've stayed in bed."

"Colonel," Walkingstick said, "we're going to be lucky to get out here with Diehl…"

He let his words trail off, not speaking the rest out loud.

…there's no way we could do it with prisoners.

"Blast!" Col. Crowe said. He looked over at Diehl. "Can you manage on your own?"

Diehl took a breath, slid his arms away from Crowe and Cleburne's shoulders, and stood up straight. Swaying, but straight.

Rather than say anything, he gave Crowe a weary salute.

"Good," Col. Crowe said. He pulled his Bull Dog from his pocket again and started angling toward the door. "We're going. You vile, treasonous piles of filth will give us one full minute before you follow. If I look back and see any one of you before—"

Something sitting on a side table caught his eye as he passed, and he slammed to a stop beside it.

It was a plaque with words engraved on it.

With Malice toward None, with Charity for All.
ABRAHAM LINCOLN
February 12, 1809 – April 15, 1865

Col. Crowe gave a little snort, shot a hate-filled glare back at Senator Cleburne, then picked up the plaque, tucked it under his left arm, and carried on to the door.

When he opened it, the hotel manager shrieked again. The stout man beside him joined in this time.

The hallway was filled with black smoke.

"Out out out!" Col. Crowe said to Diehl and Walkingstick. He pointed up the hall. "That way! Service stairs! Go go!"

Diehl lurched past and disappeared into the smoke. Walkingstick backed out behind him, moving his Smith & Wesson from the senator on one side of the sitting room and Hosmer and the rest on the other. Then he dashed off up the hall leaving Col. Crowe alone in the doorway.

For a moment, the little man looked tempted to fill the room with flying lead. He settled for spitting on the faded red carpet.

"You will wait one minute!" he said. "Do not test me!"

He started to go, but stopped.

"Rebel scum!"

Then he popped out into the hall and slammed the door behind him.

———

Everyone left behind in the suite—Hosmer, Senator Cleburne, Garland Dockery, Una, Mayor Bewley, Stowers the hotel manager —looked at each other.

"One-one thousand, two-one thousand, three-one thousand..." Stowers said.

"Surely we don't have to stand here for a *minute* while the hotel burns down around us...?" said Dockery.

"There's one way to find out." Una held a hand out toward the door, palm up. "Garland? Mr. Mayor? Major Hosmer? Daddy?"

None of the men moved.

Una sighed theatrically, then got up from the settee and started toward the door.

"Like that wee pixie of a man would want to linger here any more than us," she said.

"She's right," said Mayor Bewley. He cut in front of the lady and hustled to the door. "We'd be crazy to wait."

He jerked open the door and stepped into the hall.

There was a *crack* of gunfire, and he staggered back, then toppled forward onto the floor.

The mayor of Joplin, Missouri, lay face down, dead, as smoke billowed above him.

"Well…" said Una, "how about that?"

The others began coughing but didn't move.

"Twenty-seven-one thousand," said Stowers. "Twenty-eight-one thousand. Twenty-nine-one thousand…"

———

There was almost no smoke in the claustrophobically narrow service stairwell Walkingstick and Diehl were trying to go down. Smoke wasn't the problem.

The problem was that the stairwell *was* filled with Knights of Keziah.

Every squeaking, scuffed step had at least one man in a business suit standing on it. A few had two, though it was a tight squeeze for them.

"Move!" some were shouting as they pushed against the men ahead of them.

"Hurry!" shouted others.

"We're all going to die in here!" shouted one.

"Shut up!" a couple shouted back.

"Did anyone hear a gunshot?" said one. Fortunately, the rest ignored him.

"What's the delay?" Col. Crowe asked as he hurried down the steps to join Walkingstick and Diehl at the end of the line.

In the thirty-four seconds since they'd made their escape from the senator's suite, they'd managed to get down only half a floor's worth of stairs.

Walkingstick and Diehl turned to answer.

The man standing in front of them did, too. He spoke first.

"Something's blocking the way further down."

He was a balding man with spectacles and a thick accent from the deepest of the Deep South.

When he noticed that bloody, disheveled Diehl was the first person behind him, his eyes widened.

When he noticed that beyond Diehl were a tall, goateed Cherokee and a scowling runt, both holding guns, his eyes nearly popped from their sockets.

He glanced down to take in the plaque the little man held pressed against his chest—the same plaque he'd seen men fighting over in the hotel restaurant the night before. Then he pressed his lips together and turned around and tried to act casual. Quite a challenge under the circumstances.

"He's right," Walkingstick told Col. Crowe. "We've barely gone down a step since we stopped."

"Damn and blast!" Col. Crowe spat.

He leaned left and tried to peer down through the rectangular opening by the stairwell's rickety center handrail, but the shaft was so narrow he could only see the thinning hair atop more middle-aged men's heads one level down.

"You below!" Col. Crowe roared. "Why aren't we moving?"

Fleshy faces turned to frown up at him.

"We don't know!" one of the men yelled back.

But an answer came from further down the stairwell.

"The doormen are trying to come *up*!"

"Damn and blast," Crowe said again, though he sounded more resigned than angry now.

A few steps down from him, the balding man was surreptitiously tapping another Knight on the shoulder.

"Isn't that the Yankee spy they caught last night behind me?" he said, voice low.

The Knight in front of him on the stairs—a heavyset man with a bushy black beard—swiveled to glower up at Diehl.

Diehl, who'd heard the whole exchange, met his gaze and gave his head a weary shake.

"Don't worry. I'm not me," he assured the man. "I'm somebody else."

The two Knights gave each other a meaningful look while Diehl turned to Col. Crowe and dropped his voice to a sing-song whisper.

"We need to get ooouuuuut of heeeerrrrre…"

"Fast," Walkingstick added. "I don't know who you dealt with in the hall a second ago, Colonel, but if it wasn't Hosmer he's going to be on us any second. That old bastard doesn't give up."

"Right," Col. Crowe said.

Down the stairs, the bearded man was giving the Knight in front of *him* a conspiratorial nudge.

"Hey," the bearded Knight said quietly, nodding back at Diehl. "Look's who's behind—"

Col. Crowe shushed him. Then he pointed his Bull Dog up and slightly back and squeezed off a shot into the chipped, peeling ceiling.

Men up and down the creaking staircase jumped at the blast, and here and there the screws holding the stairs to the wall broke free.

"Gentlemen!" Crowe bellowed as plaster rained down behind him. "I have already killed one traitorous scoundrel in this hive of treachery, and I will gladly kill more if you do not GET YOUR FAT ASSES OUT OF THE WAY!"

The sound of the gunshot had been deafening. Yet somehow Col. Crowe managed to be even louder—and scarier.

The Knights of Keziah trapped in the stairwell—seventy-two well-fed men in heavy wool suits on rotting stairs winding up four floors—tried to stampede. Mostly, though, they just pressed themselves into the broad backs in front of them. Broad backs which were still barely moving thanks to the bottleneck near the bottom.

Diehl, Walkingstick, and Colonel Crowe managed to get down three more steps before they were blocked again.

"I SAID *GO*, VERMIN!" Crowe roared.

There was another gunshot. This time it was Walkingstick firing, though, shooting at the door behind them—the one out to the fourth floor.

Somebody had started to push it open.

Up and down the stairwell, Knights of Keziah screamed and rammed into each other even harder. Many of them tried to wriggle past the men in front of them, jamming themselves against the rough walls and pushing with all their might.

Steps splintered. The center guardrail broke free. More screws popped from the wall.

"Out of my way!" Knights shouted.

"Out of *my* way!" Knights shouted back.

"Stop! Stop!" a panicked voice screeched.

Then there were twin shrieks from the first floor as the logjam broke, and the two burly doormen trying to push their way up were swept backward off their feet. They were quickly trampled by pair after pair of brightly shined Oxfords on two hundred-plus pound men.

"Finally," Diehl said as the line twining up the stairwell began to tramp downward.

No one heard him. The sound of stomping on wooden steps filled the stairwell like the chugging of a locomotive.

Slowly but now steadily, Crowe, Walkingstick, and Diehl moved down to the third floor. Then there were new sounds.

Cracking wood. Shattering plaster. More screams from down below as the staircase — cheaply built in 1873 for underfed maids toting folded linens, not a herd of pancake-packed politicians in 1894—separated from the crumbling walls.

"Get out!" someone yelled. "It's going to—!"

The zigzagging staircases from the third floor to the second collapsed onto the stairs from the second to the first, which then also flattened. In the span of a second, the long sections of wood smashed together like an accordion squeezed tight, crushing the men between them into splinter-filled jelly.

"Oh my lord oh my lord oh my lord," panted the balding man in front of Diehl.

He was standing by the door out to the third floor gazing down into the abyss that had suddenly opened up before him. The bearded man he'd tapped on the shoulder had plummeted into the pit with the other Knights. Now he was a bloody splotch atop the wreckage forty feet below, the bright red cherry on a rubble sundae.

The balding man clasped his hands together, amazed and grateful for the miracle that had spared him.

"Oh my lord," he said again.

Diehl pushed up beside him to peer down at the carnage below. He was normally an articulate man, with poetry quotes at his beck and call. But only one word seemed to suit what he saw.

"Whoa."

"Go, go!" Col. Crowe barked. "This is no time for sightseeing!"

"Right."

Diehl turned away and yanked open the door to the third floor. It smacked into the balding man's back and sent him flying off what was left of the landing.

The scream was brief. It was already over by the time Diehl, Walkingstick, and Col. Crowe had all hurried out into the third floor hallway.

The *smoke-filled* third floor hallway.

"You know, diversions are supposed to divert," Diehl said between coughs. "Not kill everyone, including yourself."

"Feel free to return to Senator Cleburne's room while Walking-stick and I make our escape," Col. Crowe shot back.

"No, that's all right," Diehl said. "I want to see how you do this."

"Me, too," Walkingstick muttered.

Doors were open up and down the hall—left ajar by fleeing Knights of Keziah. Col. Crowe headed for the nearest one.

"Follow me! And close the door behind us!"

Diehl and Walkingstick did as they were told as Col. Crowe went striding through the doorway and into the room beyond. He passed the unmade bed and the opened valise on the floor, not stopping until he reached the window on the far side of the room. He stuffed his Bull Dog into his coat pocket and reached out for the window sash.

Walkingstick lingered by the door, head cocked, listening.

"I think I heard someone come into the hall behind us," he said.

There was a *bang*, and a hole punched through the door four inches from his head. The shot zipped through the room and shattered the window Col. Crowe had just finished raising.

"Shit!" cried Diehl, who'd felt the bullet zip over his left shoulder.

Both he and Walkingstick ducked.

Col. Crowe just leaned out to coolly take in the scene below. The sound of shouts and gasps rose up from the street, as well as the whinnying of horses and the clanging of a bell.

Walkingstick took cover behind the bed, then pointed his forty-five at the door and blasted another hole in it, this one dead center. There was no indication it hit anyone on the other side.

A hunched Diehl, meanwhile, scurried over to the window, broken glass crunching beneath his boots.

"We're still on the third goddamn floor, you know!" he said to Col. Crowe. "If we jump, we'll break our legs if we're *lucky*!"

The colonel brushed that aside with a flutter of his little hand. "Not at all. Did you know I've become captain of a volunteer fire brigade in Ogden?"

Diehl furrowed his brow. "Uhh...no, but I'm not surprised. How does that—?"

Another shot blasted through the door, this one plowing into the mattress and sending puffs of cotton and feathers flying. Walking-stick took aim at the fresh hole in the door but didn't pull the trigger.

"That you, Major?" he called out. "You're not gonna hit anything firing blind like that. You need to get a look in here."

Solmon Hosmer's deep, gravelly voice came rumbling out from the hallway.

"Oh, I don't know, Henry. I think I've got a good chance of hitting *something*."

Smoke was swirling in now through the three holes in the door.

A hand holding a gun appeared in one of the holes, as well. It was angling toward the sound of Walkingstick's voice.

Walkingstick fired at it, and there was a grunt and a clatter from the hallway.

"Good, good," Colonel Crowe said. "Keep up the covering fire, Captain."

"Three more shots, and I'll need to reload," Walkingstick whispered back.

"Oh, we'll be long gone by then," Colonel Crowe replied.

He turned back to the window and leaned out so far Diehl grabbed him by his suit coat so he wouldn't tumble over the sill.

"You there! You! Up here!" the colonel shouted at someone down below. "That's a fine-looking steam engine you have there! Surely you have a Browder life safety net as well...?"

CHAPTER 39

Bowlegs Charlie Durant didn't want to be in Joplin any longer than he had to be. He was the sort of man who drew attention, what with his long, thin, hooped legs and big beak of a nose and cocked top hat and draping cape. He was light-skinned enough to pass at a glance—a gift of the white Durants who'd mixed with the Cherokees in the family line—but a longer look might bring doubts. And trouble. So there'd be no lollygagging or detours for Bowlegs.

Go to the Joplin Hotel. Find Major Hosmer. Tell him someone had killed their friends guarding the wagon and made off with Lincoln's body. Weather the major's reaction. Be ready for whatever came next—hopefully an immediate departure for the Cherokee Nation. That was Bowlegs's plan.

The first complication was the kids. A pack of them attached themselves to him on the outskirts of town, throwing rocks that bounced off his back and annoyed his horse. If he'd been in the Indian Territories he could whip out his rifle and give the brats a good scare. But he couldn't risk that here. The kids were white. So he had to put up with it—until he finally figured out they were just trying to knock off his hat. The next time a rock came close he gave his head a jerk that sent his top hat tumbling into his lap, and the kids peeled away laughing.

The second complication was getting directions he could follow. "The county road turns into Schifferdecker Avenue, which runs into Perkins which'll take you to McCoy which runs down to Seventh after a little jog around the cannery and the lumberyard. Once you're on Seventh you just go east to Ozark, and there you are," an old man told him, waving indistinctly to the south. The problem being that Bowlegs had never been in Joplin and couldn't read. So he just wound his way into the city bearing southeast and tried again three more times, and finally the man he asked said, "Take a right at the corner. Six blocks and you're there."

The third complication was the hotel itself. Which was on fire.

It wasn't a little fire either—not a single room going up in flames because some dumb SOB nodded off smoking a cigar. Bowlegs could see a huge mushroom plume of black smoke rising up when he was still three blocks away. By the time he got to the hotel, one whole end of it—all four stories—was a wall of fire that threatened the stables and other buildings around it.

A crowd had gathered to take in the spectacle, and Bowlegs hitched his horse a safe distance away and joined them. A different kind of smoke—white—was coming from a red wagon parked in front of the hotel, and when Bowlegs craned his neck to peer at it he could see a gleaming brass boiler on the back and men in black helmets dragging off a heavy-looking hose. The men braced themselves, shouted something, and a thick arc of water spouted out.

The crowd applauded as the firemen angled the water onto the flames.

"I'm Republican to the core," a fiftyish man standing in front of Bowlegs said to no one in particular, "but you've got to give it to Mayor Bewley. *That* is how a modern American city fights a fire."

He affirmed his own opinion with a satisfied nod, then glanced around searching for more.

When he saw Bowlegs staring at him, he frowned and went back to watching the fire.

There was a loud *pop* from inside the hotel, then another.

"Was that gunfire?" asked a woman holding a squirming, whining baby.

The Republican shook his head.

"Gas expanding in the burning timbers," he said.

"Oh. Right."

There was another *pop*, then yet another.

They didn't sound like gas expanding in burning timbers to Bowlegs.

"Look!" a man yelled.

"Oh, no!" another cried.

"Sweet Jesus!" said the woman with the baby. "There's a little boy trapped up there!"

Bowlegs followed her gaze and saw a small figure leaning out one of the windows on the third floor, about halfway down the length of the building.

The Republican looked that way, too.

"I don't think that's a little boy," he said. "Not in that suit."

This time, Bowlegs agreed.

The little *man* seemed to be shouting directions at some of the firemen. A cluster of them ran back to their wagon and pulled out something long and beige that looked like a rolled-up carpet. There were two more *pops* from inside the hotel as they hurried back toward the little man.

"I think he's going to jump!" a gray-haired lady said.

She sounded pretty excited.

"Ooo, there's someone with him!" said the lady beside her.

Indeed, a larger man in a dirty white shirt appeared in the window. He looked down and shook his head as the firemen took position on the sidewalk below, spreading out into a circle with the tarp they'd been carrying stretched between them.

The little man yelled something at him and pushed him up onto the windowsill.

The crowd gasped.

The taller man shook his head again.

There was another *pop*.

The man jumped.

There was a moment of near silence as everyone watching held their breath. Then cheers erupted from the spectators closer to the building, and someone shouted, "He made it! He's all right!"

"Well, I'll be goddamned," Bowlegs said to himself as applause broke out all around.

"Here comes the kid!" someone said, and the smaller figure in the window came plummeting earthward clutching something that glinted in the sunlight as he fell.

The applause died away—then roared back even louder along with cries of "Thank god!" and "He made it, too!" and "That ain't no kid!"

Yet another figure appeared in the window—a tall, dark-skinned man with a goatee holding something in his right hand.

"Is that a gun?" said the woman with the baby. Her child was full-on writhing and crying now, but she wasn't going to leave and miss the show.

"I think it's a candlestick," said the Republican.

The tall man stuffed his "candlestick" into its holster and thumbed down the fastening strap as the people below began chanting "Jump! Jump! Jump!"

"I'll be god*damned*," Bowlegs said again.

He'd recognized the latest man in the window.

Everyone in the Cherokee Nation knew Capt. Henry Walkingstick. That he was here now, with the hotel the major was supposed to be at burning down around him, did *not* bode well.

Walkingstick jumped.

Bowlegs hoped to hear a *splat* this time, followed by shrieks of horror.

Instead cheers erupted yet again, and a few men even threw their hats in the air.

"Fantastic!" the Republican enthused. "Huzzah for Joplin, I say! The fire brigades in St. Louis and Kansas City couldn't have done any better!"

This time when he looked around for nods of agreement, he got them.

Bowlegs nodded along just to fit in—then swept his hat off his

head and bowed his legs even more than usual to drop himself
down behind the Republican's back.

The crowd was parting to let three men through—the three
they'd just seen leaping from the third-story window. Bowlegs stayed
squatted down behind the Republican while they swept away from
the hotel collecting back-pats and handshakes and questions they
clearly didn't want to answer.

"...back on the road west and find Hoop and...yes, ma'am,
we're very lucky..." Bowlegs heard one of them saying in a clipped,
high-pitched voice. "Find Hoop and...no, ma'am, it didn't feel like
flying...find Hoop and...yes, sir, we certainly do owe those firemen
a round of beers...find Hoop and..."

Then they were out of earshot. Just to be safe, Bowlegs stayed
crouched with his hat in his hands for a minute, ignoring the suspicious glances he was getting from the Republican and the woman
with the baby. Another shout from the crowd drew him up straight
again.

"Look! There's still someone up there!"

It was true. Another figure had appeared in the window — a
white-maned man who stared gravely down at the crowd.

Bowlegs recognized Major Hosmer immediately. And despite
the distance between them, he was sure that the major recognized
him. The long, steady stare Hosmer gave him seemed to give an
order.

Wait there. I'll be right down.

"Jump! Jump! Jump!" people began chanting again.

Major Hosmer turned away, though. He stepped back into the
shadows holding his hands out toward the window in a way that
seemed to say *Ladies first.*

CHAPTER 40

Eskaminzim kneeled by the riverbank and stared at the hoofprints pressed into the soft soil. He reached down and touched the ground with his right hand, as if examining something. He was really steadying himself. He was in pain from his shoulder wound, weak and woozy. But he was determined not to show it.

Ow. I was shot in the shoulder, and it hurts. Boo hoo.

That was not an Apache warrior's way. Eskaminzim could have a spear going in one side and out the other, and he'd just frown down at it and say, "A *spear*? Must be Navajos. Give me a minute to go kill them." Or so he hoped.

"They watered their horses, but not for long," he announced to Pixley, his voice as strong and clear as he could make it. "They didn't let them drink much before they pulled them away."

"Because they know we're following them?" Pixley asked.

He was twenty yards off holding back the horses that he, Eskaminzim, and Hoop had ridden up on. The horses strained against the reins, trying to reach the river. They were thirsty, too.

"Maybe. But it's not just that," Eskaminzim said. "I think they didn't *need* to let the horses drink much."

"Because...they're going to keep following the river?"

Eskaminzim didn't answer. He just stood slowly—hoping the wobble in his knees wasn't noticeable—and walked past Pixley and the horses, into the little clearing where the wagon had stopped.

Hoop stepped out of the forest to his left, near the tree Eskaminzim had marked with a broken branch—another signpost for Diehl—when they'd arrived a few minutes before. (Reaching up to twist the branch until it snapped had hurt like hell, even using his good arm, but Eskaminzim had still insisted on doing it himself, of course.)

Eskaminzim and Hoop locked eyes on each other, communicating without words.

Something bad had happened in the woods. But Onawa was alive.

Eskaminzim saw pain in Hoop's eyes, too. The dizzying, blinding kind that can linger after a blow to the head. But Hoop wouldn't acknowledge it out loud.

Eskaminzim's brother-in-law wasn't an Apache, but he understood about pain. It didn't count. Where they had to go, what they had to do—that's what mattered.

Eskaminzim turned away and followed the ruts of the wagon wheels as they headed back onto the road. He trotted along beside the tracks for a moment, eyes down, then spun around and returned.

"She's not leaving any more hair," he told Hoop. "She doesn't have to now."

His sister had found another way to tell them she was still up ahead. A way he hated.

"I know," Hoop said grimly. He looked over at Pixley. "All right —let 'em drink. But not much."

"You don't think they could use more of a rest?" Pixley asked. "They don't look good."

Eskaminzim turned toward him, about to say the horses looked fine. Then he saw the worry on the man's face and realized he wasn't really talking about the horses.

Eskaminzim snorted, both rueful and amused. He and Hoop weren't as good at hiding their suffering as they thought.

"We don't need much water or rest now," he told Pixley, "because wherever we've been going, we're almost there."

———

Onawa wiped again at her stinging nose, intentionally breaking the clots in her nostrils so that blood trickled over her fingers again. Then she drooped her head and put her bound hands to the side of the wagon as if steadying herself.

She couldn't feel the drops of blood dripping from her fingertips to plop down to the ground, but she knew they were there. They'd tell her husband and her brother not only that there was someone bleeding in the wagon but—from their color as they dried in the sun —how far ahead they were. For Hoop and Eskaminzim that would be as good as a big red arrow and a sign saying, "THIS WAY. KEEP COMING."

Wormwood and Nathaniel trotted along just behind the wagon, oblivious. Wormwood had tried taunting her some more after they'd stopped by the river, but Onawa hadn't risen to the bait, remaining silent and seemingly defeated. So the girl had given up for a while. Now she and Nathaniel were talking about what they were going to do with their share of the ransom for the body.

"I'm gonna get drunk the second we get to Mexico," Nathaniel said, "and I ain't gonna sober up till Christmas. Then I'll get drunk some more!"

"Why wait till Mexico?" said Wormwood. "Blaze says no booze till we have the money. Fine. But once we got it, we'll still be in New Orleans. The biggest party town in the South. You're gonna have to carry me onto the boat for Veracruz, cuz I'm gonna be soused already."

Onawa could feel Wormwood's eyes on her. The girl was hoping Onawa would look up so she could rub it in some more.

There was only one reason they'd talk in front of her about their future.

They didn't think she had one.

Onawa kept her eyes down. The last time she'd taken a peek at the terrain, it had been because the sounds around her had changed. No more flowing water, different birds. When she'd looked, she saw that the trees weren't pressing in close around the road like before, and the river wasn't visible. Instead the wagon was rolling past clearings filled with high grass and weeds, the ramshackle remnants of rotting fences around them. Abandoned farmland.

Now she felt the wagon angling up slightly, gaining elevation. She heard a kingfisher and geese again, too, and though she couldn't hear the river she could smell it. Then another sensation told her something had changed.

The feeling they were being watched.

It didn't come from anything specific. No tingling of the skin, no sour pit in the stomach, no raising of the hairs on the back of the neck. It was simply an uneasiness—one Onawa had learned to listen to over the years.

She raised her head just enough to get a look around.

They were moving past a shattered building. It had been two stories tall, but the top floor had caved in on the first. It looked like it had been a home.

A little further up was another building, then another and another—about a dozen that Onawa could see, all in various states of decay. Most were simply falling apart. Some were splintered and battered, as if by giant fists. A few had burned down to their foundations, leaving nothing but toppled chimneys in broad brick squares.

"Welcome to Hope's Landing," Wormwood said. "Go ahead, squaw. Take a good look." She pointed straight ahead. "That's where you're headed."

Onawa turned to face forward.

Blaze Bad Water was still out in front on his big black mare. He was leading the group up an incline, toward another abandoned building, this one with a distinctive outline. Rectangular base, steepled roof, door in the front, belfry on top.

A church on a hill. But Onawa wasn't sure that's what Wormwood had been pointing at.

Scattered to one side of the church, on a little slanted plateau that eventually dropped off to a steeper slope down to the river, were gray humps that jutted from the grass and weeds.

A forgotten graveyard.

That's what the whole town was, in a way. Rotting monuments to people long gone. There'd been a community here once, but something—the whites' big war, from the look of it—had destroyed it. Now there was nothing left but crumbling edifices and whatever ghosts might still haunt them.

"Welcome back, *Mr. Smith*," someone said.

Onawa turned toward the voice and saw a slender young mixed-blood man—a combination of Indian, black, and white lines from the look of him—stepping out from behind an old blacksmith's shop.

Bad Water stiffened and reined up. The rest of the group stopped behind him.

"Thank you, *Mr. Jones*," he said. "Do we have company?"

"We do. Over here." "*Mr. Jones*" jerked his head to the left, then squinted at Onawa. "And you brought another...? *And* the guest of honor?"

"Never mind them," Bad Water said. "I want to meet your guests. Bring 'em out."

"Right."

Mr. Jones stepped back behind the blacksmith's shop. When he returned a moment later, he was herding two old men with worn clothes and dark, leathery skin and craggy, fear-filled faces. Their hands were bound behind their backs.

"Caught 'em looking at the road up near Honey Creek," Mr. Jones said. "Said they were Senecas just going over to the Neosho to fish."

"We *are* Senecas just going over to the Neosho to fish," one of the old men said, voice quavering. "We didn't know nobody was out here."

"And we don't care," said the other one. Like his friend, he'd noticed Onawa in the wagon but didn't let his gaze linger on her long. Instead he stayed focused on Bad Water. "Ain't none of our business."

Bad Water looked at Mr. Jones. "They have poles with 'em? Bait?"

Mr. Jones nodded. "And a bottle of whiskey."

Bad Water grunted.

"So you aren't friends of Major Hosmer?" he asked the old men.

They looked genuinely perplexed.

"Solomon Hosmer?" said the one with the quivery voice, shaking his head. "Never met the man."

"And don't want to. We wasn't no rebels," said the other. "Got burnt out by one side then the other and spent the rest of the war starving up in Kansas. To me Major Hosmer wasn't nothing but another damned—"

The old man's friend sent a bony elbow into his ribs.

He got the message—*No politics*—and clamped his wrinkled mouth tight.

"Bass and catfish—that's all we're interested in," said the first man. "Just came here cuz most folks avoid it. 'Restless spirits.' 'Cursed land.' 'Bad juju.'" He rolled his eyes. "Good place for some privacy. So we was surprised to see fresh ruts in the road, that's all. We stop to take a look, and this one..." He nodded at Mr. Jones. "...he pops out and starts waving a gun at us. Ties our hands, won't let us leave. We tried to explain we ain't nobody, but he—"

"All right, all right," Bad Water cut in. "I believe you. Just one more question."

His saddle creaked as he tilted forward toward the men.

"Do you know who I am?"

The old men threw a quick glance at each other, unsure which response would be the right one.

One just licked his lips and shrugged.

"Nobody we wanna mess with," said the other—the one with the trembling voice. It was trembling even more now.

Bad Water sat back and smiled.

"Good answer," he said. "Okay, fellas. You had a nice afternoon all planned for yourselves, and I hate to interrupt it. But you need to go home now. Stay off the river and the road and keep your mouths shut. You understand?"

The old men nodded vigorously.

"Yes, sir!"

"You don't gotta worry about us!"

"Untie 'em and give 'em back their stuff, Mr. Jones," Bad Water said. "And don't forget the whiskey bottle…which better be full."

"It's as full as I found it," Mr. Jones grumbled.

He stepped behind the old men and began untying the leather thongs around their wrists.

Bad Water turned his horse and rode slowly toward the wagon. When he was lined up beside Onawa in the back, he stopped and leaned toward her.

"See, Momma?" he said softly. "I'm reasonable. You remember that if your man comes. Help me talk to him. We can work things out."

Onawa met his gaze but remained silent.

Bad Water moved his horse on toward Nathaniel and Wormwood still mounted behind the buckboard. He said nothing to them in words, but he gave them an order all the same.

First his eyes flicked left, back toward the old men.

Then they slid to the right, toward the forest they'd have to walk through to get back to Seneca land.

Then he raised his eyebrows.

Then he put a finger to his lips.

Nathaniel furrowed his brow, not quite following. But Wormwood understood.

She watched Mr. Jones giving the Senecas their fishing poles and whiskey bottle and coffee can full of nightcrawlers. Watched the old men smile at each other in relieved disbelief as they scurried off toward the woods.

And she smiled, too.

CHAPTER 41

Senator Cleburne sat at the same table he'd eaten pancakes at that very morning, his head in his hands.

The Fontainebleau Room wasn't so opulent anymore—not with scorched walls and the back door burned away and the kitchen beyond a heap of smoldering timber and twisted metal and fractured, blackened plaster. The restaurant was dark and deserted, except for the senator and, seated across from him, Una and Garland Dockery. Despite the smoke that still hung heavy in the air, this is where Cleburne preferred to be. He couldn't stand being outside in the sunlight. Not with the fire brigade still pulling one mangled Knight of Keziah after another from the rubble of the service stairs and stacking them on the sidewalk like soggy cordwood. The senator had told the police who was responsible—a couple mad dog Northern agitators and their renegade Indian accomplice, all deadly dangerous and to be shot on sight—but the scoundrels had fled the scene quickly to stir up trouble for him elsewhere.

"Well, look at the bright side, Daddy," Una said. "Given what happened to the hotel, it really is a lucky thing that Major Hosmer didn't bring you-know-who here like he was supposed to. If he had, you might not have anything to ransom back to the government but an especially tall pile of ashes."

She smirked at her own little joke. Her face was still flushed from the excitement she'd felt leaping from the third floor and plummeting to the fireman's tarp below. It had given her a thrill like nothing she'd ever experienced. It made her wonder whether (perhaps even hope?) there were more hotel fires in her future.

"'The bright side?'" Senator Cleburne groaned bitterly. "Don't speak to me of a bright side with the bodies of so many good men still warm."

Dockery drummed his manicured fingernails on the soot-stained tablecloth.

"Where is Hosmer?" he asked his wife. "I haven't seen him since he jumped into that net thing after you."

"Oh, he wandered off into the crowd while I was waiting for you two to join us on the ground," Una said.

The senator lifted his head and let his hands drop to the table. "'Wandered off into the crowd?' We need him. Now. To get this sorted. Can we even carry on with the ransom with those Yankee lunatics running around loose? No one's going to help them around here—I can see to that. But they'll find *someone* who'll believe them unless Hosmer and his men hunt them down first. That stiff-necked son of a bitch needs to get back here, give me a salute, and get cracking."

Una reached across the table to pat her father on the hand. "Now, now. Don't you worry about the major. He's really not so indispensable. In fact, if he's gone and dispensed with himself, so much the better."

Cleburne snatched his hand away. "What are you talking about? We don't even know where you-know-who's you-know-what *is*! Why, Hosmer could just carry on without us and leave us to twist in the damn wind!"

Una sat back and smiled primly, unruffled by her father's fury.

"I don't think so," she said.

A reply came from the back of the room, in the ruins of the

kitchen. The voice was so deep and gruff, the wreckage all around seemed to vibrate.

"Oh?" it said.

"Major Hosmer? Is that you, my friend?" the senator said, suddenly smooth and cool. "I was just saying how anxious I was for you to return so we could strategize together. We have much to discuss."

"Indeed we do."

A figure separated itself from the shadows in the kitchen. As it approached, another—tall and almost impossibly slim figure, with legs that bowed so much they practically made an O—appeared behind it, following. The second man was wearing a cocked top hat and old-fashioned greatcoat that made him look like the ghost of a hotel doorman who'd died of consumption thirty years before.

"Ah. One of your fighting Cherokees has joined us, I presume?" Cleburne said as the two men—Solomon Hosmer and Bowlegs Charlie Durant—walked toward his table. "Excellent. We need to get word of what's happened back to your forces in the Indian Territories."

"We have something to settle first," Hosmer said. "Between us."

He and Bowlegs came to a stop a few feet from the senator's chair, just behind the Dockerys.

"I am as unhappy as you are with the state of things, Major," Cleburne said. "But the thing to do is regroup, counterattack, and regain the initiative. We can point fingers later."

"I prefer now," Hosmer said. "My men were ambushed last night. By a large party in the Cherokee Nation. They took the wagon...and the body."

"What?" the senator roared. "Damn it, Hosmer! If you'd listened to me, we'd be sitting back right now waiting for word that the money was on the way! Instead you tell me you've gone and lost Lincoln? Hell's bells, man! You've bungled everything!"

"Now, now, Daddy," Una said soothingly. "You're pointing fingers."

She didn't seem especially shocked by Major Hosmer's news.

"Well, that's that then," Dockery said. "Without the body,

there's nothing we can do but go home and hope none of this ever gets connected to us."

"Aren't you curious about *who* took the body?" Hosmer said.

Dockery had to swivel awkwardly in his seat to look up at him.

"I should think that's obvious," Dockery said. "It must have been more friends of that man 'Diehl.'"

Hosmer shook his head. "They came from inside the Cherokee Nation, and they went back that way, deeper into it. Not out toward Missouri and Illinois."

"Well, that just means you've bungled it again!" the senator said. "Obviously it was the Cherokee tribal police. Or some of your own men betrayed you."

Bowlegs spoke then for the first time. He directed his words at Senator Cleburne. There were two of them. The second word was "you." The first made the senator gasp.

"There is a lady present, you damned savage!" he snapped.

Bowlegs repeated his first word followed by "her, too."

This time the senator was so flabbergasted he couldn't even work up the breath to gasp.

Dockery pushed back his seat and started to come to his feet.

"Come along, Una," he said. "We're not going to sit here and let—"

Hosmer put a hand on his shoulder and shoved him back down.

"You have quite a reputation as a defense attorney," the major said, his fingers still pressing down hard on Dockery. "I've read about some of your cases in the papers. Didn't you represent Blaze Bad Water and Gerty Wormwood a couple years ago? On a charge of attempted murder? Before they were so famous."

"I don't know. I have so many—"

Dockery squealed in pain.

Hosmer's fingers were digging into the tendons at the base of his neck.

"Yes! Yes, I remember now!" Dockery cried, writhing but unable to escape Hosmer's hold. "I got them acquitted!"

Hosmer lightened his grip but didn't move his hand.

"And did they stay in touch?" he said. "They must have known they'd need a good attorney again sooner or later."

"What are you driving at, Hosmer?" Cleburne said.

Dockery let out another yelp, though not as loud this time.

The major's fingers were tightening on him again.

"I'm not the one who bungled it," Hosmer said. "I'm not the one who was betrayed by someone close to me. Isn't that right, Mr. Dockery?"

"No! It's not true! I would never—!"

Dockery's words turned into another howl of pain.

"Stop it! Let him go!" Una said. "I'll tell you everything!"

Hosmer's hand slid away from Dockery's neck.

"Una...don't," Dockery panted, slumping.

"Oh, why not? He's guessed most of it anyway," she said. For a moment, real emotion—real fear—had shown on her face. But now she sat up straight and smoothed it away like an unwanted crease in the folds of her dress. "Now we can talk it over like civilized people."

Her father gaped at her. "Una...are you saying it's true? Garland betrayed us?"

"Not exactly, Daddy. *We* betrayed *you*."

"*Una...*" Dockery said again.

His wife ignored him.

The senator, meanwhile, was shaking his head, speechless.

"It was for your own good," Una told him. "This silly little club of yours. Resurrecting the Confederacy. So stupid. And so unnecessary! Is the South really so different than it was before the war? Aren't things moving back to the old ways already? We can't call the Blacks our slaves anymore, but they may as well be in shackles for all the freedom they have. And the carpetbaggers and darkie lovers were kicked out ages ago. So why waste all that beautiful ransom money on a war that's already won?"

"And what about *my* war?" Hosmer said. "To preserve the sovereignty of the Cherokee Nation?"

Una gave that a flippant shrug. "I'm sorry, Major. But it's a waste to throw money away on a war that's already *lost*, too. A million dollars isn't going to stop the coming of the state of Oklahoma."

"So you told Blaze Bad Water what we were doing," Hosmer growled. "And you were going to split the ransom with *him*."

Una nodded calmly, seemingly unfazed by the barely restrained rage in the major's voice. "That's right. So you see—the money was going to the Cherokees in a sense. We were just sharing it with a different Cherokee. Of course, I understand how vexing all this must be for you. To have ridden so far, braved so much, only to have the fruits of your labor snatched away and your grand plans dashed. But I can supply a powerful palliative."

"Oh?" Hosmer said.

"Oh?" said Senator Cleburne.

Dockery raised his eyebrows.

Bowlegs, having no idea what a "palliative" was, had no discernible reaction. He just kept glaring at the haughty White lady with obvious contempt.

"Indeed. The perfect balm for your wounds, Major," she said. She looked over at her husband. "You should show Major Hosmer and his friend that document we were discussing earlier."

"Document?" Dockery said.

"Yes, silly! The document! The one I wanted you to show to Mr. Diehl."

"Una, what are you talking about?" the senator said.

But Dockery's eyes widened, and he said, "Oh. Of course. That. Yes. I have it right here."

He slipped a hand into the right pocket of his suit coat.

Major Hosmer grabbed him by the hair and slammed his face into the table. Dockery still managed to get his hand from his pocket —the hand he'd wrapped around his little five-shot twenty-two revolver—but Hosmer just reached down, yanked the gun away, and put the muzzle to the back of Dockery's head.

Una started to scream, but Bowlegs stepped up and clamped a hand over her mouth. His other hand whipped out a knife that he pressed to her throat.

"Don't!" Senator Cleburne cried.

Hosmer pointed the twenty-two at him and pulled the trigger. The gun made a sharp, high *pop*, and the old man's head jerked back.

When Cleburne brought his head forward again, there was a dark hole in it just above his left eye. There was a look of frozen surprise on his face that disappeared from view as he slumped forward onto the table.

Una let out a muffled shriek that might have been "Daddy!"

Hosmer put the gun to Dockery's head again.

Dockery yelped at the touch of the hot metal.

"Do you know where Bad Water's taking the body?" Hosmer said.

"Yes! Yes! We know!" Dockery said.

Hosmer pulled the trigger again.

Blood and brains splattered over the tablecloth, and Dockery's suddenly limp body toppled sideways to the floor.

Again, Una tried to scream, and again Bowlegs stifled it.

Hosmer turned to them. For a moment he did nothing but listen to see if anyone had heard the gunshots outside. When he was satisfied that no one was coming to investigate, he spoke.

"Your husband said, 'We,' Mrs. Dockery. So *you* know where Blaze Bad Water is, too. Tell me, and I won't do to you what I did to him and your father."

Una was panting now beneath Bowlegs's grip, her eyes as big and round as silver dollars.

Hosmer gave Bowlegs a nod, and the other man slowly loosened his grip on Una's mouth.

She stared up at the major, trembling, tempted to scream but stopped by the blade that still pushed in close beneath her chin.

"There's an abandoned town..." she said, her voice whisper-quiet. "In Cherokee country..."

She told them the name and where it was, so far as she knew, though she needn't have bothered with the location. They knew the place.

When she was done, Major Hosmer kept his word. He didn't

shoot her. Instead, he gave Bowlegs another nod, and the knife pressed to Una Dockery's throat moved from left to right.

After it was over, the two men hurried from what remained of The Fontainebleau Room and the Joplin Hotel. There weren't many hours of light left, and they had a lot to do.

Return to the Indian Territories. Find their friends. Turn them south, along the Neosho River.

To Hope's Landing.

CHAPTER 42

There were only five of the gang there at Hope's Landing: Blaze Bad Water, Wormwood, Nathaniel, "Mr. Jones" (real name: Greer, Onawa eventually learned), and the one who'd been driving the buckboard, an old man (compared to the others) of perhaps twenty-five they called Pigeon.

It wouldn't be easy for Hoop and Eskaminzim to kill so many who were so mean and so hard though so young. But Onawa figured it wouldn't be that difficult either, with some luck. Not that they'd had any on this trip.

Then the boat arrived, and the odds got worse.

Onawa wasn't surprised by it. They were keeping her in the dilapidated sanctuary of the old church, on the floor in front of the altar, beside the box they'd been hauling. But she could see out the smudged and warped windows that faced the river. Bad Water kept returning to the hilltop cemetery, clearly watching for someone to arrive on the water. Then Onawa saw the gray smoke of an engine on the horizon, and a little later, Bad Water's gap-toothed friend Gootch came up the hill with the two young men who'd ridden off with him and the ice cream wagon hours before. With them was another man—white, scruffy, with dirty hands and even dirtier clothes—who glared at Onawa unhappily when the gang reunited inside the church.

So now there were nine. That made things trickier, but not hopeless. Onawa had snuck away from more bastards than that in the past. Even bastards have to sleep.

The sun was sinking behind the distant hills on the other side of the river. When it was dark, she might have her chance.

Bad Water was talking to Gootch and the grimy white as they came inside, but he gave Onawa a long, steady look that seemed to say he knew exactly what she was thinking.

"…the telegram to Dockery?" he was saying.

"Yes, Blaze," said Gootch, round head bobbing on his spindly neck.

"And you hid the ice cream wagon?"

"Just like you said, Blaze," Gootch said, still nodding.

"And you loaded enough coal to get us to New Orleans?"

The White answered this time.

"Of course."

They'd been walking up the center aisle of the church sanctuary, the other gang members—the ones who'd arrived with Bad Water —sprawled here and there around them on the rotting pews.

The White stopped and jerked his chin at Onawa.

"What about her?" he said. "She wasn't part of the plan."

Bad Water carried on toward the altar and Onawa sitting before it, her face crusted with dried blood, bound hands in her lap.

"We're just keeping her for tonight. In case someone she knows shows up." He gave Onawa a little smile that was perhaps meant to be reassuring. It was hard to tell. "She'll stay with me in the whatchamacallit back there. Where the preacher kept his shit."

"The sacristy," Nathaniel said from one the two pews at the front, nearest Onawa and the pinewood box. He looked over at Wormwood, who was on the other. "I was an altar boy."

"You ain't one anymore, that's for damn sure," said Wormwood.

She and Nathaniel had been gone for a while, after Greer let the two old Senecas go. When they'd returned, Wormwood was wiping a knife on her dirty trousers. She'd walked up the aisle and taken a seat as close as she could to Onawa so she could tear pages from an old hymnal and wad them up and throw them at her.

"You don't have to worry about the woman," Bad Water went on with a glance back at the White. "I'll keep an eye on her myself. If we have a quiet night, we'll let her go when we leave in the morning."

Wormwood snorted. Maybe at Bad Water "keeping an eye on" Onawa for the night. Maybe at letting her go the next day. Probably at both.

Whichever, it was bad news for Onawa. Trying to sneak out of the sanctuary when the gang nodded off—that would be one thing. Dangerous, but not impossible. But being alone with Bad Water all night? Just that one set of eyes on her, focused, fixed, strangely intent? That felt far worse.

She had to try something *now*.

"You only need me," Onawa said, "if this is worth something."

She jerked her head at the box on the floor beside her. She was close enough to rap on it with her knuckles or kick it with an outstretched foot, but she didn't want to touch the thing.

"If it's not," she went on, "you could just let me go right now and get away while you've still got time."

"What are you talking about?" Wormwood snarled.

Bad Water shushed her…then smiled at Onawa and said the very same thing.

"What are you talking about?"

"So you stole a box from some old men," Onawa said. "What is a box worth? I haven't seen any of you look inside it. How do you know what you think you have is there?"

Wormwood and Nathaniel threw each other quick glances that told Onawa she was right. No one had checked inside the box.

"Maybe the old men didn't really get the body," Onawa went on. "Or maybe they got it but hid it somewhere else before you attacked them. If either of those things is true, you're about to go a long way and take many more risks for nothing. You'd be better off letting me go and finding some other way to get the money you want."

Wormwood and Nathaniel glanced at each other again, and the other gang members up and down the aisles traded nervous looks, too. The White ran a hand through his greasy hair and hissed out a "Shit." They were all thinking the same thing.

What if she's right?

"This," Bad Water said, shaking a finger at Onawa, "is a clever, clever woman."

He turned away from her to face the White.

"McNite," he said, "there must be a crowbar or hammer or something in the boat."

"Yeah," the White said.

Bad Water spread out his arms.

"Well...go get it."

———

Diehl's butt hurt. His back ached. His head throbbed. His sides—where he'd taken one blow after another while tied to that damn chair in the Joplin Hotel—screamed in agony. But he kept riding, leading Walkingstick and Colonel Crowe deeper and deeper into the Cherokee Nation.

"You're sure this is the right way, Diehl?" Crowe asked.

He'd asked the same question five times already, sounding more skeptical with each repetition.

"I'm sure," Diehl replied (again). He'd sounded less *certain* each time.

And now they were losing the light, so even the signals Diehl thought he was seeing—dangling branches every mile or so—would soon be lost in the gloom. They'd have to stop for the night, and he'd finally be able to rest. But Diehl preferred the pain.

He didn't believe in premonitions or sixth sense or second sight. He did believe in his gut. And his gut—sore as it was—told him something had gone terribly wrong for Hoop, Eskaminzim, and Onawa.

"Well, I hope you're right," Crowe said unhelpfully.

The horse the colonel had bought for himself in Joplin was a big

Morgan gelding with a simple McClellan saddle, and perched atop it the little man looked like a child riding an elephant.

"Do you know where this road leads?" he asked Walkingstick.

Walkingstick nodded. "Nowhere anyone goes anymore. There were a few farms and a little town out this way once, but that all got chewed up in the war. Some bad things happened out there. Things some people think left a mark on the land." He looked over at Diehl. "Perfect place to hide out, actually."

"Good. That means we probably know where we're going." Diehl rubbed his eyes. "And I can stop staring at trees."

"We will *all* keep staring at the trees," Col. Crowe said. "I needn't tell you, Diehl, what a perfect spot this little lane would make for an ambush."

"No," Diehl said wearily. "You *needn't* tell me."

"Oh yeah?" someone said from the growing darkness of the forest. "If you knew that, how come you didn't see *me*?"

Eskaminzim stepped out into the road. He looked rough—sweaty and haggard, with his right arm bound in a bloody sling—but he managed to give Diehl a small smile.

"What happened to you, anyway?" he said. "You look terrible."

Diehl shrugged. And winced.

"Complications. What happened to you?"

Eskaminzim shrugged—but only with his left shoulder. "Complications."

He shifted his gaze to Col. Crowe, who'd reined up alongside Diehl and Walkingstick.

"The Little Badger!" Eskaminzim said. "How did *you* get here?"

"When I realized I needed to come take charge myself I was able to cobble together a sort of special express. One accumulates quite a few friends who owe favors working for the Southern Pacific Railroad as long as I did," Crowe said. "Now…where are Hoop and Onawa and Mr. Pixley, and what's the situation?"

Eskaminzim took a deep breath. There was clearly a lot to tell—so much it was hard to know where to start. So he began with what was foremost on his mind.

"My sister has been taken prisoner," he said. "By men who

attacked the old Cherokees and took their wagon. They brought it and her to a deserted town at the end of this road. We got there a couple hours ago, less than an hour behind *them*. Hoop and Pixley are watching the place now, and I came back to look for Diehl and Walkingstick before we did anything."

The colonel balled up a fist and gave his saddle horn a thump. "Damn. Onawa a prisoner of who-knows-who. Why I let you three start dragging a woman around, I don't know."

Eskaminzim stiffened. "Because she's as tough as any of us. It could've been me or Hoop or Pixley they captured if things went different. They didn't get my sister because she's a woman."

"No," said Diehl. "But I bet that's why they didn't kill her. A woman's a more appealing hostage. One they're more likely to underestimate, too." He held Eskaminzim's gaze solemnly, making a promise. "Either we'll get her back, or she'll escape on her own."

"I know," Eskaminzim said.

"These men...how many of them are there?" Walkingstick asked.

"Eight or nine altogether. They split up a while back—"

"Where this trail forks off from the road," Walkingstick said. "We noticed that."

He and Diehl exchanged a quick look. *They'd* noticed that. The colonel hadn't been sure he believed them and almost insisted they stick with the obvious tracks on the main road.

"We think they're all back together again now," Eskaminzim said. "The ones who left with the ice cream wagon came back...in a boat."

"A boat?" Crowe said.

He turned to Walkingstick.

"A *boat*?" he said again.

Walkingstick nodded slowly. "That abandoned town, Hope's Landing...it's on the river. The Neosho. It connects with the Arkansas..."

"And *it* connects with the Mississippi," Diehl said.

Walkingstick kept nodding.

"So that's their escape route," Crowe said. "They're taking their prize somewhere south. Perhaps as far south as New Orleans."

"And the New Orleans Mint," Diehl added. "The perfect place to collect a fat ransom from the federal government."

Crowe gave his saddle horn another thump—one of satisfaction rather than frustration this time. "Capital! We have them just where we want them!"

"We do?" said Walkingstick.

Crowe nodded confidently. "I know the Neosho. It runs all the way up into Kansas. It's barely big enough for a boat of any real size. They won't risk taking theirs downriver in the dark, running aground, capsizing, spilling their precious cargo. No, they'll wait until dawn…which gives us plenty of time to lay a trap."

"One that won't get my sister killed?" Eskaminzim said.

"Don't worry about her," Crowe told him. "We'll have surprise on our side, and there'll be six of us and only a few more of them."

"Maybe more like five-and-a-half of us," said Diehl, giving Eskaminzim's right arm a pointed look.

Eskaminzim puffed out his chest. "I count for two even with an arm in a sling. But you don't look so good. Maybe *you're* half today. And what should Pixley count for? Two-thirds?"

"He's a full man," said Diehl.

"Six and a half, four and two-thirds, five and three-quarters, it doesn't matter," Col. Crowe snapped. He drummed his little fingers on his thigh, plans swirling in his head. "We'll have enough. With the right strategy, waiting for the right moment, nothing can go wrong."

————

Eli Lizzenbe led the exhausted, dispirited Cherokees slowly down the darkened road, heading southeast. Back the way they'd come.

The five men had spent most of the day following the ice cream wagon's tracks away from the spot near the Missouri border where their friends had been killed the night before. The stolen wagon was moving fast—far faster than they'd dared driving it on their way down from Illinois for fear of busting a wheel or shaking apart the box in the back. They were catching up, though. The horse turds on the road—getting steadily fresher—told them that. But then they reached the outskirts of the little town of Wyandotte, and the trail abruptly stopped.

They found the wagon abandoned in the forest nearby, not far from where Lost Creek flows into the Neosho River. There was nothing inside it and no clue where the men with it had gone.

Lizzenbe tried asking around in town about men arriving from the southeast—men with tired draft horses to get rid of and perhaps a long crate? But all he got in response were shrugs and sly smiles.

Lizzenbe and the other Cherokees didn't have any friends here. They were north of the Cherokee Nation, in the clump of little tribes jammed into an upper corner of the Territories. These were Wyandottes, Ottawas, Quapaws, Senecas. And they weren't inclined to help strangers, even Indian ones, find whoever it was they were tracking.

Which gave the Cherokees no choice. They'd failed. All they could do now was head back the way they'd come and worry about what the major would say when he saw them again.

They found out a few hours later, just after night fell.

Two dark figures rode toward them in the soft starlight. One was tall and straight and steady in the saddle despite the sagging of a weary horse. The other rode with stooped shoulders and long, spindly legs jutting out on each side.

One of the Cherokees behind Lizzenbe stated the obvious.

"It's the major and Bowlegs Charlie!"

As the two groups converged on the road, Lizzenbe felt the urge to salute—just like in the old days of the 1st Cherokee Mounted Rifles. But before he could bring up his hand or report their failure, Hosmer's deep, rough voice rumbled out.

"It's Blaze Bad Water we're after. He and his gang took the body to Hope's Landing. There'll be others sniffing around after him. The ones who followed us from Illinois. We'll have to deal with them, as well. Then we can move on with the plan without any 'partners' to get in our way or share with."

Lizzenbe listened intently, then spoke for the rest of the men.

"Yes, sir," he said.

The major and Bowlegs rode on, and Lizzenbe and the others quickly fell in behind them.

The turnoff for Hope's Landing wasn't far away.

———

The church was lit by two lanterns and some candles Bad Water brought out of the sacristy. It wasn't much light, but it would be enough.

The gang gathered around the box that they'd lifted up onto the altar, and McNite began working at the edges with a crowbar he'd fetched from the boat. They let Onawa stand there and watch with them, Bad Water on one side of her, Wormwood crowding the other, a hand resting on the pearl grip of her big Remington.

Wormwood made sure that her bony elbow dug uncomfortably into Onawa's side, but Onawa ignored her. She kept her eyes on the box, both repulsed and fascinated by it. Whatever its contents might turn out to be—a pile of worthless dirt or dead relics of a sad past that were better off left alone—it could determine her fate.

The wood squealed as McNite made his way around the lid, loosening the nails that held it in place. When he'd gone all the way around, he set down the crowbar and took the lid in both hands and lifted.

Gootch and Nathaniel were holding the lanterns, and they moved them in closer the second McNite got the lid out of the way.

All the light revealed was straw.

The gang gaped down at it a moment, then slid their gazes over to Bad Water, watching him expectantly.

He reached into the nearest end of the box with both hands and parted the straw there. Beneath it were two black humps.

Gootch and Nathaniel laughed.

"I'll be damned," whispered the man across from Onawa, the older one they called Pigeon.

They were staring down at the toes of a man's boots.

Bad Water shifted to his left, forcing Onawa and Wormwood and the young man called Greer to step back out of his way. They quickly moved in again as Bad Water stopped at the other end of the box and began pushing aside the straw there.

A dark oval came into view. Gootch and Nathaniel extended their arms, bringing the lanterns closer, and features became visible.

Shriveled, discolored skin. Dark hair. Closed eyes, pruned mouth. A beard along a prominent jaw. A mole on the left cheek.

"I'll be damned," Pigeon said again.

"It's him!" said Greer. "It's actually him!"

"So those old bastards really got him," Wormwood marveled.

Two of the other gang members—the ones whose names Onawa still didn't know—began jumping up and down, whooping while Gootch and Nathaniel went back to cackling.

"How is he still so…him?" Onawa said.

She knew it would be better to stay quiet, but she was so horrified she had to ask.

"Embalming, Apache Momma," Bad Water said. "Don't you know whites like to pickle their dead?"

Wormwood snorted. "And they'd pay millions to have that one back. They're crazy…but I'm glad."

"It's not that old thing that's worth millions," Bad Water said, nodding down at the withered, almost copper-colored face. "It's the idea of him. That's what we're selling back to them. So they can keep thinking of him as a saint in heaven instead of a nasty old bag of bones someone could throw to the dogs."

"Maybe we should do that!" Nathaniel laughed. "He doesn't need all his arms and legs, right? Let's take him out and have some fun with him!"

He started to put his free hand into the box.

Bad Water slapped it away.

"Nail it shut again," he told McNite. "We've had our look."

"Right, Blaze."

Nathaniel put on an exaggerated pout, like a child denied a peppermint stick, as McNite brought the lid back up and covered the dark face below.

"Wert. Acorn," Bad Water said to the young men who'd been hooting and jumping. "You got so much spunk left, you can take first watch. Up in the belfry. Do *not* let each other fall asleep. You can trade with Wormwood and Nathaniel at midnight, then it'll be Greer and Pigeon's turn after that."

"What about Gootch and McNite?" either Wert or Acorn whined. "They get to sleep all night?"

"Yeah, they do," Bad Water said. "On the boat. That way it's watched, too. We leave at dawn…got it?"

Everyone nodded.

Nobody asked when Bad Water would take a turn on watch.

He wrapped a hand around Onawa's upper arm and began steering toward the sacristy at the back of the church.

CHAPTER 43

"Do you think it was wise?" Pixley whispered. "Dividing our forces like this?"

Diehl didn't bother looking over at him. He wouldn't have been able to see his face.

Dawn had yet to arrive, and it was pitch black at the edge of the forest where the two men kneeled.

Colonel Crowe had sent Pixley and Diehl to the east of the church and the graveyard and the grassy slope down to the river. Crowe and Walkingstick were in the woods somewhere opposite them, to the west, to set up a crossfire when whoever was in the church made their way down to the boat in the morning. Hoop and Eskaminzim, meanwhile, were hunkered in the little half-collapsed house nearest to the church—perhaps the rectory once. They'd watch for signs of Onawa and grab her if they could.

All of them were to stay as still and quiet as possible once they got into place. They knew there were two lookouts up in the church belfry: They could see their silhouettes against the stars. And there could easily be more men guarding the boat or patrolling the woods.

"'Our forces?'" Diehl whispered back. "That's a generous description of six men, half of whom are beaten to hell."

"Well, that hardly makes me feel better about this."

"It's not my job to make you feel good. It's my job to do what the colonel tells me. You should know that. You were a soldier."

"Three decades ago. Now I'm a 54-year-old accountant about to attack some kind of outlaw gang in the Indian Territories. So I think I'm allowed some doubts."

"I probably shouldn't say this, but if you've got doubts, why are you here sticking your neck out for a corpse? You're the client now."

Diehl and Pixley were leaning against an oak tree, one on each side of the trunk. Diehl brought up the Winchester in his hands and held it out before him, brandishing it for Pixley's benefit though he knew to the other man it would just be a vague shape in the dark, if that.

"You don't have to be out here with one of these if you don't want to be," Diehl said.

"Yes, I do," Pixley replied. "I swore an oath to my friends and my country. If this is where that takes me, I accept that, like it or not. It's not the why I have doubts about. It's the how."

Diehl opened his mouth to respond, then closed it. His own why was simple. He needed money and had never figured out a better way to get it than fighting for it. Pixley's why, on the other hand, struck him as foolish. Maybe even insane—though it was a brand of insanity that was common enough. But this wasn't the time to debate it, so he kept that thought to himself.

"'Brave hearts bend not so soon to care—firm minds uplift the load of fate,'" Diehl recited instead. "'They bear what others shrink to bear, and boldly any doom await.'"

Pixley mulled that over a moment.

"That's a fancy way of telling me to shut up, isn't it?" he said.

Diehl laughed softly. "Pretty much. I'll feel better about our strategy if we don't give our position away and get ourselves shot. If you want me to tell you all about C. Kermit Crowe and why I've been following his orders for nearly twenty years, I'd be happy to. When this is over. For now, if you're going to be here, just accept that he knows what he's doing and wants what you want—Abe back in his crypt and the country none the wiser he was messed with."

"Fine," Pixley sighed.

For a while, the only sounds were the chirping of crickets, the croaking of frogs, and the smooth, steady burbling of the river.

"But I still think dividing our forces was a bad idea," Pixley said.

———

"With so few of us, and so many of us in bad shape," Walkingstick whispered, "I wonder if maybe we should've stayed—"

"A crossfire is just the thing," Col. Crowe said. He managed to make the words firm but keep them quiet. "With us under cover in multiple positions, it'll be all the harder for them to figure out just how few and weak we are. Fighting Apaches taught me that."

"But with a crossfire we're more likely to hit the woman, too. If they bring her out with them, and she makes one step in the wrong direction—"

"Which is why Hoop and Eskaminzim are where they are," Crowe snapped.

Walkingstick heard the little man swivel toward him. It was too dark in the woods to see your own hand in front of your face, but that didn't mean Crowe wouldn't try to glare at him.

"If there's a chance to get her before the shooting starts, they'll do it," Crowe said. "And if there's not a chance, they'll do what they can for her after it starts. We've been over that."

"If only there were time for me to go to Tahlequah for rein-forcements…"

"But there's not. We've been over that, too."

Walkingstick conceded with a grunt, then went silent. For a minute.

"I just wish we knew who was in there."

He was looking up the hill, at the church. There was no light from inside. It was just a silhouette against a starry sky.

"Whoever it is seems to be pretty clever and pretty organized," Crowe said. "Pretty well-informed, too, to know what Hosmer and the senator were up to and strike at the right moment."

Walkingstick grunted again, drawing the sound out this time so it sounded more like a long "Hmmm."

"You're wondering if they're Cherokee, aren't you?" Crowe said.

"Yes."

"Would it change anything for you if they're not?"

Walkingstick went silent again.

"Maybe," Crowe said, "you're thinking if they're whites or Creeks or Choctaws or Osages, it's not really your problem. You could go home to a warm bed and let them sail off with President Lincoln and take all this trouble with them out of the Cherokee Nation."

"Yes. I was thinking that," Walkingstick admitted. "For a moment. But it was Cherokees who brought the trouble here. Cherokees who've been killed because of it. So whoever that is in the church, they're murderers and thieves and kidnappers in my jurisdiction. Which makes it my problem."

Crowe reached out into the darkness and managed to clap a hand on Walkingstick's shoulder.

"Bully for you, Captain," he said. "I admire your dedication to duty, and I'm grateful you're with us."

The hand slid away and wrapped itself again around the stock of Crowe's rifle.

"Now shut up," the colonel said, "and let's get ready to finish this thing."

———

Eskaminzim rose up, took a quick a look at the church fifty yards off to make sure nothing was different—no lights inside, no change of watch for the lookouts in the belfry—then sank back down behind the half-demolished wall at the back of the little abandoned house.

"You know—" he whispered to Hoop.

Hoop shushed him.

"Right," Eskaminzim said.

That was the end of the conversation.

There was a bed in the sacristy—a four-post one with a drooping canopy top and a rotting mattress. It had obviously been moved in from one of the old houses nearby. It took up half of the little chamber tucked away beyond the altar at the far end of the church.

Onawa lay atop it on her back, her bound hands tied by an extra loop to one of the posts. Whenever Bad Water slept—curled on a mound of ratty blankets on the floor rather than in the bed with her—she worked at the rope. If she pulled hard enough and long enough, she thought, she could snap the old post she was tethered to, but there was no way Bad Water would miss the sound of it. So instead she was swiveling her hands back and forth, back and forth, against the rough rope. Wearing away the skin and slicking it with blood. If she could get the rope wet enough and just a little more loose…

Bad Water stirred again. Onawa froze.

He'd been restless all night. Gentle when he'd tied her up—"Sorry…it's almost over"—but full of violent nightmares that had him whimpering and kicking his legs like a dreaming dog.

For the fourth time since he'd settled down by the foot of the bed, he rose and went to the little sacristy window. It was still just a dark-gray rectangle barely visible in the gloom.

"Come on, come on, come on," Bad Water said, peering up at the stars. "Go away, go away."

"Dawn will come soon," Onawa said.

Bad Water must have known she was awake. He wasn't startled.

"I'd like now better than soon," he said.

"Not me," said Onawa.

Bad Water lowered his head.

"There's still time to let me go," Onawa said. "You could tell the others I escaped while you slept. I won't tell anyone where you're going. What do I care about some dead White man?"

Bad Water took a deep breath. He seemed to be considering it.

Then he shook his head.

"I can't risk it. I don't really know what you'd do. And my

friends…" He scoffed bitterly at the word. "…they're hard to control. I can't make mistakes. I can't be weak. Wormwood…"

He shook his head again.

"Why does she hate me so much?" Onawa asked.

"For the same reason I like you. You're a reminder that we all have a mother."

"If that's how you truly feel, then you should let me go. For your m—"

"Shut up," Bad Water snarled. "Shut up, or I swear to god I'll kill you right now."

Onawa went quiet.

For a moment, Bad Water was quiet, too. Then he looked out the window again, and when he spoke his voice was soft and sad.

"God, I hate this place. 'The Cherokee Nation.' It's more like a garbage dump. Where the whites threw their trash. Just look what it's done to us. I can't believe that old asshole Hosmer—getting so many people killed so he can say this junkheap is still his land, his 'nation.' Well, when the sun comes up, we can finally leave, and we'll never have to fight over the scraps here again."

Onawa said nothing. There was no point. She knew she wasn't part of the "we."

"Just a few more minutes of dark and quiet," Bad Water said to the stars. "Then we're free."

———

Gootch wasn't a light sleeper. Quite the opposite. Once asleep, Gootch was practically comatose. A herd of buffalo could mosey past in the dark unnoticed by him. Blaze Bad Water knew that.

But Bad Water knew something else, too. Bill McNite snored. Loudly. Really, *really* loudly. Which was reason enough to send him down to the boat for the night. The racket he made would shake the walls of the church. Every so often he'd even snore loud enough to wake up somebody like Gootch. So Bad Water had sent the two of them to the boat together, knowing he had a guarantee that, from time to time, at least one of his lookouts on the river would actually be awake.

To make matters worse for Gootch, the trickling-swirling-gurgle of the river made him want to piss. So every time McNite let out a particularly thunderous snort, Gootch would lie there a while trying to ignore his bladder as he drifted off again. If he could.

This time he couldn't. Dammit. The pressure in his bladder was too strong.

He was on his side at the bow of the boat, just beyond the boiler in the middle, while McNite had the wider, roomier stern section to himself. Gootch got up grumbling, stumbled to the gunwale, and spat into the water off the dock through the gap in his teeth—permanent reminder of a fistfight he'd lost to his stepfather at the age of ten. McNite let out another rumbling roar of a snore as Gootch unbuttoned his frayed and filthy trousers and took himself out.

The sound of piss hitting the water caused McNite to stir, snorting and muttering and turning over.

Good, Gootch thought.

McNite had woken him up half a dozen times. Turnabout is fair play.

Gootch ripped a fart and began moving his member in circles so his stream hitting the river would make more noise.

A smile started to stretch over his gummy mouth…then wilted as something on the riverbank caught his eye.

A little way off, just beyond the end of the dock—was that a shape that shouldn't be there? *Two* shapes that shouldn't be there?

Gootch blinked, then blinked again.

The shapes remained. Unmoving, just like him. Upright, lean, just like him.

Men, just like him. Standing there staring at him from the darkness hoping he was too bleary-eyed to notice.

Gootch's whizzing came to a sudden stop.

"McNite!" he cried.

He instinctively slapped at his side, reaching for his pistol.

The pistol that was in the holster curled up at the bow of the boat where he'd been sleeping.

But the two old Cherokee rebels didn't know that. The major had told them to take care of anyone guarding the boat as quietly as possible, with hands over mouths and blades across throats. That wasn't an option now, though, with (they thought) the gangly man with his pecker out about to draw his gun. So they drew theirs, and they used them.

Gootch flew backward into the boat with a hole in his chest— dead before the first shot of the battle was done echoing across the river.

Chapter 44

Solomon Hosmer saw the flash of the gunshots a quarter of a second before he heard them. He was in the woods to the east of the church with two of his men—Bowlegs Charlie Durant and Eli Lizzenbe, his final reserves—while the rest either went down to secure the boat or crept through the forest looking for the Northerners or stray members of Blaze Bad Waters's gang.

This part was supposed to be quiet. By the time the sun came up, the boat would be theirs and any rivals hiding in the woods would be bleeding to death. Then, when Bad Water and his friends came out of the church with the box, the shooting could start.

It wasn't going to work out that way. There was another gunshot —this one not toward the boat but *from* it — followed by a flurry of shots in return.

His men by the river had failed to take the boat without a sound, and now it looked like they were in a gunfight with someone on board. It was unfortunate, but not a disaster. In fact, it could be an opportunity.

"Get ready," Hosmer said. "Watch."

Bowlegs and Lizzenbe raised their rifles.

———

McNite popped up over the side of the boat and fired another shot at the riverbank.

"Bastards!" he hollered.

He ducked down again.

He heard scurrying footsteps—on soft soil, not the planks of the dock, which was good—then more shots came his way. One of them thunked into the gunwale between Gootch's splayed legs.

McNite rose up again and pointed his gun at no particular target.

"Sons of bitches!" he yelled.

He pulled the trigger.

———

"Who do you think it is?" Pixley asked. "Hoop and Eskaminzim?"

He stood and leaned out from the tree he'd been sitting against and craned his neck for a better look at the flashes of light by the river.

Diehl reached out and grabbed his arm.

"Stay—!"

There was another gunshot—not a distant *pop* but a big, closer *boom* quickly followed by another. Bullets screamed through the trees slicing off leaves and twigs as they went.

Pixley grunted and dropped to the ground.

Diehl flattened himself, then reached over and put a hand on the other man's back.

"Are you all right?"

"I...I...think so," Pixley said. "I think..." He slowly brought a hand up to the side of his head. "I think they shot off my ear."

"Don't worry." Diehl gave Pixley a reassuring pat on the back. "That's why God gave you two."

Pixley sucked in a sharp breath as he gently probed his wound.

"No...no, it's still there," he said. "Mostly."

There were two more blasts from somewhere nearby, and bullets whistled past directly above them.

Diehl pressed himself even flatter against the ground.

Pixley brought his hand down and peered at it in the dark, unable to make out the blood he knew was smeared across it.

"Still…of all the things to forget from soldiering," he muttered. "*Keep your head down.*"

"Just don't forget it again," Diehl said into the soil.

A second later, there was another volley in their direction.

The gunshots sounded closer.

———

"Dammit," Walkingstick said. "It's Hosmer. It must be."

He and Colonel Crowe were crouched two hundred yards away, watching helplessly as someone in the woods to the east—two some-ones, to judge by the side-by-side flashes of orange light—fired on Diehl and Pixley's position. For all Walkingstick and Crowe knew, there was no need for them to keep at it. Maybe Diehl and Pixley were already dead. But the shots kept coming.

The gunfight by the boat was continuing, too, with one figure stretched out flat near the dock, another lifeless in the boat, and the two remaining participants throwing wild pistol shots at each other.

Walkingstick brought up his Winchester, waiting for the next rifle flares in the forest to the east—nice, bright targets.

Crowe grabbed the Winchester's barrel and pushed it down.

"We don't know who's shooting or where Diehl and Pixley are now," he said. "We can't fire blind."

"Dammit!" Walkingstick spat again, jerking his rifle away from Crowe's hand. Furious because he knew the colonel was right.

He eyed the grassy hill that ran from the church and the grave-yard south down to the river.

"I could get across that in thirty seconds," he said. "Circle around behind whoever's over there. *Then* shoot if it makes sense… hopefully while Diehl and Pixley are still alive."

"A half minute is a damn long time to be in the open right now, even in the dark," Crowe said.

But Walkingstick was already taking a step out from the trees.

There was another gunshot, but not from the east this time.

A spray of sod exploded out of the ground a yard in front of Walkingstick. He spun around and went diving for cover again as another shot shrieked past a few feet behind him.

"Where the hell did that come from?" he said.

Crowe hunkered down behind a tree and jerked his head toward the north.

"The high ground!" he said.

———

Hoop and Eskaminzim peeked up at the lookouts in the church belfry taking potshots first at Walkingstick and then, when that target darted back into the forest, at the man exchanging gunfire with whoever was on the boat.

"They're just shooting at shapes, shooting at the shooting," Eskaminzim said. He shook his head disapprovingly. "When they don't even know who else might be nearby."

"Not very smart," said Hoop.

Eskaminzim jabbed his revolver at the belfry. "So teach them a lesson."

Eskaminzim couldn't handle a rifle with his right arm in a sling, so all he had to fight with was the Colt in his hand and a knife at his side. No good for picking off would-be sharpshooters. But Hoop had his Sharps rifle.

Hoop raised it, aimed, and fired.

One of the men in the belfry jerked backward into the bell that still hung there, bounced off, and rolled out. The bell clanged dully as he and his rifle slid down the roof then fell the twenty feet to the ground. The other man in the belfry ducked out of sight before Hoop could fire again.

Hoop and Eskaminzim dropped down behind the half-collapsed wall at the back of the abandoned house. All the furnishings had been taken out, but it was obvious they were in what had once been the master bedroom of a small residence.

"The ones in the church—they're going to be distracted, maybe panicking," Eskaminzim said as Hoop reloaded his single-shot rifle. "Might be a good time to use the back way in, through the window. If they held onto my sister to use as a hostage—"

"They'll make that play soon, and we'll have lost our chance to get her first," Hoop said. "Agreed. I'll take out that other one up top, then we go."

Eskaminzim nodded.

Hoop slinked over to a different part of the wall and got ready to pop up Jack-in-the-box style. Hopefully he'd get a clear shot at the man on top of the church looking for Hoop in the wrong spot.

Hoop cocked the hammer on his rifle and started to stand.

A noise from behind froze him halfway up.

He looked at Eskaminzim. Eskaminzim was already looking at *him*. He'd heard it, too.

The creaking of a floorboard.

A footstep. Inside the house.

They'd been shooting at the shooters without knowing who else might be nearby. And now someone was coming to teach them a lesson.

———

Blaze Bad Water strapped on his gun belt as he burst out of the church's back room into the sanctuary. His friends there—Wormwood, Nathaniel, Acorn, and Wert—were all gazing out the side windows facing the river, their pistols in their hands. The church had been too small and poor to afford stained glass, but the windows were still hard to see through—grimy and smeared. So all that was visible outside was darkness and, both to the left and straight ahead, blurred here-and-gone flashes of gunfire. There'd been shooting from the belfry and the little house over to the right, too, but that had stopped after one of their friends—either Pigeon or Greer, it was impossible to tell which — had rolled off the roof and landed in a heap, dead.

"What the hell is going on?" Bad Water said.

"No idea," said Wormwood, and she started busting out glass with the long barrel of her pearl-handled Remington.

Nathaniel copied her, then Acorn and Wert.

"Stop it!" Bad Water said.

But they couldn't hear him over the sound of shattering glass, and then they were making even more noise—firing wildly this way and that into the night.

Bad Water stalked over to the nearest of them—Nathaniel—and yanked him away from the broken window he was shooting through.

"I said stop it, dammit! Who the hell are you even shooting at?"

"I don't know!" Nathaniel said. "But they ain't us!"

Bad Water shoved him away in disgust. He stalked over to Wormwood and pressed himself against the wall beside her.

"Stop!" he roared. "All of you! Stop shooting!"

Wormwood glared over at him, but then nodded and lowered her Remington.

Acorn and Wert stopped firing when they noticed Wormwood had.

Bad Water took a deep breath.

"Get away from the windows," he said quietly. "You're making easy targets of yourselves."

"Oh. Right," said Acorn, hopping away from the window frame.

Wormwood and Wert stepped to the side, too, and Nathaniel pressed his big body against the wall like Bad Water.

"You think it's her husband?" Wormwood asked with a nod at the open door to the sacristy and, beyond that still tied to the bed, Onawa. "With friends?"

"Let's ask," said Bad Water.

He leaned in close to the window to his left.

"Hey! You out there! Who are you? What do you want?"

The sporadic blasts of gunfire outside petered to a stop. There was a moment of silence, then a deep, rough voice boomed out from the darkness like sudden thunder.

"You know what we're here for! We had it first, and we want it back!"

Bad Water and Wormwood looked at each other.

Bad Water laughed softly.

"That's gotta be him," he said. "Major Solomon Hosmer himself."

"Give it back to us, and we'll let you go!" Hosmer shouted from somewhere in the woods.

Wormwood snorted.

"You may have stolen it first, old man, but we stole it last!" she shouted back. "That makes it ours!"

"It doesn't belong to either of you!" someone else called out.

It sounded like another man around Hosmer's age—one from up north somewhere—but with a thinner, weaker, wobbly voice. It seemed to be coming from somewhere just beyond the cemetery.

Bad Water and Wormwood peeped out through the broken windows, trying for a look at whoever it was. The sun had finally started coming up, giving the treetops to the east a pink-purple halo. But the men hiding in the shadows of the forest were still out of sight to them.

"It belongs to the American people!" the voice beyond the graveyard added.

"*We're* American people, asshole!" Wormwood yelled. "So we're keeping it!"

She gave Bad Water a self-satisfied grin.

He shook his head at her, frowning.

He wanted the conversation to continue. He wanted more time to think, calculate, plan.

He didn't get it.

A shot from the forest slammed into the window frame inches from Wormwood's face. Then someone else near the woods shot back at the shooter. Then the gunfire started up again down by the boat, and whoever was still in the belfry joined in, and shots came back at *him* from the trees to the east *and* the west.

The battle was on again, and there was no stopping it now.

"*Dammit,*" Bad Water said.

There was a flicker of light to his right, and he turned to find Wert at the end of one of the pews, firing up the lantern sitting there.

"Turn that down, you idiot!" he snapped.

"But, Blaze," Wert whined, holding up his pistol, "it's dark in here and I gotta reload my— "

A bullet smashed through glass and kept going through Wert's head and carried on into the wall on the opposite side of the church.

Wert toppled sideways, his instantly lifeless bulk carrying the lantern with it as it hit the pew, bounced off, and crashed to the floor. The lantern's glass globe shattered beneath him, and burning oil quickly spread across the floorboards. The blazing puddle flowed under the next pew over, and the old, dry wood burst into flame.

Within seconds, the sanctuary began to fill with fire and smoke.

CHAPTER 45

Eskaminzim and Hoop watched with alarm over the half-crumbled wall as smoke started coming from the church. They were crouched down, listening to the gun battle that had erupted again, waiting for whoever was inside the little house with them to make their move.

They couldn't wait any longer. Not with Onawa still a prisoner in an old building that would go up like a struck match if it caught on fire.

Eskaminzim elbowed Hoop. Then he pointed at Hoop's Sharps with his pistol, nodded at the closed bedroom door, touched the barrel of his gun to his chest, nodded at the door again.

You shoot through the door, then I'll bust out and see who's there, he was saying.

It was a reckless plan. But reckless would have to do.

Hoop nodded.

He gave Eskaminzim all of three seconds to ready himself, then he brought up his rifle and fired.

The shot blasted a hole dead center in the door, and there was a cry and a clatter from the other side.

Eskaminzim leaped up, threw the door open, and rushed out to see what awaited him.

Two men were there, closer to the door then he expected a couple of the old Cherokee soldiers they'd followed down through Missouri. One was on his back on the floor, bloodied but not dead, and he started to lift the pistol he still gripped in his right hand. The other Cherokee had an Enfield rifle that was up but pointed off toward the wall, probably jerked to the side when the man had jumped in surprise.

Eskaminzim's momentum brought him hurtling straight at them. He shot the man on the floor through the forehead then swung his gun toward the one with the rifle as they came practically face to face. Before Eskaminzim could pull the trigger again, the Cherokee knocked the gun from his hand with the barrel of his Enfield. Eskaminzim reciprocated by jerking the rifle away, but with his right arm in a sling there was nothing he could do with it but fling it to the floor.

Eskaminzim leaped back in case the Cherokee had a knife. Which he did—a big Bowie he whipped out from under his jacket. As Eskaminzim drew his own knife he heard rifle fire coming and going from the bedroom behind him.

Hoop was dueling with the lookout in the belfry again. Perhaps pinned down. Eskaminzim would have to finish this fight on his own.

"Been a long time since I gutted anyone," growled the old Cherokee—who wasn't really *that* old. He looked to be in his early fifties, only a few years beyond Eskaminzim himself. "Gonna be a pleasure to get back into practice."

"I gutted a bony old Cherokee two days ago," Eskaminzim replied. "It's going to be a pleasure to stay in practice."

The Cherokee scowled and took a lunging step forward, his Bowie knife out in front of him like a lance.

Before this, Eskaminzim would've boasted that he could kill a Cherokee with one arm tied behind his back. Now he'd have to prove it.

———

"Put it out! Put it out!" Wormwood shouted, pointing at the fire.

Acorn and Nathaniel stripped off their jackets and hurried toward the flames and began beating at them. But the blaze was already too big to be smothered—two pews were engulfed, and the ones around them were starting to catch—and all they succeeded in doing was smearing their coats with burning oil.

"Stop it!" Bad Water yelled at them. "You're making it worse!"

Nathaniel gave up and tossed his jacket into the flames and darted away. But when Acorn tried to do the same, one of the greasy sleeves of his shirt caught fire.

"Oh, god! My arm! My arm!" he howled.

He began beating at the burning fabric with his other hand, a perfect silhouette in front of the blaze behind him.

A shot burst through one of the windows and knocked him into the fire. He fell, shrieked, kicked, writhed, while Nathaniel and Wormwood and Bad Water watched in helpless horror.

After a moment, the screaming and struggling stopped.

"Jesus…" Nathaniel said.

Wormwood turned to Bad Water.

"We can't stay in here!" she said, shouting to be heard over the growing roar of the fire. "We've gotta get out!"

Bad Water tore his gaze away from Acorn's burning body. He looked at Wormwood, blinked, then stared off at the long pinewood box sitting on the floor in front of the altar.

"Forget about that!" Wormwood told him. "We've got to go!"

Bad Water blinked again, then shifted his gaze to the open door at the back of the sanctuary. Heavy black smoke was drifting through it.

Bad Water started toward the door.

"Forget about *her*!" Wormwood yelled.

But Bad Water just went faster, racing past the box and the altar toward the sacristy.

He wasn't going to leave the Apache woman to the flames, he knew that. But what *was* he going to do? Drag her outside with them as a human shield? Shoot her and spare her the agony of Acorn's death? Cut her loose and let her go? He'd decide what to do—who he was—when he saw her.

He ran into the sacristy and skidded to a stop before the bed.

The *empty* bed with a snapped bedpost.

The little window at the back of the sacristy was open. The woman had freed herself and slipped off while Bad Water's friends were blasting away at gunfire and shadows—back when it was still pitch black out and there was no fire to backlight a fleeing figure.

There'd been but a moment when easy escape was possible, and she'd waited for it patiently, then seized it.

"Good for you, Momma," Bad Water said. "Good for you."

He looked at the window—a rectangle of dim dawn light, the woods beyond starting to take shape—and considered following the woman through it. He'd been an easy target for whoever was out there now. Halfway out he'd probably be shot, dropping to the ground lifeless and alone. But it was a chance.

"Blaze!" Nathaniel called out. "What's going on?"

"We're running out of time, Blaze!" Wormwood added. "How are we getting outta here?"

Bad Water turned away from the window and walked calmly back to the burning sanctuary to tell his friends what to do.

———

Diehl dared a peek around a headstone at the church, and Pixley slowly did the same around the other side. After taking fire for minutes at the edge of the forest, they'd risked a belly-crawling escape to the graveyard that had bought them a brief respite from constant close calls. Pixley could have given them away when he felt compelled to join the conversation between Hosmer and the man in the church—dazed from the oozing wound to his ear, he'd remembered to keep his head down but not to shut up—and though the gunfire had started up again, none of the bullets were headed their way.

Yet. With the sun coming up they wouldn't stay out of sight for long.

Behind them, at the bottom of the slope, the battle by the water was over. Two Cherokees lay near the riverbank, one dead and one dying, while another corpse was stretched out in the boat and yet another drifted south down the Neosho River.

Almost all of the shooting now was going back and forth between the east and west sides of the clearing, with the surviving lookout in the belfry popping up to join in from time to time.

And now, Diehl and Pixley saw, the church beneath the lookout had caught fire.

"My god," Pixley said hoarsely. "Lincoln's in there."

"And Onawa. And bastards with guns," said Diehl. "*Dammit.*"

Diehl gave himself a second to think—knowing from the way the smoke was growing that even a second of planning might be a luxury Onawa couldn't afford.

"I have to get inside. Quick, before we're spotted again." He pointed at the back of the church. "I might be able to get in there if I run like hell, and you give me cover with—"

The top of the headstone between him and Pixley exploded, sending stone shards spraying.

Both men yelped and hit the ground.

Another bullet whizzed past above them, then yet another slammed into one of the headstones nearby, cracking it in two.

"They've seen us," Pixley said.

Diehl wiped at the blood that was flowing into his eyes from a deep cut across his forehead.

"I noticed," he said.

———

The Cherokee with the Bowie knife hopped back, and Eskaminzim's swipe at him missed by inches. Again.

The Cherokee smiled grimly and kept circling slowly to his left, keeping himself lined up with Eskaminzim's right arm—the one in the sling. Eskaminzim had to stretch his good arm out across his body to reach the man with his knife, giving his opponent the extra split second he needed to jump away.

Every so often the Cherokee would make feints himself, starting a roundhouse stab or a quick forward jab but stopping himself, assessing Eskaminzim's reactions. He may have been an older man, but whatever he'd done for a living—blacksmith, farrier, cooper—had kept him fit, with hands that looked steady and strong.

"You're right-handed, ain't ya?" he sneered with a quick flick of the eyes at Eskaminzim's sling. "It shows."

"Left hand, right hand...it doesn't matter," Eskaminzim replied. "I once killed a Mexican Federale with nothing but the little toe of my left foot. I think I'll do the same for you."

The Cherokee snorted and faked the beginning of a lunging slash with his Bowie knife.

Sooner or later the lunges and slashes wouldn't be fake.

The two men kept circling each other.

The little house had been stripped bare long ago, and the only obstacles for them other than the walls were the dead man splayed out on the floor and the pistols and rifle lying near him. That was all behind Eskaminzim now, near the door to the bedroom.

Somewhere beyond that door, out of sight from the front part of the house, Hoop was still trading rifle fire with the lookout in the belfry. Eskaminzim intended to give Hoop a *really* hard time about taking so long to kill the man. Assuming he *did* eventually kill the man, and the Cherokee with the Bowie knife didn't kill Eskaminzim.

There was another one-two exchange of rifle shots, followed by a grunt and a thump and clatter that might have been Hoop's heavy Sharps hitting the floorboards.

"Sounds like your friend got it like mine did," the Cherokee taunted.

Eskaminzim half-turned his head, cocking an ear at the doorway behind him, looking alarmed and distracted.

The Cherokee dove in at him—just like Eskaminzim wanted.

Eskaminzim pivoted to the side and leaned back, and the blade of the Bowie knife swished past his stomach, slicing open his shirt rather than his belly. At the same time Eskaminzim stuck out his left foot and jabbed his knife into the Cherokee's back.

The Cherokee cried out, tripped, and went flying. He landed flat on his face, and instantly Eskaminzim was landing on *him*, driving a knee into the man's lower back while his knife opened the sides of his neck.

Blood splashed out over the floorboards, and the Cherokee struggled to rise for a moment, then let go of his Bowie knife, sagged, died.

Eskaminzim hadn't killed him with nothing but the big toe of his left foot. But the big toe had helped. Just as it had with the Federale years before.

There's nothing wrong with a little exaggeration when you're telling a man how you're going to kill him.

Eskaminzim wiped his knife on the dead man's jacket, then stuffed it away and started toward the back of the house, scooping up his pistol as he passed it. When he reached the doorway he crouched and peeked cautiously into the room beyond.

The Sharps was lying on the floor, and Hoop was a few feet away, stretched out against what remained of the crumbling back wall. He was on his right side with a hand pressed against his left, just above the hip. His face was sweaty, and blood trickled between his fingers.

"You let him shoot you?" Eskaminzim said.

"Not…on purpose," Hoop panted. "What took…*you*…so long?"

Eskaminzim started to reply, but Hoop cut him off with a weak "Never mind."

Hoop swiveled his gaze skyward.

"The church," he said.

Through the big hole where part of the upper wall and ceiling used to be, Eskaminzim could see that dawn had fully arrived now —which made it easier to see that the smoke swirling up into the brightening sky had grown thicker and more black.

There was no more time for rifle duels or knife fights or strategy. Not even time to start a death song. Only time for Eskaminzim to find Onawa or die trying.

He took a breath, steeled himself, then sprinted toward the gap in the shattered wall and leaped through into the new day.

———

Colonel Crowe and Walkingstick were watching the belfry as they worked their way up the hill along the edge of the forest. The lookout atop the church had an annoying habit of hopping up at just the right (for them wrong) moments—whenever they or Hoop and Eskaminzim exposed themselves. He never seemed to need more than a second to draw a bead and fire before ducking down again, and the closest they'd come to hitting him was bouncing a couple shots off the bell he hunkered down under. But the man wouldn't be able to stay up there menacing them much longer.

"Looks like the fire's spreading fast inside the church," Crowe said. "The whole north side must be...look!"

A familiar figure had come hurtling out of the little house at the top of the hill — Eskaminzim, charging the church with a revolver in his hand.

Right on cue, the lookout in the belfry shot to his feet and took aim.

"Get him! Get him!" Crowe shouted as he slammed to a stop and brought up his rifle. "Now now now!"

Walkingstick was already firing.

The man in the belfry jerked back, then dropped out of sight again.

He wouldn't be getting up this time. The glistening of the blood and brains splattered on the bell made that plain.

"Finally!" Crowe said, lowering his rifle.

Walkingstick gave him an annoyed look, about to suggest that "Nice shot" was the more appropriate thing to say. But the sound of shattering glass jerked his attention back to the church.

Three people were leaping through what remained of the windows facing the river, a wall of flames behind them. One was hulkingly large, one was small, one medium. None were Onawa.

"It's them!" Crowe shouted.

"It's who?" Walkingstick said, squinting at the trio as they landed hard, scrambled to their feet, and started a hunched, wobbly, weaving dash toward the graveyard—and Diehl and Pixley hiding there—with guns in their hands. Something about them seemed familiar, hinted at a memory, but they were too far off and moving too erratically to see clearly.

He'd heard the voice shouting out from the church. Youthful, cool, unafraid, defiant. A young leader, intelligent and daring, who'd accrued followers in the Territories.

Could it be…?

"It's whoever took Lincoln from Hosmer!" Crowe said. "And now they've left him in the church! Come on!"

Crowe ran out into the open, heading straight for the church door two hundred yards away.

Walkingstick didn't follow him.

Hosmer and the last of his men were still somewhere in the woods on the other side of the clearing. They could easily escape if they slipped away now and let the body burn. But would they, after all they'd been through? Or would they—like Crowe, apparently—literally hurl themselves into a fire to try to get it back before it was ashes?

High, yipping howls from the forest to the east, like the yowling of a pack of coyotes, provided the answer.

The old battle cry. The rebels were going to charge the church, too.

They'd have to pass the cemetery—and Pixley and Diehl and maybe Blaze Bad Water and Gerty Wormwood and Nathaniel Pumpkin, if that's who'd just jumped from the sanctuary—to get to the front door. There was about to be a free-for-all gunfight among the headstones, and Walkingstick was too distant and the light too dim for clear shots once the battle was on.

Eskaminzim and Crowe kept heading for the church door. If anything was to be done for Onawa and Abraham Lincoln, they could do it. Pixley and Diehl, meanwhile, were pinned down in what would soon be a battlefield, with Indian outlaws and rebels doing the fighting all around them.

It was clear where a Cherokee lawman should go. Dammit.

Walkingstick cursed and started running toward the graveyard.

———

Bowlegs bayed out the battle cry again as he ran through the trees, and Eli Lizzenbe joined in beside him.

Years before, during the war, they'd heard the cry taken up by hundreds of comrades up and down the lines. It had created a terrible, awe-inspiring, exhilarating noise, more fearsome than the roar of a tornado. It had bonded them together and torn the men facing them apart. But now it was a lonely, pathetic sound, thin and wheezy and weak.

Bowlegs didn't think about that. You couldn't let yourself think during a charge at all. Not if you wanted to keep charging. You had to just fix yourself to a point in the distance and keep moving forward forward forward to reach it, killing whoever got in your way.

"Onward! Onward!" Major Hosmer boomed out behind them. "To the church!"

"To the church!" Lizzenbe yelled.

Bowlegs just cut loose with the battle cry again. Words were too close to thoughts. And if he let himself think "To the church" that might lead to "Really?" which might lead to "What hope is there now?" which might lead to "I'm going home."

Bowlegs and Lizzenbe burst out of the trees, their rifles held out before them, and angled toward the graveyard and the burning church beyond it. There was movement in the headstones— crouching shapes dodging for cover. Bowlegs took aim at one as he ran. Hopefully it would be like the best of the old days, their charge sweeping them over the enemy's position quickly, splayed bodies strewn behind them as they sprinted to victory.

"Onward!" the major shouted one more time. And Bowlegs didn't let himself think, *He sounds farther behind us now.*

I can't hear his footsteps anymore.

Did he stay in the forest?

That dirty old son of a bitch...

Instead he started shooting, and beside him Lizzenbe did the same.

Diehl tried to wipe the blood out of his eyes again—the gash on his forehead was still bleeding freely—as he peeped in disbelief around the nearest headstone. Three men had already been coming at him and Pixley from the church to the north, and now at least two more were rushing out of the forest to the southeast, yipping and howling like coyotes?

The dawn light was still too dim to read the engraving on the headstones, but Diehl half-suspected he was cowering behind one with his own name on it. God definitely seemed to be telling him something.

"Play dead," Diehl whispered to Pixley two graves over.

"But the president—"

"Forget that. Just pray they kill each other instead of—"

The men charging out of the woods started shooting. At Diehl and Pixley. One shot shattered the gravestone Diehl was hiding behind, while another caught the edge of a marker near Pixley and ricocheted away.

Diehl rolled to the side, holding tight to his Winchester. When he was behind an unbroken headstone again he stopped and looked toward the forest, eyes blinking madly to keep his own blood from blinding him. It took him a second to focus. When he did the first thing he saw was a skinny Cherokee in a stovepipe hat closing the distance between them—no more than thirty yards now—on long, bowed legs.

"Shit!" Diehl said.

He jerked up his Winchester and took aim.

The Cherokee aimed at *him*.

Pixley rose up with his rifle and fired before either of them.

The Cherokee arched back as if admiring the purple-gray clouds becoming visible overhead. His hat dropped off, his arms flew out to his sides, his rifle dropped to the ground. His bent legs managed to carry him three more steps forward before they gave out, and he collapsed into the tall grass at the cemetery's southeastern edge.

The old Cherokee who'd been charging with him howled out another battle cry—it sounded almost like a wail of despair now—and ran past his fallen friend, his rifle swinging toward Pixley. Diehl put a round in his side that slowed but didn't stop him, and the man got off a wild shot that skimmed screaming through the cemetery as he stumbled sideways.

That was when the three who'd escaped from the church joined in, firing wildly with their revolvers.

"You want this? You want this?" one of them shouted, the voice so high-pitched it almost sounded like a girl. "Come and get it!"

Most of their shots whistled past overhead as Pixley dropped down behind the headstones again. But one caught the staggering Cherokee in the shoulder. He jerked back then sagged forward onto his knees, yet still somehow kept hold of his rifle. He raised it high enough to get off one more shot—at the biggest of the three figures outlined against the still-spreading fire.

"Nathaniel!" the high voice shrieked as the big silhouette toppled into the darkness of the earth.

Then she—and it actually was a she, Diehl realized—fired again at the man on his knees. The shot caught him in the stomach, and he dropped his rifle, curled forward into a ball, and lay still.

"Nathaniel?" the girl said.

She got no reply, and when she spoke next she was raving.

"Who else needs to die? Who else? Come on, you sons of bitches! I'll give it to you!"

Her voice was growing louder, and Diehl could hear her quick footsteps as she stalked into the graveyard.

There were other footsteps, too. Heavier ones circling around the edge of the cemetery.

Both would reach the row Diehl and Pixley were in within seconds.

Diehl looked at Pixley a few graves over. The little man was lying on his side, back to Diehl, bloody half-ear in the air. There was no time to get his attention and signal some kind of plan. No time to do anything but choose who to go up against—Diehl didn't want his last act to be shooting a girl, so he picked whoever the other one was—and think one quick, final, blasphemous prayer (*So You finally got me, damn You*). Then he swiped at his eyes one more time and started to push himself onto his knees, readying himself to take—or receive—his final shot.

"Bad Water! Wormwood!" someone shouted.

Diehl peered back toward the river and saw Lt. Walkingstick fifty yards off, in a crouch with his rifle raised. He was out in the open on the slope, no cover at all. He'd been trying to skulk up unnoticed, probably, when he saw Blaze Bad Water and Gerty Wormwood—Hey, they were famous! It was almost an honor to be murdered by them!—closing in on Diehl and Pixley in the flickering light of the burning church.

"Hold it right there!" Walkingstick said. "It's over!"

The approaching footsteps stopped.

"You hear that, Wormwood?" Diehl heard Bad Water say. "It's over."

"I know," the girl replied.

There was a crash behind them as a church window shattered from the heat, then a whoosh and a crackle as flames spread up onto the roof.

Bad Water sighed. "Well…shall we?"

"Why the hell not?"

Diehl rose up and tried to get his Winchester on them—he knew what they were going to do from the resignation in their voices—but it was too late. They were already swinging their revolvers toward Walkingstick.

Walkingstick's rifle boomed, then Wormwood's big Remington and Bad Water's Colt, then the rifle again, twice more, all within the span of three seconds.

Bad Water and Wormwood dropped out of sight—dropped in that way that said they weren't getting up again.

Diehl turned and looked down the hill and saw Walkingstick wobble and lower his rifle. Then Diehl couldn't make out anything but a blur of red.

"Goddamn all this *blood*…" he said, rubbing a sleeve across his eyes.

When he could see again, Walkingstick was already lying on his side, his rifle on the grass beside him. Diehl started toward him and realized there was an obstacle in his way.

Pixley was still stretched out on the ground by a grave marker, in the same position he'd been in a minute before. Diehl went to his side and rolled him onto his back knowing what he'd see.

Open but blind eyes. A bloody hole over the heart.

Diehl wasn't even sure who'd got him—Bad Water or Wormwood or the last of Hosmer's men.

Diehl decided to believe it was the old Cherokee, and that Pixley had died bravely facing the final rebel charge.

Maybe it wasn't true. So what?

Diehl stepped over Pixley's body and started down the hill to see if anything could be done to keep Lt. Henry Walkingstick from joining him wherever he'd gone.

———

There were flames everywhere, yet Eskaminzim kept searching.

"Sister! Sister!" he called, peering this way and that under burning pews as he raced up the center aisle of the sanctuary.

At the end of the aisle stood the altar and a long wooden box on the floor before it. Both on fire.

"No!" Colonel Crowe cried.

He was a few steps behind Eskaminzim, and when he reached the altar, he took off his coat and began beating at the flames consuming the box.

"Help me with this!" he said.

Eskaminzim ignored him. He carried on around the altar and then, seeing nothing there, angled off toward the door at the back of the sanctuary.

"Sister!"

He burst through into the little room beyond the door.

All he saw was a bed with a broken post and an open window. But that was enough.

He spun around and ran back into the sanctuary.

"Help me with this!" the colonel shouted at him again.

He was still flailing at the burning box, though it was clearly a losing battle. Half of it was on fire, and the whole thing was smoking. Even if Eskaminzim didn't have an arm in a sling, it would be too late for him to help put out the flames or drag the box outside.

There was a crash from the front of the church. The rafters were starting to come down there. Any second, more would fall. On *them*.

There was only one way Eskaminzim could help Colonel Crowe now.

He grabbed the little man by the collar and dragged him toward one of the big, busted-out windows on the south side of the church.

"What are you doing?" Crowe yelled. "Stop it! We can't leave him like this! We can't!"

"He doesn't mind!" Eskaminzim shouted back.

When he reached the window, he whipped the colonel around and shoved him through, then went diving after him as the roof came down behind them.

CHAPTER 46

So…it was over. Again.

Well, over wasn't over. A lost war had taught Major Solomon Hosmer that.

You fight another day. And if you lose then, you just wait for yet another day. The men who win are the ones who never stop.

Hosmer watched as the Indian—an Apache, by the look of him—pulled the man he'd just pushed out the window away from the burning church. The man resisted, and as he bellowed and waved his stubby arms Hosmer realized he recognized him.

It was the arrogant little Yankee he'd briefly encountered at the Joplin Hotel…before *it* burned down. Wherever the man went, an inferno seemed to follow.

Hosmer knew it would be gratifying to pull his old Colt revolver from its holster and point the long, dark barrel at the man and pull the trigger. But he was too far off for a sure shot, and though the sun was coming up he was still hidden in the shadows at the edge of the forest. The survivors didn't know where he was. Best to keep it that way.

The major surveyed the carnage on the battlefield—Bowlegs and Lizzenbe stretched out by the cemetery, two more old veterans lying by the riverbank, the last two of his men most likely dead somewhere to the west. Like him, he assumed they were Protestants. Methodist or Baptist, one or the other. So they were in Heaven now, with God, not lost like the stubborn old pagan Cherokees who still insisted on believing that the spirits of the dead lived on in the land or went on a journey through some dark night realm.

Hosmer hoped that Henry Walkingstick had believed that gibberish. Hoped he was in Hell now as a result. Seeing the way the other Yankee, Diehl, slumped over Walkingstick's motionless form was one of the few victories of the day to savor.

Hosmer soaked it in a moment, then turned and headed into the forest, toward the horses hidden among the trees a half-mile to the east.

He'd recruit young men in the future. That would make the difference. This time, he'd relied on old loyalties, old skills, old men. And though they'd achieved something remarkable—Abraham Lincoln burned to a crisp by the banks of the Neosho River!—it wasn't a triumph.

That would come some other time, some other way. With the fire and force of youth—guided by his wisdom and wiles—the major could still ensure that the Cherokee Nation had a future, sovereign and separate and strong. He'd return to his land, watch the sharecroppers spread their spring seeds, and think and wait and prepare. Planting seeds of his own.

Hosmer stretched a long leg out over a fallen tree. Before his foot could come down firmly on the other side, something hit him hard from behind. He stumbled forward, and his other foot caught the dead wood, tripping him even more.

He plunged face-first into the underbrush, his broad chest slamming into the ground, knocking the air from his lungs. Before he could refill them with a breath or get stock of what was happening, a weight came down on his back, and something rough slid down over his forehead and face to settle around his neck.

Whatever it was yanked back, biting into his flesh, squeezing his throat.

Hosmer tried to reach back and grab whoever was behind him,

but his arms were pinned down against the earth. He groped at his holster, but it wasn't low enough, and all he could do was scratch at the black leather tip.

He began jerking his head this way and that, trying to shake free. The pressure against his throat didn't let up, though. It came from two hard knobs on either side of his neck, with a short length of coarse cord between them.

Hands, he realized, bound with rope.

The weight on his back shifted, bearing down even harder on his spine as the person choking him leaned in close to his left ear.

"Die..." a woman whispered, her voice both bitter and somehow soothing, coaxing—like a mother shushing a squalling baby into sleep. "Die...die..."

He did.

CHAPTER 47

"Sister!" Eskaminzim called again into the forest. "Where are you? It's over!"

As before, he got no answer.

"I'll help look for her when Diehl's done pawing at me," Hoop said. He'd staggered out of the little house a minute before, hands pressed to his side. He'd made it as far as Walkingstick's body before his legs gave out.

Diehl had pulled Hoop's hands away to give the bloody wound beneath them a quick once-over. Now he shrugged out of his coat, folded it, set it over the gash, and put Hoop's hands back.

"Keep up the pressure," Diehl said. "We'll need to clean it out, but I don't think it's gonna kill you."

"Very reassuring," Hoop said, looking up at Diehl.

Diehl's face was covered with drying blood—a dark red mask all the way from the cut across his forehead down to the collar of his shirt.

"Stay still for now," Diehl said. "Wherever Onawa is, you're not gonna help her by stumbling around bleeding to death."

Hoop looked like he might argue, but instead he just gave Diehl a grim nod.

He glanced over at Walkingstick's body, then Pixley's, and his expression turned even grimmer.

Not far off, Colonel Crowe was pacing back and forth at the edge of the graveyard, as close to the church as he dared to go. It had almost entirely collapsed in on itself now, and everything inside the sanctuary was engulfed in flame and smoke.

"Utter failure. Defeat. Disaster," Crowe muttered. "All for nothing."

"Not at all," Diehl said. "I'd call it a miraculous success against nearly impossible odds."

Crowe shot him a scowl. "I don't need your sarcasm right now."

"I'm not being sarcastic," Diehl said. "We prevented Abraham Lincoln's body from being used for extortion, which headed off who knows what kind of trouble the ransom was going to pay for. Success."

Crowe spun to face Diehl fully. "We were supposed to save him!"

"He's been dead thirty years. It's a little late for saving."

"You know what I mean! It's the principle of the thing! The sanctity of a great man...the honor of the nation...they've been besmirched. Sullied. Stained."

Diehl shrugged. "Your honor's only stained if people think it is."

"Spoken like a man with no understanding of honor!" Crowe spat.

He turned his back to Diehl...then instantly whirled around again.

"What are you suggesting?" he said.

"Other than us, who knows that Lincoln's body was taken from its tomb?"

Crowe let his gaze drift for a moment to the three young outlaws —Blaze Bad Water, Gerty Wormwood, and Nathaniel Pumpkin— sprawled among the tombstones. Then he looked off at the old men lying dead on the eastern side of the cemetery.

His eyes narrowed.

"Solomon Hosmer," he growled. "He knows. Everyone else is dead."

"And Hosmer's going to keep his mouth shut," Diehl said. "Why admit he was part of a huge, failed conspiracy when he can slink away and lick his wounds?"

"And bank on us staying quiet, too," said Hoop.

Diehl nodded. "Exactly. Colonel, if you go back to Springfield with a body in a box and you seal it up tight—hell, pour concrete over it this time so it can never be messed with again—then you stick that plaque back up and just carry on as if all this never happened..."

He waved his hands in the air like a stage magician saying, "Voilà!"

"All this never happened," said Hoop.

Diehl gave him another nod. "And there's no stain on the national honor."

"I'll know there's one!" Colonel Crowe said.

"Who cares?" said Diehl.

That rendered the colonel speechless.

"There are plenty of bodies to choose from," Eskaminzim said, moving from the edge of the woods into the cemetery. He still looked worried, but clearly he was warming to the conversation. "Not one of these, though." He gestured down at Bad Water and Wormwood and Nathaniel. "They'll have bounties on them."

"How about him?" said Diehl. "He earned a spot under a monument."

He jerked his chin at Pixley.

Hoop shook his head. "I got the feeling he has a wife waiting for him in Illinois. Who knows—maybe kids, too. Even if they can't know the truth, they deserve to know that he's dead and buried where they choose." He took a deep breath, grimacing at the pain it brought him, and nodded at Walkingstick. "Same goes for him, if that thought crosses your mind."

"An Indian buried in Lincoln's tomb, though..." Eskaminzim said with a little smile. "I like it."

He swerved toward the dead Cherokee rebel with the long, bowed legs.

"Maybe this one? He's tall. Lincoln was tall, right?" he said.

He cocked his head, sizing up the dead man.

"No, probably not him. Those legs…" he said. "We couldn't squeeze him into a normal coffin." He shifted his gaze a little to the right. "Good taste in hats, though."

"Oh, stop it," Colonel Crowe said listlessly.

He turned back toward the church, clasped his hands behind his back, and stared into the flames.

Eskaminzim walked toward the other old rebel who'd been shot down near the graveyard.

"This one's got too much fat on him," he said. "He wouldn't rattle around in the box like—"

A noise from the woods behind him—the sound of movement through the brush—whipped him around, his left hand shooting to the revolver he'd stuffed under his belt.

"Sister?" he said.

The sun was high enough now to send shafts of bright light through the trees, and a figure emerged from the shadows to step into one.

"It's me," Onawa said.

Eskaminzim rushed over to her as she walked out of the forest.

"Sister!" he said again, joyfully this time.

They didn't hug—not Apaches in front of outsiders—but they paused to gaze into each other's eyes.

Onawa lifted her hands. They were still tied with a length of rough rope.

Eskaminzim stuffed away his gun and drew his knife and cut through the rope.

Onawa looked up into his eyes again, then leaned to the side to peer past him.

"How is my husband?" she said.

"He's fine," said Hoop. "I'm glad to see you."

Onawa smiled. "I'm glad to see *you*."

Her smile faded into a frown as she made her way toward him.

"Is that the best you could do?" she asked Diehl, jabbing a finger at the folded coat Hoop was holding to his side.

"We've been busy," Diehl said. "I was going to do something better in a bit."

Onawa snorted in disbelief.

"The Little Badger," she said to Colonel Crowe as she passed him. "I haven't seen you in a long, long time."

Crowe gave her a respectful nod. "Mrs. Hoop."

"Find the dead men with the cleanest shirts," she told him. "We need bandages."

"Yes, ma'am," said the colonel.

Not many people could bark orders at Colonel C. Kermit Crowe. Onawa was one.

Crowe started toward Blaze Bad Water's body. Bad Water's clothes looked cleaner than his friends'.

Onawa gave Bad Water a long look, too. Then she came sweeping up to where Diehl and Hoop sat, near Walkingstick. She grabbed Diehl's blood-covered face in her hands, inspected the gash across his forehead, then let him go with a dismissive grunt.

"I like you with a red face," she said. "Makes you more handsome."

Diehl ran his fingers over the crusted blood on his cheeks.

"Maybe I'll keep it," he said.

Onawa kneeled beside Hoop.

"Hello," she said softly.

"Hello," said Hoop.

She gave the lump on his head a disapproving look, then pointed at his side. "You're not supposed to let that happen."

"You're not supposed to get captured."

Rather than answer that, Onawa turned to see if Col. Crowe was following her orders.

He was. He was undoing the buttons on Bad Water's white cotton shirt.

Again, Onawa's gaze lingered on the dead bandit. Then she tore it away.

"What were you talking about a minute ago?" she said. "With the bodies?"

"Lincoln was still in there," her brother told her, waving a hand at the church as it turned to ashes. "Diehl thinks we should just lie and pretend he was never stolen in the first place. I was looking for the right body to take his place."

"Ah," Onawa said, nodding, thinking. "I have a good one for you. In the woods. It would do."

All four men—Eskaminzim, Hoop, Diehl, Crowe—gaped at her.

"Is it the major?" Diehl asked. "Hosmer?"

He'd been wondering where the old bastard was.

Onawa nodded.

Diehl shook his head in amazement.

"My god..." he said. "How did we ever get along without you?"

"*You* will have to find out again," Onawa said. "I quit." She looked down at her husband, then at her brother. "And you should, too."

Eskaminzim spread out his arms and grinned at the burning church and scattered cadavers. "And miss out on all this?"

Onawa frowned at him, then turned back to Hoop.

"Stay on the reservation with me," she said. "There are other ways to live."

"We'll talk about it," Hoop said.

"Yes. We will," Onawa replied. "Right now."

She threw a quick glance over at Diehl.

He got the hint.

Diehl cleared his throat and pushed himself to his feet and walked off as Onawa and Hoop carried on their conversation in low tones. He glanced back once, catching Hoop's eye. Hoop looked like he wanted to walk off with him.

Diehl returned to the cemetery. He sat by the grave at the southwest corner and leaned back against the headstone and took in the view. It struck him as a nice one, if you ignored all the corpses.

The Neosho River wound its way through lush green springtime trees, fertile farmland to the east, rolling hills to the west.

Songbirds chirped. A heron swooped past.

Eskaminzim stepped up beside the headstone.

"I know the Cherokees aren't happy about how they got here,"

Diehl said with a nod at the horizon. "Losing their lands in the east, the Trail of Tears here. But I can see why Hosmer would fight to keep this for them. It's a beautiful place."

Eskaminzim gazed out over the hills, the river. The forests, the farms. The grass, the birds, the clouds.

"Meh," he said.

A Look At: Holmes on the Range: A Western Mystery Series (Holmes on the Range Mysteries Book 1)

SHERLOCK HOLMES MEETS THE OLD WEST IN THIS THRILLING MURDER MYSTERY ON A KILLER RANCH.

It's 1893, and wandering cowboy brothers Big Red and Old Red Amlingmeyer are down to their last few pennies. When a job becomes available at a ranch run by a confident and enigmatic foreman, neither brother can say no.

Although the work is tiresome and their boss is bad-tempered, they have a welcome distraction—the Sherlock Holmes stories Old Red has come to love so much.

But when someone discovers a dead body on the ranch, a menacing game is afoot. Old Red is determined to catch the killer using Holmes' infamous methods, and Big Red is dragged along for the wild ride—whether he likes it or not—while his brother tries to deduce his way to the truth.

Can Old Red and Big Red solve the mystery with stampedes, rustlers, Holmes-hating aristocrats, and a cannibal named Hungry Bob standing in their way?

AVAILABLE NOW

ACKNOWLEDGMENTS

In the acknowledgments for the first book about Diehl, Hoop, and Eskaminzim, *Hired Guns*, I thanked a lot of people. This time I'm going to thank a lot of books. Which might seem a little goofy, since it's not like the books care one way or the other. But what the heck —I feel like I owe them, so here goes.

Stealing Lincoln's Body by Thomas J. Craughwell planted the seed for *No Hallowed Ground* years ago. It's a fascinating nonfiction account of the real-life attempts to snatch Honest Abe from his grave. If you thought the conspiracy in *No Hallowed Ground* was far-fetched, I can assure you, the stuff that really happened was just as wild.

Caught in the Maelstrom: The Indian Nations in the Civil War, 1861–1865 by Clint Crowe provided historical context for my depictions of Solomon Hosmer, Henry Walkingstick, and conditions in the Territories during and after the Civil War. If you want a deep dive into the back and forth of the war in the Indian Nations, you couldn't ask for a deeper one than this.

Black, Red, and Deadly: Black and Indian Gunfighters of the Indian Territories by Art Burton was, as you can probably guess from the title, an influence on my thinking about Blaze Bad Water and his gang. Burton's *Black, Buckskin, and Blue: African-American Scouts and Soldiers on the Western Frontier* is a fascinating read, as well, and helped shape my approach to my heroes.

The way I wrote Eskaminzim and Onawa was partially shaped by *The Apache Wars* by Paul Andrew Hutton, *Apacheria: True Stories of Apache Culture 1860 – 1920* by W. Michael Farmer, *The Mescalero Apaches* by C.L. Sonnichsen, *I Fought with Geronimo* by Jason Betzinez with W.S. Nye, and *In the Days of Victorio* by Eve Ball. I also just wanted to write Apache characters of a kind I'd rarely seen elsewhere: funny, quirky, decorous (in Onawa's case), distinctive. If I mischaracterized Mescalero Apache culture in any way, please let me know and—as with all things—I will endeavor to do better in the future.

Steve Hockensmith
    Alameda, California
    June 15, 2024

ABOUT THE AUTHOR

Steve Hockensmith's first novel, the western mystery hybrid *Holmes on the Range*, was a finalist for the Edgar, Shamus, Anthony and Dilys awards. He went on to write several sequels—with more on the way—as well as the tarot-themed mystery *The White Magic Five* and *Dime* and the *New York Times* bestseller *Pride and Prejudice and Zombies: Dawn of the Dreadfuls*. He also teamed up with educator "Science Bob" Pflugfelder to write the middle-grade mystery *Nick and Tesla's High-Voltage Danger Lab* and its five sequels.

A prolific writer of short stories, Hockensmith has been appearing regularly in *Alfred Hitchcock* and *Ellery Queen Mystery Magazine* for more than 20 years.

Learn more about Steve and his books at *stevehockensmith.com*.

Made in the USA
Las Vegas, NV
15 October 2024

96900634R00184